Her lips twisted. "Let me guess, if you tell me what you do—"

"I'd have to kill you." He captured her wrist in his hand. "I think you've done enough. We should finish the work and get back to the B and B."

Jillian stared into his eyes.

A few short inches separated them, but all Chance could think about was those pretty pink lips and what they might taste like if he dared kiss her.

Jillian ran her tongue around those pink lips, sending Chance's control flying.

"Do you realize how crazy you're making me?"

She shook her head, her eyes rounding, her gaze shifting to his mouth.

Like a moth drawn to the flame, Chance couldn't resist the temptation. He slipped his hand beneath her hair at the back of her head and dragged her forward until their lips almost touched. "Tell me to stop and I will," he breathed, praying she wouldn't when the temptation to kiss her threatened to overwhelm him.

If you're on Twitter, tell us what you think of Harlequin Romantic Suspense! #harlequinromsuspense

Dear Reader,

We're back in Cape Churn! I thought *Deadly Allure* would be the last in the series, but when I told my editor I wanted to write more Devil's Shroud books, I was thrilled she agreed.

Some of my fans asked for Jillian the real estate agent's story, so I took the chance to bring her back and to introduce a new character. And it's all because of a wedding. And since the area has its own spook factor, I gave Jillian her very first fixer-upper home. Not only does the home have a past, it helps Jillian learn more about the past she could never remember.

Enter former warrior turned Stealth Operations Specialist Chance McCall, and things heat up in Cape Churn.

Hang on for a bumpy and often creepy ride!

Elle James

DEADLY OBSESSION

Elle James

 HARLEQUIN® ROMANTIC SUSPENSE

Recycling programs
for this product may
not exist in your area.

ISBN-13: 978-0-373-27988-3

Deadly Obsession

Copyright © 2016 by Mary Jernigan

All rights reserved. Except for use in any review, the reproduction or
utilization of this work in whole or in part in any form by any electronic,
mechanical or other means, now known or hereinafter invented, including
xerography, photocopying and recording, or in any information storage
or retrieval system, is forbidden without the written permission of the
publisher, Harlequin Enterprises Limited, 225 Duncan Mill Road,
Don Mills, Ontario M3B 3K9, Canada.

This is a work of fiction. Names, characters, places and incidents are
either the product of the author's imagination or are used fictitiously,
and any resemblance to actual persons, living or dead, business
establishments, events or locales is entirely coincidental.

This edition published by arrangement with Harlequin Books S.A.

For questions and comments about the quality of this book,
please contact us at CustomerService@Harlequin.com.

® and TM are trademarks of Harlequin Enterprises Limited or its
corporate affiliates. Trademarks indicated with ® are registered in the
United States Patent and Trademark Office, the Canadian Intellectual
Property Office and in other countries.

Printed in U.S.A.

New York Times and *USA TODAY* bestselling author **Elle James** is a former IT professional and retired army and air force reservist. She writes romantic suspense, mysteries and paranormal romances that keep her readers on the edges of their seats to the very end of every book. When she's not at her computer, she's traveling to exotic and wonderful places, snow-skiing, boating or riding her four-wheeler, dreaming up new stories. Learn more about Elle James at ellejames.com.

Books by Elle James

Harlequin Romantic Suspense

Deadly Reckoning
Deadly Engagement
Deadly Liaisons
Secret Service Rescue
Deadly Allure
Deadly Obsession

The Adair Legacy

Secret Service Rescue

The Adair Affairs

Heir to Murder

The Coltons of Oklahoma

Protecting the Colton Bride

Visit Elle's Author Profile page at Harlequin.com, or ellejames.com, for more titles.

This book is dedicated to my son, who has a heart bigger than the state of Texas, has a great sense of adventure and would do anything for you. He's the kind of guy with the ability to make friends everywhere he goes and keeps in touch with all of them. I wish him a happy, healthy life, full of the love he so richly deserves. I love you, Adam!

Prologue

Excitement rippled through her. She could barely wait to get home from school. Instead of taking the road as she'd promised her mother, she cut through the woods. She carefully balanced the treasure her teacher, Mrs. Tillman, had given her. It was a thank-you gift for staying late every day after school the entire year to help straighten the classroom, clean the boards and check papers.

A gift hadn't been necessary, and that wasn't the reason she'd stayed after school. She loved helping her beautiful young teacher. The added bonus was access to all the books on the shelves in the classroom. They were filled with wonderful stories and picture books of places Mrs. Tillman had been—Germany, Russia, Italy, China—exciting, exotic places in all parts of the world. Reading about those places was all the thank-you she could ask for.

But the gift had been special. A beautiful black porcelain music box from Russia. Painted with colorful women in flowing ball gowns dancing with handsome men in military regalia. The pictures told a story of another time, of richness and beauty. And when she opened the pretty little box, music spilled out. *The Nutcracker*, her teacher had told her.

Mama would love it as much as she did. When she was younger, Mama had played the piano and sang in the church choir. Now she barely had time. Since her daddy had moved out, her mother had gone back to teaching, and she didn't play the piano anymore. But she loved music and made sure her daughter grew up with the same love.

Her attention was on the pretty black box, and she was in such a hurry to get home, she didn't see what tripped her until she flew forward. She tucked the little box against her body to keep from breaking it when she hit the uneven ground. She landed hard, the wind knocked from her lungs, her head bouncing off a big rock. For a moment she lay still, trying but not succeeding at dragging air into her lungs. Darkness gathered around the edge of her vision, closing in…swallowing her.

How long she lay there, she didn't know. Cold seeped into her skin, making her shake. No matter how hard she tried, she couldn't open her eyes. The darkness was inside her, gripping her like a hand, squeezing so tightly it wouldn't let go.

Shivering turned to violent tremors. Pushing against the grasp of the black abyss, she cracked open an eyelid. Fog closed in around her. Nothing looked familiar. She didn't know where she was, or where she'd been going.

"I want to go home," she cried. But she couldn't remember where home was.

Sobs rose up her throat and tears ran down her cold, damp cheeks. She lay curled in a ball, trying to warm herself but failing miserably. Maybe, if she went to sleep, she'd wake in her bed…where she belonged.

Closing her eyes, she lay as still as her trembling body could. Soon a warm blanket was wrapped around her. By the coarseness of the fabric, it had to be wool. It covered her body, her face and her head, making it harder to breathe and blocking out any daylight that managed to filter through the fog. Then she was lifted into strong arms and carried. How far, she didn't know. But it seemed like forever.

She would have kicked, screamed and cried for her captor to release her, but she didn't have the strength, and she didn't want him to take away the warmth of the blanket. He kept going and going.

At last he stopped and fumbled with something. A screeching sound could have been a rusty hinge. She couldn't see through the thick wool of the blanket, wrapped so tightly around her that she couldn't move.

They were going down steps; the musty scent of dirt and decay filtered through the blanket. It was the same dank smell she could remember from visiting someone's earthen root cellar in the country. She grasped at the memory, but before she could identify whose basement she'd visited, the thought drifted away like smoke in the wind.

Finally, she was deposited onto cool, damp earth. She struggled to free herself from the blanket. By the time she did, her captor was already up the wooden steps leading out of the ground where he'd brought her.

Her heart hammering, her voice lodged in her throat, she pushed to her feet and stumbled on wobbly legs toward the light. As her foot hit the first step, a heavy metal door dropped down over the opening, shutting out the light, plunging her into darkness so complete, it had to be hell.

Chapter 1

Chance McCall pulled the rented SUV into the parking area in front of the McGregor Bed-and-Breakfast and shut off the engine. The flight from the East Coast to the West Coast had been long, with a four-hour layover in Chicago. Now that he was in Oregon, he could relax and enjoy seeing his friends and take in the peace and calm of the stunning seaside town of Cape Churn.

He dropped down from the vehicle and stood for a long moment, taking it all in: the craggy coastline, the steely blue waters of the cape and the sprawling old mansion the McGregor siblings had converted into a successful bed-and-breakfast. Already, he could feel the tension of his last assignment easing from the muscles in his neck and shoulders.

Dragging in a breath of the salty sea air and evergreen-scented forest, he filled his lungs. He could see why Nova had chosen to stay in Oregon instead of heading back east to Alexandria, Virginia, where the Stealth Operations Specialists headquarters resided.

This was heaven.

"Amigo!" Casanova Valdez burst from a screen door onto the wide front porch. "We didn't expect you for another hour."

"Traffic was in my favor in Portland." Chance crossed the yard and met Nova at the bottom of the steps in a bone-crushing bear hug. From a large Hispanic family, Nova wasn't shy about displaying his affection for his family and friends. And Chance was about as close to Nova as Nova's own siblings. Closer. They'd been in combat together and survived.

"I'm glad you concluded your assignment in time for the wedding," his friend said. "I would have postponed if you hadn't."

"That's crazy." Chance pounded Nova's back and stepped away. "The way you've been talking about Molly, I would think you'd have eloped by now."

"No way. Molly is special. She deserves the works." Nova flung out his arm, grinning. "The bigger the wedding, the better. *Muy grande!*"

"I tried to hold him back, but between Nova and my wedding planner, this simple ceremony is taking on a life of its own." A beautiful redhead dressed in a white button-down blouse and well-worn jeans that hugged her long slender legs and curvy hips stood at the top of the stairs, a smile tugging at her lips and a twinkle in her green eyes. She held out a hand. "You must be Chance."

Chance climbed the steps and took her outstretched hand. "And you must be the Molly Nova can't shut up about." Chance winked and shook her hand.

"Oh, no, you don't. I feel like I know you already. Come here and give me a hug. You're practically family." She dragged him close for a quick hug and stepped back.

Nova slipped an arm around her waist and kissed her. "What did I tell you?" he said. "Isn't she gorgeous?" He beamed at Chance, his love for his fiancée shining from his eyes.

Molly blushed. "Nova, stop. You're embarrassing me."

Chance chuckled. "No, really. He's right. You're as pretty as he said. Congratulations on your engagement."

"Thank you." She nodded toward the rental. "Do you need help with your luggage?"

He shook his head. "All I have is a duffel bag."

"I'll get it," Nova offered. "Molly can show you to your room. Oh, and just so you know, the McGregor mansion is haunted." Nova left Chance with Molly and hurried to the SUV.

Molly clucked her tongue. "Don't let him scare you. The ghosts here are benevolent. They rarely make a nuisance of themselves."

Chance followed Molly into the old mansion. "I never knew Nova believed in the supernatural."

"Oh, neither one of us did at first. It took some hocus-pocus on the ghost's part to convince us. He can tell you all about it. After I show you to your room, I have to get back to my kitchen. I'm baking bread and need to get a start on it to let the dough rise."

"You don't have to show me around," Chance assured her. "Just point. I can figure it out."

She looked at him, her brows coming together. "Are you sure?"

"Absolutely."

In the large front gathering room, Molly pointed to

the top of the massive staircase. "Hang a left at the top
and your room is the third door on your right. I gave
you the room with the view of the cape. The bathroom
is down the hall. Let me know if you need anything."
Molly hugged him again. "Nova is thrilled you made it.
I believe he really would have postponed the wedding
if you couldn't have come."

"I take it his family will be here for the wedding?"

She laughed. "He said as many as could make it. I
think there will be at least twenty of them." Molly held
up a hand. "Don't worry. Not all of them are staying
here. We have several vacation cottages reserved. His
parents and grandparents will be staying at the B and
B. Siblings, aunts, uncles and cousins will be scattered
along the shore in the cottages." She waved her fingers.
"I'll be in the kitchen if you need me."

The front screen door banged shut behind Chance.

"Molly isn't used to large family gatherings," Nova
said. "It's just her, her brother, Gabe, his wife and two
kids. You'll like Gabe and his wife, Kayla. She's a re-
nowned artist and he works for the local police department." He hefted the duffel bag onto his shoulder. "Come
on, I'll show you to your room."

Chance didn't bother telling Nova he'd just informed
Molly he could find his room on his own. Instead, he
climbed the staircase, following Nova to the top.

"I just got back from an assignment in Los Angeles.
Molly was getting worried *I* wouldn't be here for our
wedding."

"What did Fontaine have you working on?" Chance
asked.

"I tailed a suspected terrorist for a couple weeks. Long

enough to know he was plotting to blow up one of the major movie producers' lots during a big social event."

Chance frowned. "And why was SOS called in for that?"

"The terrorist was the new husband of the California senator's daughter. The senator is up for reelection and they wanted everything to be kept on the down low." Nova opened a door and stepped back. "This is your room for the duration. It's the largest guest room and has the best view."

Chance entered. The room was nicely decorated with antique furniture, a large mahogany bed with a matching chest of drawers and a full-length floor mirror. But it was the French doors leading out onto a balcony that captured Chance's attention. He pushed through the door and stepped outside.

"Molly calls that the Juliet balcony." Nova stepped up behind Chance. "She says I'm the romantic, but she's just as much so. That's why I love her so much."

"You're a lucky man."

"I know. I never thought I'd find the woman of my dreams in some obscure town in Oregon."

"About that." Chance turned to face his friend. "How is it there are enough SOS agents in this town to start a regional office?"

Nova shrugged, a grin spreading across his face. "There's something about this place that draws you in. And once you come to Cape Churn, you can't leave for long. It keeps calling you back."

Chance clapped a hand on his back and smiled. "Or is it the people you meet here that keep you coming back?"

Nova nodded. "It's a combination of both, with the

people we meet at the top of the list." He winked. "Watch out. You might be the next to fall victim to the magic."

"First you tell me there are ghosts here. Now you're telling me there's magic, too?"

Nova turned back into the room. "Just saying you never know what surprises might happen in Cape Churn."

"Well, I'm not here to find a wife. I'm here to see that you get married and settle down. And if I can get a little R & R, even better. I could use it." Chance ran a hand through his hair.

"You still battling PTSD?" Nova asked.

Chance nodded.

Nova's lips pressed together. "Sorry to hear it. I have dreams, but for the most part, I'm managing."

"I'm sure it helps having someone like Molly to keep you grounded."

That ready grin spread wide on Nova's face. "*Sí.* Not only is she *muy bonita*, she's smart, tough and a fighter."

"You need a woman like that when you're in the business we're in." Their SOS assignments took them all over the world.

Chance's last assignment had been to Syria to rescue a missionary surrounded by an organization by the name of the Islamic State of Iraq and Syria, or ISIS. Had Chance not arrived when he had, the missionary would have been tortured and killed as a warning to other Christians. Luckily, he'd arrived on the outskirts of the small village as a twenty-man contingent raided the missionary's hideout.

By staging an explosive distraction, Chance had been able to slip in, free the missionary and get him out. But it had cost him.

The explosion and the resulting gunfire threw his mind back into his final mission in Afghanistan before he was medically retired from the army rangers. It was all he could do to keep his head on straight and pull the missionary out while his mind played tricks on him, making him think he was fighting the Taliban.

Everything that could have gone wrong did on his final active-duty mission. No matter how much his gut told him it was a bad deal, he'd had no choice. The intelligence guys had gotten a hot lead. One of the most notorious Taliban leaders had taken refuge in a small village. His team had to move quickly, but from the moment they'd put boots on the ground at the drop zone, everything had gone to hell.

Rappelling from the chopper, one member of his squad hit hard on a big rock, rolled his ankle and broke it. The chopper was forced to land to retrieve him and two other teammates had to help get him back into the helicopter, thus slowing the entire mission.

They'd scaled the village wall and moved in, seeking their quarry. The village was quiet. Too quiet. Chance had opened his mouth to tell his men to fall back when all hell broke loose.

An explosion rocked the walls around them, and automatic gunfire filled the air, tracer rounds lighting the night.

Too late to turn back, the men had to fight their way out, outnumbered two to one. One by one, his men were picked off. All Chance could do was get as many out as possible.

His radio communications man called for reinforcement before he took a hit that rendered his radio unusable, and he nearly didn't make it out with his own life.

Chance felt a sting in his right hip, but pushed on, adrenaline pumping, the safety of his squad on his shoulders. He was responsible for those men. He'd have to face all their wives, mothers and children if they didn't come home alive.

A hand on his shoulder brought him out of Afghanistan and back to the McGregor B and B.

"Thinking about it again?" Nova asked.

Chance shook himself to clear the images that filled his memories and dreams. He gave Nova half a smile. "Sometimes it creeps up on me."

"I know. It does me, too. But you can't let it run your life. We did everything we could to get them out alive."

So they said. Chance still felt he could have done more. Again, he focused on the present, the way his therapist had taught him. "I'm here to help with the wedding preparations. What can I do?"

Nova clapped a hand to his back. "That's more like it. I'm not really sure what we need to do. Molly's friend Jillian has the plan well in hand, or so they say. They won't let me do anything except fetch and carry."

"So you're telling me we just sit on the front porch and drink beer while the women do all the work?" Chance's lips quirked. "I'm all for relaxing and drinking beer, but I can't stand by while others are working hard."

Nova laughed. "Same here. I've been doing repairs to the B and B and some touch-up painting. Molly wants to have the wedding out near the cliffs with the cape as the backdrop. I think it involves setting up chairs and an arched trellis I have yet to see or be tasked with going to the rental shop and acquiring."

"When does your family arrive?" Chance asked.

"Some are coming in the day after tomorrow and the

rest arrive a couple days before the wedding. We have a few days of relative peace until that time. Then all bets are off."

Chance chuckled. "I remember." He'd visited Nova's family while they'd both been on terminal leave, having been discharged from the army. His mother had welcomed him like one of her own. And she probably wouldn't have noticed he wasn't one of them, considering all the people moving through his parents' home.

Nova was one of eight children. Some of his siblings were already married with children of their own. It had been overwhelming for Chance, whose one brother rarely contacted him. And their parents were retired and traveling all the time.

"I look forward to seeing your family," Chance said, and meant it. The Valdezes were close-knit, valuing the time they spent together.

"Once you get settled, come down to the kitchen. Molly will have a list of things for us to do before dinner." Nova hugged Chance again. "Damn, it's good to see you."

After Nova left, Chance stood in the room with a knot in his throat, his chest tight. Nova had his head on straight. PTSD wasn't ruling his life, and he had a lot going for him—a hot fiancée, living among some of the most beautiful scenery Chance had ever encountered and having a home to go to when he finished assignments.

Chance found himself wanting what Nova had, knowing he never could. Not when he was struggling with violent dreams and having the feeling he needed to be moving all the time. He was afraid if he stopped for too long, the memories would come crashing in.

Chance had no business starting a relationship with

a woman. He wasn't what he considered good boyfriend material, much less husband material.

Getting the itch to move, stretch his legs and walk off some of the pent-up energy he'd had to contain en route, he tossed his duffel bag in a corner and went in search of the communal bathroom. A splash of cool water on his face did a lot to restore his focus. After drying his hands and face, he headed down to the kitchen.

The great room had a huge fireplace with hearty leather sofas positioned to take advantage of the warmth of a fire. The nights would be cool enough for a crackling blaze.

The scent of cookies drifted across his senses. Something with chocolate, like his mother used to bake. The McGregor mansion seemed to wrap around Chance and make him feel at home.

Passing through the large dining room with small tables scattered around, he heard the rattle of pans and a giggle behind a swinging door.

He paused for a moment before pushing against the wood panel. With the door half-open and the strong, rich scent of baking luring him inside, Chance opened his mouth to ask what was cooking.

A loud *bang* sent him diving for the floor, covering the back of his head. The swinging door slammed against the wall and bounced back to hit him in the ribs.

For moment, Chance was back in that village in Afghanistan, his side torn open in a gaping wound caused by an explosion. He felt for the blood but came away with a dry hand. Then he realized he wasn't in Afghanistan. He was lying on the kitchen floor, a large stockpot resting on the floor beside his head.

"I'm so sorry, Chance." Molly snatched the pot off

the floor and set it on the stove. She bent over Chance, her brow making a V over her nose. "Are you all right?"

His heart racing and heat rising in his cheeks, Chance sprang to his feet and shoved a hand through his hair. "I'm fine."

Nova shook his head. "Brother, you are *not* fine. Your face went completely white, and now it's burning red. You don't have to pretend everything is okay when it's not. You're with friends here."

Chance's jaw tightened, and he squared his shoulders. "I said I'm fine. Is there something I can help with?" He needed to keep busy, or his heart would explode out of his chest.

"As a matter of fact," Nova started, "I'm supposed to be over at Jillian's today helping her unload."

"Jillian who? And unload what?" After making a complete idiot of himself, he would do anything to get out of the house.

Molly smiled. "Jillian's my maid of honor and wedding planner. She just bought her first house and is in the process of moving in. She needs help with the big stuff."

"I'm your guy." Chance nodded toward Molly and Nova. "You probably have other things to do." Like more giggling and holding each other. He thought it, but he didn't say it out loud.

Nova's ready grin filled his face. "If you're sure…"

"Positive," Chance said. "All I need are directions."

Nova walked Chance through the door and out onto the wide front porch. "I can join you in an hour."

"By then, we could be done. Don't worry. I'll help Molly's friend get moved in."

Nova laid a hand on Chance's shoulder. "We didn't invite you here to put you to work."

"I need something to keep me moving."

Nova nodded. "I understand. It took six months for me to stop hitting the dirt when I heard loud noises."

Chance shrugged. "Yeah. I'll get over it."

"You don't have to work through it on your own, you know."

"I know." Chance hadn't come to Cape Churn for sympathy. He came to help a friend get ready for the biggest day of his life. He'd be damned if he ruined it for him by coming unglued in front of his fiancée and guests. All he needed to do was focus and keep his head on straight for five days. Five days of rest and relaxation that would go a long way toward restoring his body and soul. "Where is this friend?"

Chapter 2

Jillian drove the truck and trailer into the yard, by-passed the two vehicles parked there, made a big circle and backed the trailer to the porch. Excitement rippled through her like a shiver.

Though she'd been a Realtor for the past six years, she had never actually owned her own home. When she'd started selling real estate in Portland, she was content to live in an apartment and build her savings.

Then she'd discovered the quiet seaside village of Cape Churn. Something about the beauty of the coastal town called to her, as if telling her it was home. She'd packed her belongings and moved, promising to purchase a house when she found one she loved. Her plan was to purchase a fixer-upper with good bones and make it her own. But it took money for a down payment and closing costs, and still more money to renovate. So she'd saved for the past two years.

When the bank had come to her, asking her if she could sell one of their properties that had been sitting unoccupied for the past seventeen years, she'd agreed. Located just beyond the edge of town, the quaint Victorian house was tucked away into the woods, quiet, beautiful and…perfect. Yes, it was neglected, it needed to be brought up to electric and plumbing codes, but Jillian couldn't contain her excitement.

She'd offered the bank a ridiculously low price, knowing it would take every bit of her savings to restore the structure and the interior to a livable condition. The bank had snapped up her offer, grateful to unload an albatross they'd paid property taxes on for too long.

Jillian climbed out of the truck her friend Dave had loaned her and stood staring at the old house with the charming dormer windows, wide wraparound porches and so much charm, it looked like a place she could love and restore to its former glory.

Something about it made her feel as though she belonged here. Sure, many of the windows needed to be replaced, the porch sagged and she needed a new roof. But the house was hers and she had plans for it.

Now all she had to do was transfer her belongings from the trailer to the house. Everything would go into the small sitting room at the back until the workers completed the remodeling effort.

Jillian had hoped to sleep in her new home while they worked, but she couldn't until they completed the plumbing and electrical work they'd begun a week before. Her lease was up on the cottage she'd rented, and the owner wanted to have it ready for the summer season. So she was moving things into her house before it was ready for her.

Thankfully, Molly had a room for her at the McGregor B and B, which worked out fine. As Molly's wedding planner, Jillian needed to check with the bride on all the last-minute details leading up to the big day scheduled for the following Saturday. For the most part, the preparations had been made. All she had left to do was make certain everything was delivered on time, as promised. There was to be a combined bachelor and bachelorette party, rehearsal dinner and the wedding. Then Jillian could concentrate on her own life and getting her house in order.

"Ah, Miss Taylor, I'm glad you're here." Bob Greer, the contractor, stepped onto the front porch. "We ran into a problem with the septic lines."

Jillian bit back the urge to say, *What now?* Instead, she followed Bob around the porch to the rear of the building.

He pointed to a damp, mossy spot on the ground. "You have a leak."

With a nod, she smiled at the man. "I know. That's why I have you here. To fix all the issues this house might have."

"If the septic lines are damaged, it'll cost more than I originally budgeted for inside the house. And depending on the condition of the septic tank, you might need to have it dug out and replaced."

Her heart sank. Already her savings had taken a huge hit for the down payment and closing costs. She hoped the bigger issues would settle out soon so that she could see what she had left for the interior upgrades. "How much will that be?"

"Another eight to nine thousand." He stared at her, expectantly. "What do you want me to do?"

"If it's broken, fix it. Just let me know how much before you start replacing big-ticket items."

Bob nodded. "Yes, ma'am." He followed her to the front of the house. "Well, I'll be going. I'll be back tomorrow afternoon."

Her heart sank deeper into her belly. "Why not in the morning?"

"We're finishing up on another job in town. Then I have to arrange for a backhoe to dig up the lines, and order more parts for the interior. It'll take a day for both of those to make it out here, so the plumbing issues won't be resolved for a couple days."

Jillian sighed. "I was hoping to move in as soon as the plumbing and electricity were turned on."

He nodded. "If I don't have to replace the entire septic system, it's possible to be in in a couple days. But don't bank on it." He tipped his ball cap. "Night, Miss Taylor."

"Please, call me Jillian," she said.

"Yes, ma'am." Bob hurried toward his four-door truck with Bob's Building written in faded red lettering across the side panel. His team of carpenters was already inside, ready to go home.

Jillian opened the screen door. Every time she did, she had the tingly sensation of déjà vu.

A loud thump was followed by a string of curses at the back of the house.

Following the sounds, Jillian arrived in the kitchen, where Mitchell Knowlton held one thumb with his other hand, dancing around the yellowed linoleum floor.

"Are you all right?" Jillian asked.

Mitchell turned so fast he didn't take into account the corner of the old upper cabinets, which had yet to be thrown out, and smacked his head on the sharp edge. He clamped his lips tightly together, his face turning a bright red. "Smashed my thumb," he finally grumbled, alternating between pressing his fingers to his forehead and his battered thumb. "Should have listened to my wife."

Jillian chuckled. "Did she tell you not to hit your thumb?"

"No." He frowned. "She told me not to take this job."

"Why?" Jillian asked, taken aback by Mitchell's revelation.

"She says the place is haunted. Something bad happened here almost two decades ago. When the last owners moved out, no one would buy it. All the old-timers think it's because it's haunted."

This wasn't the first time she'd heard the stories. No matter what everyone else said, the house called to her like no other. She'd be damned if she was scared off by tales of ghosts. "You're not an old-timer, Mitchell." Jillian crossed her arms over her chest. "Do you believe this place is haunted?"

He shrugged and gathered his hammer. "No offense, but I think you're crazy trying to restore this big ol' house. It's more than a single lady can manage on her own, much less maintain the yard."

"You didn't answer my question." She tapped her toe, her brows raised in challenge.

Mitchell shoved a hand through his sandy hair. "Don't know about ghosts, but I have a weird feeling about this place. None of the other old houses I've rewired made me feel like that."

"Well, I think it's a grand ol' house. And if there are ghosts, I bet they're just as grand as the house. If it makes you feel any better, plan your work when there are others in the house. Maybe ghosts don't like crowds."

"Ah, now, Miss Taylor."

"Jillian," she corrected.

"I better stick to Miss Taylor. If my wife hears me callin' you Jillian, she'll let me have it."

Mitchell wasn't much older than Jillian, but he and his wife had been married for seven years and had two small boys.

"In fact, I should leave if you're going to be here for a while. She doesn't like me to hang around after hours. Especially…"

"If I'm here." Jillian smiled. "Don't worry. I don't plan on stealin' Caroline's man." She winked. "I'm not in the market for a relationship, legitimate or clandestine. I just want my house fixed so I can move in as soon as possible."

Mitchell's face reddened. "Sorry. Being eight months pregnant, Caroline's a little jealous when I'm working around pretty single women."

Jillian beamed. "I'll take that as a compliment. Tell Caroline she has nothing to worry about. I have too much to keep me busy to bother with men right now. Between renovating this house, running my real estate business and planning Molly McGregor's wedding, I barely have time to sleep."

"Ever think you might have taken on too much?"

A slightly hysterical giggle left Jillian's lips. "Yup."

Mitchell shook his head. "When is the construction crew going to start the demolition of the kitchen and bathrooms?"

Jillian's mouth twisted and she glanced around. "They were supposed to start today. But I can see nothing's been done."

"What time is it anyway?" Mitchell glanced at his

watch and blinked. "Holy smokes. I have to pick up the boys at Mother's Day Out." He gathered his tools and slung them into a tool bag.

"Mitchell, don't let the stories keep you from rewiring my house. I have it from one of the top Realtors in Cape Churn that you're the best electrician for the job. I'm counting on you to bring the house up to code without burning it down."

Mitchell paused with his hand on the door. He stared past her, his gaze taking in the sweeping staircase and the rooms at the front of the house. "I'll do the job. With a baby on the way, I need the money. Hopefully it won't take long."

Otherwise he wouldn't be doing the job. Jillian heard the unspoken words. She didn't care, as long as the job got done. "Thank you, Mitchell. Say hello to Caroline for me." If it helped, she'd stop by with some fresh-baked cookies for the family. When she had a kitchen to bake them in.

Mitchell drove away in a cloud of dust. Someday, when she could afford it, she'd have the driveway paved. That particular upgrade was way down the list of priorities.

Finally, she had the house to herself. Jillian wandered around, with a keen eye for what flooring, cabinets and countertops would be best in each room. She'd been a real estate agent long enough to know what she liked and what fit with the style of house she'd purchased. As she went through the kitchen, she stopped in front of the window over the sink and stared out at the overgrown backyard, reminding herself that the house came first, then the yard.

A movement in the corner of her eye made her turn

her head. Had Mitchell or Bob forgotten something and returned to the house? Jillian stepped out the back door to check, a salty breeze lifting her hair off the nape of her neck. No one was there. She reentered the house, shaking her head. Mitchell and some of the older residents of Cape Churn, with all their talk about ghosts and missing persons, had her spooked.

Determined to shake it off, Jillian opened and closed the kitchen cabinet doors, checking one last time for any leftover items that needed to be removed before demolition started. All she found was an old soda bottle.

With one last glance at the kitchen, Jillian was in the process of turning to leave when she noticed the door to the basement standing ajar. She didn't remember the door being open when she'd first entered the kitchen. Perhaps the breeze from the back door had opened it.

Jillian strode across the kitchen, grasped the doorknob and started to push it closed when she heard the plaintive cry of a kitten.

She froze with her hand on the knob and tilted her head, listening.

Again, she heard the puny mewling. This time she could tell it came from somewhere below her. Though she didn't believe in ghosts and she had big plans for a wine cellar in the basement, Jillian hesitated at the top of the steps. She stared into the darkness, her hand fumbling for the light switch. When she found it, she flipped it and the small yellowed bulb hanging over the top landing flickered once and then glowed to life, providing illumination only halfway down the steps.

Every scary movie Jillian had seen in high school came back to haunt her. Every lone female who ventured into a dark basement met with a terrible fate.

The kitten mewed again, startling Jillian into leaving the top landing and taking several steps downward. "Here, kitty," she whispered, disappointed in herself for her sudden aversion to going downstairs. Why had she let Mitchell's words affect her? She was a grown, independent, well-grounded woman who'd been living on her own since she left her parents' house to go to college. She had never been afraid of living alone in the big city, where crime was a given, and being a lone woman meant taking extra precautions to remain safe.

Since coming to Cape Churn two years ago, she'd never felt the sense of dread that now invaded her body as she crept down the stairs into the basement of her own house. Perspiration beaded on her upper lip, despite the cool dampness of the cellar.

She could wait to explore the basement until the next day, when there were more people there who could be her backup should she fall and twist an ankle. Or be attacked by a serial killer hiding out, waiting to pounce on her once she descended to the bottom step.

The cry of the kitten dragged her out of her morbid thoughts and made her feet move, one step at time, to the bottom. If there was a kitten in the basement, it might be in trouble. Perhaps its mother had brought the baby in through one of tiny basement windows and the wind had blown the window shut, thus trapping the poor creature. It could be hungry, maybe even starving.

The needs of the kitten outweighed Jillian's fear of exploring the creepy, dark basement by herself. She'd have Mitchell lay in the wiring to lighten up the darkest corners and give new life to the dingy space. But for now, she had to find the kitten and rescue it or leave the house worrying about a little animal incapable of fending for itself.

At the bottom of the stairs, the chill air of the basement permeated Jillian's skin, sending shivers creeping across her arms and making the hairs on the back of her neck spike upward.

All her life she'd had an aversion to dark, dank spaces. In high school, at a slumber party with a friend, they'd played truth or dare. Her friends had dared her to go down in the basement of her friend's house and stay for five minutes.

Jillian's parents didn't have a basement. Having lived in a town house, Jillian couldn't remember a time when she had been down in a basement. Accepting the dare, she'd gone down the steps into a dirt basement, where her friend's parents stored old mason jars, lawn chairs and a couple of bicycles. The place was dark, damp and chilled Jillian to the bone. After the first minute, she must have blacked out.

She came to with her friend shaking her shoulders, shouting into her face. "Jillian!"

They'd told her she lay there wide-eyed and shaking, in a catatonic state, neither out cold nor coherent.

Jillian didn't remember any of it, except going down into the basement. Her parents came to take her home, her friends more than happy to see her leave, all shaken by the experience.

That had been eleven years ago. Why think of that now? This basement was constructed of concrete block walls, not dirt. A little cleaning would remove the cobwebs and old crates.

The chill and the dampness filled her pores. For a moment, she forgot why she was there.

Then the meow of the kitten penetrated the haze of memory and forced her to lift her feet, to move and find the source of the sound.

Wrapping her arms around her middle, Jillian shivered, going deeper into the basement. Something moved among the old boxes. Jillian fought the urge to jump up on one of the wooden crates, her mind conjuring images of giant rats. If there were giant rats, they could easily kill the kitten.

Jillian had a soft spot in her heart for kittens and puppies. She couldn't leave the animal in the basement. Not even for a night.

As she stepped away from the staircase, the dull yellow light flickered and suddenly blinked out, plunging her into a darkness so very deep, she couldn't see her hand in front of her face.

A soft click sounded above and what little light that had come from the open door above was erased.

Jillian screamed and spun toward the staircase, her pulse beating so fast it made her dizzy. Her chest seized and she couldn't drag in a breath to feed her airless lungs. With no sense of what was right or left, up or down, the ground seemed to rise up to greet her.

Armed with directions and a promise to be back with Miss Taylor by dinner, Chance set off. Lowering all his windows, he took the coastal highway back toward Cape Churn. In less than fifteen minutes, he was bumping along a gravel road, wondering if he'd taken the wrong turn.

Chance couldn't believe Molly's friend planned to live on a creepy, isolated road that had seen far better days maybe a century before. At the end of the road, the trees seemed to part and an old Victorian house appeared, tucked into a wooded glen. Like the road, the house had seen better days. The paint was peeling and a couple of the windows were broken. The yard hadn't been maintained and the porch sagged. A truck and trailer sat in front of the dilapidated structure, the doors wide-open.

Chance parked his SUV beside the truck and climbed down. His feet had barely touched the ground when he heard the scream. At first he thought it was a figment of his imagination. The setting was perfect for a horror story; perhaps his mind had conjured a muffled scream to add to the ambience.

"Miss Taylor?" Chance called out.

No response.

He climbed the stairs and entered through the open front door, treading softly, holding his breath and listening for any sound.

Nothing moved. The old house didn't even creak, as if it, too, held its breath. Chance passed through the wide center hallway all the way to the back of the house, peering through the open doors into what appeared to be a living room, study and dining room. At the other end of the house, he emerged onto the back porch. Lumber lay in neat piles against the side of the house. But there was no one around.

Chance's gut tightened. Molly's friend wouldn't have abandoned her truck, leaving the truck doors and the trailer wide-open.

He returned to the entrance and climbed the stairs to the second story. Cobwebs hung from the corners and the wooden floors were covered in a thick layer of dust. This home hadn't been lived in for a very long time.

After determining each room was empty, Chance returned to the first floor, passed a stack of clean white drywall leaning against a wall in the living room and entered an old-fashioned kitchen. Some of the upper cabinets had been ripped from the walls, and the countertop had been removed from the lower cabinets, making their remains appear skeletal.

"Miss Taylor?" Chance called out.

A plaintive, bleating cry of a small animal, muffled by walls, reached him, and he turned toward a door at the far end of the kitchen.

Chance twisted the knob. The door didn't budge. Inspecting the door, he noticed a rusty hook near the top, threaded through a metal eye loop. Forcing the hook out of the loop, he flung open the door and flipped the light switch. A yellow bulb blinked to life, illuminating a small portion of the stairs nearest him.

The weak cries of a tiny animal sounded again, only louder.

Chance descended the stairs, the pitiful amount of light diminished by the time he reached the bottom. In the gloom, he almost tripped over a pile of rags. When his toe connected with them, the rags moved and a low moan rose from the floor.

Chance dropped to his haunches, his vision adjusting to the darkness. A figure dressed in jeans and a faded plaid flannel shirt rolled over and light blue eyes stared up at him.

"Who are you?"

"Chance McCall. Molly and Nova sent me over. You must be Jillian Taylor." He scooped his hands beneath her, lifted her into his arms and rose with his burden.

She blinked and stared around the basement, her pale

blond hair tousled, strands falling across her forehead. "What happened?"

"I'd like to know that myself. But first, let's get you out of here." Chance started up the stairs.

"I can walk," she protested.

"Yeah, but if it's all right by you, I'd like to get you into the light without worrying about someone pushing you down the stairs again."

She shook her head, her silken hair brushing against his arm. "I wasn't pushed."

"No?"

Her frown deepened. "Why would you think that?"

At the top of the stairs, Chance set her on the dingy linoleum floor, keeping an arm around her waist to steady her. "If you weren't pushed, why was the hook engaged at the top of the door?" He tipped his head toward the hook.

Leaning against him, she glanced up at the door, her eyes widening. "Why would the hook be engaged? I was the only one in the house. All the workers left."

"That was my question."

"Maybe it fell into place when the door closed."

"Let's see…the door was closed, the hook engaged, and when I opened the door, the light was off. Are you telling me you turned off the light, as well? And if you weren't pushed down the stairs, you must have fallen."

"I didn't fall down the stairs." She pinched the bridge of her nose.

"Then why were you lying on the ground?"

She stared up at him. "I don't know."

"Well, one thing's for sure."

"What's that?"

"You can't stay here alone."

Jillian stiffened. "This is my house."

"Yeah, but something's not right here."

She glanced around as if still getting her bearings. "Some say it's haunted."

"And you?"

She shrugged. "I think it needs work, but it's my home."

"Lady, you're crazy. The best thing that could happen to this dump is to run a bulldozer over it."

Jillian's chin lifted. "That is not going to happen. I have workers scheduled to restore the house to its former glory. You wait. It's going to be beautiful."

Chance snorted. "It's your funeral."

"The only way I'm going to die in this house is from old age." She pushed away from him and headed back to the front of the house. "You can go back to the B and B. I don't need your help."

"Can a ghost help you unload that couch off the trailer?"

"No. But I'd dump the damned thing on the ground before I let you touch it."

Chapter 3

Anger forced back the last vestiges of the fuzzy gray mist that had clouded Jillian's head when Chance had found her lying on the basement floor. "Don't you have a bachelor party to plan?"

"I'm told you have everything to do with the wedding completely planned."

"I do."

"Good, because I came to help. Now stop being stubborn."

"I might be stubborn, but you are a jerk." She stepped through the open front door and marched down the steps. On the last one, the rotted board gave way. She pitched forward and would have landed on her face had Chance not been right behind her and caught her, pulling her back against his front. He wrapped his arms around her middle and held on.

Her pulse pounding, Jillian inhaled a long, steadying breath. Then she pried the arms from around her. "Thank you," she said grudgingly. "But I still don't need your help."

"Maybe you don't, but I'm not leaving without you. So while I'm here, you might as well let me help you carry that couch."

She'd had two high school boys help her load the couch from her apartment into the trailer. The best she could do by herself would be to scoot it to the edge of the trailer and dump in on the ground. Alone, she'd never get it up the porch stairs and into the house. Even with a hand truck, she wouldn't be able to get it through the door. God, she hated letting Chance help. After he'd called her stubborn and said those awful things about her house, she really disliked the man.

"Okay. But just the couch," she muttered.

Together, they lifted the couch out of the trailer and carried it up the porch steps.

Jillian lost her grip twice on the heavy piece of furniture and had to stop. By the time they had it in the house, her back hurt. When they finally got it to the back of the house, Jillian was questioning the couch's very existence. Why hadn't she sold it in a yard sale rather than move it?

With the couch shoved up against a wall in the room at the back of the house Jillian had designated to store all her boxes and furniture, she straightened, pressing a hand to the small of her aching back.

Chance stared across the sofa at her. "Why were you in the basement?"

Jillian closed her eyes, trying to remember why she'd gone down there in the first place. When it came to her, she opened her eyes wide. "I heard a kitten." She spun on her heels and hurried to the kitchen.

"No way." Chance caught up with her before she reached the basement door. "You're not going down there."

"But I heard a kitten. It might have been separated from its mother. I couldn't leave it down there."

"Then let me look for it." Chance stepped in front of her, blocking her path. "You don't need to fall down the stairs a second time."

"I didn't fall," she insisted.

"Okay, so you didn't fall. You were just taking a nap on the floor when I found you."

Jillian hiked her brows. "The kitten?"

"Promise you'll stay put?"

She glared at him.

He didn't budge.

At that moment, the animal's cries sounded from the darkness.

"Okay," Jillian said. "I promise to stay here. Now, will you go?"

He grinned for the first time since they'd met. The expression lightened his face and made her heart flutter. When he wasn't scowling, Chance was an incredibly attractive man.

She shook herself, pushing back that errant thought.

When he turned toward the stairs, her breath caught and she blurted, "Wait."

"Why?"

Jillian didn't answer. She spun and raced out the front door, dived into the passenger side of Dave's truck and retrieved the flashlight she'd seen on the rear floorboard.

Back into the house she skidded to a stop in front of Chance, breathing hard.

"Here." She grabbed his hand and slapped the flashlight into his open palm.

"Thank you." He closed his fingers around the light and squeezed her hand. Then he disappeared into the basement's shadows, the beam of the flashlight marking his course.

Jillian stood at the top of the stairs, her throat tight, her breathing ragged.

She found herself praying he would hurry. "You sure you don't want me to help?"

"You promised to stay up there."

"Yeah, but two could find the kitten faster."

"And if a ghost locks the door again, who would rescue the both of us?"

Jillian bit down on her retort. "There are no such things as ghosts."

"Then explain the hook," Chance's disembodied voice said from the darkness.

She couldn't, so she remained quiet in the kitchen, throwing a glance over her shoulder every so often as chills rippled down her spine. She didn't believe in ghosts, but she couldn't help feeling she was being watched.

A miniature, snarling whine echoed off the walls below.

"Come here, you little poltergeist," Chance muttered.

More spats from the kitten were followed by a hearty curse.

"Damn it!"

A minute later, a light shone at the bottom of the stairs. Chance started up with a bundle of rags in one hand, the flashlight in the other. "I found one of your ghosts."

Jillian reached for the wriggling wad of cloth.

"Careful," Chance said. "He's got some sharp claws."

A small gray head poked out of the fabric and big blue eyes shone up at her.

Jillian gathered the cloth-wrapped kitten in her hands and carried him into the evening light streaming in through the dirty back window. Once she unwrapped the feline, she could see the animal was scrawny, underweight and malnourished. "Ah, poor baby. Where's your mama?"

"Poor baby?" Chance snorted. "He nearly scratched my eyes out. Just like a cat. Try to help one, and what do you get? Mauled."

Jillian rolled her eyes in his direction. "Really?" His laughing eyes made her heartbeat stutter. Then she saw the line of red across his cheek. "Oh, dear, he did get you good." The kitten curled into Jillian's hands. "Come out to the truck. I have a fresh bottle of water, and I know where to find my box of towels."

"Point me in the right direction. I'm not sure I trust either one of you at this point." He led the way through the house and held the door for her as she carried the kitten through.

"I gave you the option of leaving," she reminded him.

He shook his head. "Not an option. Too dangerous for a lone woman."

Her shoulders stiffened. "I'm going to live here eventually." She deposited the kitten, rags and all, on the front seat of Dave's truck and retrieved the bottle of water in the console. "By myself." When she straightened, she was startled by how close Chance stood. She froze, her breath hitching in her lungs.

Chance took the bottle but didn't move away, effectively trapping her between the truck door and his body. "Preferably after you've had good dead-bolt locks and a security system installed."

"Ha." Jillian swallowed hard and lifted her chin. "My money might last through new dead-bolt locks, but if the choice comes between running water and a security system, I'd prefer to bathe indoors, thank you very much."

Chance's gaze captured hers for a long moment, and then the corners of his lips quirked upward. "Despite being a pain in the butt, you're kind of cute when you're passionate about your water." He chucked her beneath her chin like a kid sister and stepped back.

Jillian dragged in a steadying breath and closed the truck door to keep the kitten inside. She rounded to the other side and closed the driver's side, glad for a few seconds to gather her scattered wits. By the time she met Chance at the back of the open trailer, she was well in control. Jillian refused to let the arrogant man get under her skin again. Whether it was his high-handedness or when he softened and called her cute, she couldn't afford to let him shift her focus from all that had to be done.

Yet his mere presence with his broad shoulders and ruggedly handsome face made it hard for her to concentrate. What had she been doing?

Chance held up the water bottle. "If you'll point to the box, I'll find a towel."

She turned away from his laughing gaze as heat filled her cheeks. Damn the man. Jillian studied the neatly stacked boxes containing all of her worldly goods, some of them items her mother had treasured. "There." She

pointed to a box. "The one marked Bathroom Towels."
When she backed away, she bumped into Chance and
almost tripped over his feet.

He gripped her arm and steadied her. "Are you all
right?"

"I'm fine."

"Maybe you should see a doctor. You could have suffered a concussion in your fall down the stairs."

"I didn't fall down the stairs." She pressed to his chest,
trying to establish her balance. "I must have passed out."

"All the more reason to see the doctor."

"I don't have time to visit a doctor, and I feel just
fine." If fine was finding it hard to breathe with the man
standing so near. She tipped her head toward the truck.
"Could you get the box down?"

He held her a moment longer and she didn't breathe
until he finally let go. "Hang on to this." He handed her
the water bottle and climbed into the trailer, found the
box and carried it to the porch.

Jillian stood back, wondering what the hell was wrong
with her.

Chance pulled a fancy knife from his pocket, unfolded
a blade and slit through the tape securing the box. Inside
was a stack of freshly laundered towels.

Pulling herself together, Jillian hurried forward, se-
lected a cloth and opened the bottled water.

Chance held out his hand. "I can take care of it myself."

"No, let me. I made you go back in after the kitten."

"Yeah, but I would have gone in whether you asked
me to or not."

She wet the cloth and capped the bottle, setting it to
the side. Now she had to touch the man who'd stirred up

so many emotions since finding her in the basement. The smart thing to do would be to hand him the cloth and let him take care of his own injury. But now that she'd insisted, she had to follow through. If she treated him like a client injured on a tour of one of her home listings, she shouldn't have a problem. Squaring her shoulders, she set her jaw and commanded, "Sit."

Chance responded to the command in her voice, though he almost laughed out loud at the play of emotions crossing Jillian's face. "Yes, ma'am." He dropped down onto a porch step.

Jillian settled on one riser higher and touched the damp cloth to his cheek. "This might hurt a little," she said, leaning close.

"I've had worse injuries in the war." More than he could count. As an army ranger, scrapes, broken bones, concussions, shrapnel and gunshot wounds were expected.

As she moved nearer, the scent of herbal shampoo filled his nostrils and made him want to pull Jillian into his lap to explore further.

"That's right. You're Nova's friend from the military."

He dipped his head.

"Do you work with the same organization Nova works with now?" Jillian cupped the back of his head and gently dabbed at the kitten's mark.

With her hand tickling the nape of his neck and her breast pressing into his arm, Chance could barely breathe. "I do."

"What exactly is it you do?" She rinsed the cloth with more water and squeezed out the excess moisture.

"Whatever is needed," Chance responded, his voice

tight, desire pressing hard against the fly of his jeans. Thankfully, he didn't have to go into detail about his job. Much of what he did with Stealth Operations Specialists was classified and only those with a need to know were given the details of any operation.

Her lips twisted. "Let me guess, if you tell me what you do—"

"I'd have to kill you." He captured her wrist in his hand. "I think you've done enough. We should finish the work and get back to the B and B."

Jillian stared into his eyes.

A few short inches separated them, but all Chance could think about was her pretty pink mouth and what she might taste like if he dared kiss her.

Jillian ran her tongue around those pink lips, sending Chance's control flying.

"Do you realize how crazy you're making me?"

She shook her head, her eyes rounding. Her gaze shifted to his mouth.

Like a moth drawn to the flame, Chance couldn't resist the temptation. He slipped his hand beneath her hair at the back of her head and dragged her forward until their lips almost touched. "Tell me to stop and I will," he breathed, praying she wouldn't when the temptation to kiss her threatened to overwhelm him.

Jillian closed the distance between them, her lips brushing his. They were so soft, full and luscious. Chance increased the pressure on the back of her neck and claimed her mouth, tonguing the seam of her lips until she opened to him.

He swept in, caressing her tongue in a long, slow glide. She tasted of mint and chocolate—sweet, decadent and undeniably irresistible.

Jillian dropped the cloth on the step beside him and ran her hand up the front of his chest, linking it with the other behind his neck. She pressed her breasts against him, stirring an ever-deepening hunger inside.

Chance pulled her across his lap without breaking the kiss, drowning in the touch, taste and feel of her body pressed to his.

A loud crash sounded inside the house, bursting through the cocoon of lust surrounding them.

Chance ducked, his pulse leaped, and he would have flattened himself to the ground, but with Jillian across his lap, that wasn't an option.

Jillian squealed and pushed to her feet.

Chance rose as well, his attention on the house.

"Stay here," he said.

"Staying," she agreed.

His heart hammering from his close encounter with Jillian, Chance ran into the house. With a quick sweep of the rooms on the first floor, Chance located the source of the sound. A four-by-eight-foot sheet of drywall lay on the floor of the living room, having fallen from the stack leaning against the wall.

Chance lifted it and leaned it with the others. When he'd passed the stack before, the individual sheets had seemed to be leaning at an angle so they wouldn't easily fall. A gust of wind would not have been enough to push over one of the heavy drywall sheets. He glanced around, his gaze going to the dusty wooden floor.

There were several sets of footprints overlaying each other from where he, Jillian and the workers had all passed. Was there someone else in the house? Someone who could have slipped the hook in the loop on the cellar door and knocked one of the drywall sheets to the ground? Chance didn't like it. Something didn't feel right in his gut. And his gut was seldom wrong.

He walked back out to the porch, where Jillian stood, her hair rumpled and her lips swollen from their kiss.

"Find anything?"

"A sheet of drywall fell over." He didn't go any deeper. He could be wrong. "I set it upright."

She clapped her hands together. "In that case, let's get going."

"Right. This stuff isn't moving itself. And we need to get back to the McGregor B and B."

Jillian smiled. "Exactly. If we're late, Molly will send her brother, a member of the Cape Churn Police Department, to check on us."

Chance got to work. He wanted to get done and get back before dark—and before something else happened in Jillian's haunted house.

Chapter 4

Jillian's back ached and she counted the minutes until she could take a pain pill and crawl into bed. But she had to take the trailer back to town, drop it off and then go to the B and B where Molly kept supper for her and Chance.

Though thankful for his help, she wasn't sure she should be thankful for the kiss. Working side by side, bumping into each other in the confines of the trailer and the small room where her things would be stored had been near torture. Every time they touched, a shower of sparks set off an electrical current inside her.

Chance's broad shoulders took up a lot of space and were hard to avoid. When they carried the last two boxes into the house, she practically threw hers down. "Well, that does it." She brushed the dust from her hands and glanced at Chance. "You can head back to the B and B. I have to drop off the trailer and return the truck to my friend."

"I'll go with you," he said.

Jillian's heart did a double backflip. "That's not necessary. I'm sure you're tired from your flight and all the work you got wrangled into. I can manage it on my own."

"Just the same, I'll go with you and do the driving. Since you can't seem to recall falling down the stairs, I don't feel comfortable letting you drive."

"I told you, I didn't fall down the stairs."

"Doesn't matter. If you can't remember why you ended up lying on the floor of the basement, I have to assume you were unconscious at some point." He held out his hand. "The keys?"

She opened her mouth to continue the argument. One look at the determined set of Chance's rock-hard jaw and Jillian snapped her mouth shut. With a frustrated sigh, she turned toward the truck. "The keys are in the ignition." She climbed into the passenger side and fished the kitten out from under the seat, holding it against her chest like a shield.

Chance slipped into the driver's seat.

"What about your vehicle?" Jillian asked.

"It'll be here in the morning."

She frowned. His response implied that he would be there in the morning, as well. Something told her she'd do well to keep her distance from Nova's best man. All that testosterone and those hunky muscles could derail a girl weaker than she. Butterflies fluttered against the walls of her belly. Okay, so she wasn't so strong against an extraordinary specimen like Chance.

Jillian had been around a few of the Stealth Operations Specialists who'd moved to the area. Each one had improved the scenery—Nova with his dark, exotic looks, and Creed Thomas with his Native American high cheekbones and solid strength, were both forces to be reckoned with. Even Nicole Steele, or Tazer, as they lovingly nicknamed her, was kick-ass, with years of experience making her as much of a lethal weapon as Creed and Nova. Now Chance...

Jillian pulled at the collar of her plaid shirt, the interior of the truck suddenly too warm. "How long will you be staying?"

"Until after the wedding. Maybe longer."

Jillian swallowed hard on a groan. "Are you staying in one of the cottages?" She crossed her fingers the way she had when she was a little girl, hoping he'd say yes. If she was staying at the B and B and Chance was, too, what was the possibility of avoiding him?

Slim to none. Then again, he was the best man in the wedding she was planning.

"I'm staying at the B and B."

It was her luck. At least she'd only be there until the plumber got the water running and the electrician finished the rewiring. Hopefully, that would only be a couple more days. She could live with the dust and clutter of demolition and the rebuilding effort. Besides, Molly and Nova needed all the space they could get for Nova's family members.

As they entered town, Jillian pointed to Runyan's Convenience Store and Gas Station. "This is where I drop the trailer, and I'd like to put gas in the truck before I return it to its owner."

Chance turned in to the parking lot and backed the trailer in between other rental trailers parked at the rear of the building.

Jillian's lips twisted. "If I had parked the trailer, it would have taken a lot longer. I'm not that adept at maneuvering trailers, or driving trucks for that matter." She gave him a smile. "Thank you."

"Just trying to help. Seems like you've bit off more than a mouthful with the wedding and a total house renovation all at once."

She nodded. "I've been planning this wedding for more than a year. The house was an opportunity that just came up, and I jumped on it."

"Why that particular house? Why not something closer to town? Something that doesn't need so many repairs?"

Jillian pushed open her door and dropped down from the truck. Everyone she knew had asked the same question. Lately, she'd asked herself the same as the bills mounted and the work seemed to take forever. She met Chance at the tailgate.

While Chance unhooked the lights and hitch, Jillian stroked the kitten and thought about her answer to his questions.

"I've been in Cape Churn for two years. I didn't plan on moving from Portland, but a weekend getaway turned into a move to live here. Something about Cape Churn called to me." She shrugged. "Instinct or gut feeling, it was like coming home. I've been renting ever since, waiting for the right house."

"Doesn't make sense to rent."

"Tell me about it. And I'm a real estate agent." She laughed. "Trust me, I thought I'd seen every house in Cape Churn and the surrounding area. Somehow I'd missed this one. The bank called, wanting me to list it. They'd been sitting on it for years and were tired of paying the taxes. When I came out to see it, I fell in love with the place. Like Cape Churn, it called to me." Jillian shrugged. "That's why I bought it. I know it sounds silly and maybe a little superstitious, but sometimes you have to go with your gut."

"Yeah." Chance straightened, his lips thinning into a line, his jaw tight. "Is there some paperwork you have to sign?" he said, his voice clipped, his whole attitude changing from casual curiosity to rigid and dark.

"What?" Jillian stared at him. "Was it something I said?"

He shook his head. "No. We just need to get back to the B and B."

"Give me a minute to fill up the tank and I'll be ready to go."

"I'll get it." Chance didn't give her the chance to climb into the truck. He was in and driving around to the pumps before she could form a protest.

What the hell had happened to make him suddenly so closed off and angry?

Jillian shook her head and followed the truck on foot.

Bud Runyan, the owner of the gas station, stepped out of the building. "Miss Taylor, I expected you to use that trailer for at least another day."

She smiled at the gray-haired man with the grizzled beard and deep-set wrinkles. "I expected to use it for another day, too." Jillian tipped her head toward Chance. "I was fortunate to enlist help in unloading."

Mr. Runyan's eyes narrowed. "This your boyfriend from Portland?"

Jillian didn't remind Mr. Runyan she'd been there over two years and rarely went back to Portland. If she'd had a relationship, it would have long since disintegrated. "No, sir. Chance is here for the wedding."

Chance parked the truck at the pumps.

Mr. Runyan beat him to the nozzle and started the flow of gasoline into the tank. "I take it you didn't have any more luck talking Miss Taylor out of moving into the old Thompson house?"

Chance shook his head. "I didn't know I was supposed to talk her out of anything."

The older man leaned his back against the truck. "That house has been empty for a reason."

"What reason?" Jillian asked.

Before Mr. Runyan could answer, a four-door sedan pulled up and an older woman with salt-and-pepper hair unfolded from her sedan. She was about the same height as Jillian and, despite her age, appeared capable of bench-pressing a refrigerator.

"Good evening, Mrs. Sims." Mr. Runyan pushed away from the truck and walked to the other side of the pump.

Mrs. Sims nodded to Mr. Runyan. "Bud."

"Fill 'er up?" he asked.

"Yes. Thank you." Mrs. Sims dug in her purse for her wallet. "Good evening, Miss Taylor. I hear you bought the old Thompson place in the woods."

"I did." Jillian braced herself for yet another person telling her what a mistake she'd made.

"Personally, I'm glad the old place is getting a makeover. All that nonsense about it being haunted is ridiculous."

Jillian released the breath she hadn't even realized she was holding. "Thank you. You're the first person who hasn't tried to talk me out of it."

The older woman snorted. "Wouldn't do that. All that work you're doing to restore the building is keeping my son employed."

Jillian thought she knew everyone in Cape Churn. "Your son?"

"Daryl."

Jillian smiled. "Oh, yes. Daryl's helping out."

Mrs. Sims nodded. "He's working with the contractor. They've been involved in the demolition so far."

"Still think you're courtin' disaster with that old house. Nothing good ever happened out there," Mr. Runyan muttered.

Jillian planted her fists on her hips. "Everyone is quick to believe in ghosts and hauntings. What concrete things have happened in that house that inspires all those tales?"

Mr. Runyan glanced across at Mrs. Sims. "What was it, fifteen or twenty years ago when that little girl disappeared?"

Mrs. Sims lips tightened. "Something like that. I still think her mother had something to do with that. Especially since they found the girl a month later."

Jillian's breath caught. "Found? As in dead?"

Mr. Runyan shoved a hand through his wiry white hair. "That was the dangedest thing. She appeared as suddenly as she disappeared, with no memory of where she'd been or what had happened."

A chill slipped down the back of Jillian's neck. "Did she live in the house?"

Mr. Runyan nodded. "It was her and her mother. Her father lived in town. They'd recently divorced. He'd lost his job, started drinkin', and the wife wouldn't put up with it. She kicked him out. Anyway, the girl probably got lost."

"Or maybe she was mad about the divorce and ran away," Mrs. Sims said.

"For a month?" Chance asked. "How old was she?"

"Nine," Bud answered.

Jillian wasn't buying it. "A nine-year-old ran away and survived on her own for a month? Doubtful."

The older woman raised her hands, palms up. "Since she wasn't talking when she reappeared, no one knows what happened."

"And never will." Mr. Runyan topped off the truck's tank and hung up the nozzle. "Her mother packed her up and left the house, the town and the state, for all anyone knows. She and her daughter haven't been heard from since."

Jillian dug in her purse for the correct amount of money and handed it to Mr. Runyan. "Why hasn't any of this come up before?"

Mr. Runyan took the money from Jillian. "When Mrs. Thompson and her daughter left, I suppose people forgot."

"No use living in the past," Mrs. Sims said. "And there's no such thing as ghosts, so don't you worry about any of that. I'd love to see the house when you get done with the remodeling effort." The woman turned toward her car. "What do I owe you, Bud?"

Jillian climbed into the passenger seat of the truck, adjusted her seat belt and lifted the kitten onto her lap while Chance slipped behind the wheel.

Without a word, he started the truck and pulled to the edge of the road. "Which way?"

After giving him the directions to the marina, Jillian texted Dave to let him know they were on their way, and then she leaned back against the seat and stared out at the darkening sky. With the streetlights coming on, the stars were hard to see. That was one of the things she looked forward to when her house was finished—being able to gaze up at the sky at night and see the blanket of stars spread out in the heavens.

"Does it worry you at all that your house has a history?" Chance asked.

Jillian drew in a breath and let it out again before answering. "People are afraid of things they don't understand."

"Meaning?"

"Meaning, I need to do a little digging to find out what all the fuss is about."

Chance's lips quirked upward. "And if there was a missing girl and the house is haunted, then what?"

"Then I will at least know the truth from an old wives' tale. By the time the contractors are finished remodeling my house, no one will remember it as the place where something bad happened, and the ghosts will love it so much, they'll leave me alone. Who knows, if there are such things as ghosts, they might be mad because the place has been left to deteriorate."

Granted, she didn't believe in ghosts or places being bad. People were bad. Not places. And since she'd bought the house and planned on living in it, she refused to believe differently. A cool draft found its way into the interior of the truck, stirring the fine hairs on the back of Jillian's neck, and she shivered.

Chance shot a smile at Jillian. The woman was so feminine, yet she had a solid core and seemed perfectly capable of taking care of herself. "Nothing much scares you, does it?"

"Nope." She crossed her arms over her chest and tipped her chin. "I've been on my own for a few years.

My mother made sure I was trained in self-defense, and I'm a black belt in tae kwon do. People should be afraid of *me*."

Chance held up his hand, schooling his face to be dead serious. "I'm shaking in my boots." Then he couldn't hold back the chuckle, ruining the effect. "Sorry. You don't look very intimidating."

"Well, I am." She glared at him, though a smile tugged at the corners of her mouth. "A black belt, that is."

"I believe you." Chance pulled into the marina parking lot.

Jillian pointed. "Park near the dock."

Following her directions, he pulled into a parking space and turned off the engine. By the time he got out and rounded to the other side of the truck, Jillian was already out, the kitten in her hands, and was walking toward the long wooden wharf.

A tall, muscular man stepped out of a houseboat and waved. He crossed the dock and walked up the hill toward them, wearing sweatpants and a sweatshirt with Georgetown University embroidered on the front. "I didn't expect you back with my truck until tomorrow."

Jillian handed him the keys and hugged him. "I had help to unload, so it took half the time." She turned to Chance. "Chance, this is Dave Logsdon. Dave, Chance McCall."

Dave extended a hand and Chance took it. The man had a strong grip and a tattoo on his forearm.

"Prior military?" Chance asked.

"Army."

Chance nodded. "Same."

"Deployed?" Dave asked.

"Four times."

Dave held up three fingers. "Three." He dug in his pocket and pulled out a set of car keys. As he handed them to Jillian, he asked Chance, "Action?"

"More than I cared for."

Dave stared at Chance for a long moment.

Chance returned the stare, unwaveringly.

Finally, the tension left Dave's stance and he jerked his head to the side. "Care for a beer?"

"Would love one, but I'm supposed to deliver Miss Taylor to the B and B for dinner. We're running short on time."

"Gotcha." Dave turned to Jillian. "Everything all right at the house?"

She held the kitten beneath her chin and smiled. "Things are moving along."

Chance wondered why she didn't mention she'd passed out at the bottom of the basement steps and the basement door had been locked from the other side—and she had no idea how she'd gotten that way.

"Glad to hear you found a crew to work it. Let me know if you need anything." Dave hugged her and kissed her forehead.

A rush of heat feathered across Chance's cheeks. The longer Dave held Jillian, the warmer Chance grew. And his gut knotted. It was as if he was jealous of the other man. But then, how could that be, when he'd only known the pretty real estate agent for a few hours?

Dave glanced across at Chance. "Looking forward to that beer."

Chance muttered something, but a second later couldn't recall what he'd said.

Jillian led the way to a four-wheel-drive Jeep, opened the driver's door and got in.

Chance slipped into the passenger seat, his gaze on Dave as the man strode across the dock and entered the houseboat. "Does he live there?"

Jillian handed the kitten to Chance. "The outside looks like hell, but he refinished the inside."

Holding the tiny feline in his hand, he stroked its fur. "Are you two together?" As soon as the question was out of his mouth, he wished he could take it back. It wasn't any of his business, nor did he have a stake in the Jillian game since he had no plan to form any kind of relationship with her or anyone else. Still, he had a burning desire to know more about this woman who wasn't too terribly concerned about passing out on the floor of a basement.

She laughed. "Oh, goodness, no." Jillian shifted into Reverse and turned the Jeep around. "He's in love with Nicole Steele." Jillian glanced across at Chance. "You might know her. She works for the same organization as you and Nova."

"Ah, yes, I've run into her a couple times in the Virginia office." He pulled his gaze away from Jillian and reengaged his brain cells. "I haven't been with them long."

"She's supposed to come to the wedding. But, like you, we won't know until she shows up."

Chance snorted. "That about sums up my life. I'm glad I could be here for Nova."

"I know he was sweating it. What about you? Are you bringing a date to the wedding? Do I need to set another plate at the main table?" She didn't glance away from the road.

"No." Chance hadn't dated anyone on a long-term basis since he was in the army. Relationships didn't last when one of the parties involved was deployed more than he was home. Since he'd joined SOS, he saw no need to change his single status.

Jillian smiled. "Good to know." She navigated through Cape Churn, her confidence obvious in the directions she took and the smooth way she made the turns.

By the time they were on the highway to the Mc-Gregor Bed-and-Breakfast, Chance had settled back against the leather seat, his gaze straying to Jillian. "Have you always been a real estate agent?"

She shot a glance his way. "When I finished college with a marketing degree, the jobs just weren't available in Portland. So I put my marketing degree to work on creating ads for a real estate firm. Did the training, got my license and voilà! I've been doing it ever since."

"I'll bet you're good at it."

She tipped her chin, her cheeks darkening with a blush in the light from the dash. "I am. I have a knack for finding just the right house for my clients. Granted, the market was much larger and more lucrative in Portland than in Cape Churn, but I like it better here."

Once they left town, the road ahead climbed, twisted and turned around the cliffs hugging the coastline. When Chance had arrived earlier, he could see the water, the rocks below and the horizon. Now the darkness was also shrouded by fog, creeping in from the ocean.

Jillian slowed. "The fog's getting thick. The weatherman predicted a devil's shroud night."

"Devil's shroud?" Chance asked.

"That's what they call the thick fogs that roll into Cape Churn. I think it makes it sound mysterious. Just another thing to love about this place."

"You love a place that calls a dense fog the devil's shroud?"

"It's kind of creepy, but still adds to the ambience of the area."

As that aptly named fog thickened, the Jeep careened around a bend in the road. Chance gripped the armrest with one hand, clutched the kitten with the other and dug his foot into the floorboard, aiming for a brake that wasn't there. "Shouldn't you go a little slower?"

"Oh, sorry. I know the roads really well, but the fog is getting pretty thick." She eased up on the accelerator and continued through the haze.

At one point they rounded a curve carved out of the side of a cliff. Something big crashed onto the road and rolled in front of them.

Jillian yelped, swerved and slammed on her brake just in time to keep from falling off the edge of the road.

"Are you all right?" Chance asked, peeling the kitten's claws out of his shirt and skin.

For a long moment, Jillian didn't respond. Finally, she said, "I'm okay." She turned to Chance. "What was that?"

"I don't know, but let me take a look." He climbed out of the Jeep and checked the road in the area. He found a boulder the size of big watermelon on the edge of the road ahead. When he got back to the Jeep, Jillian stood at the edge of the cliff.

Seeing her so close to the drop-off made Chance nervous. He circled her waist with his arm and eased her back. "Do you want me to drive?"

"I can do it," she said, but her body trembled and her gaze remained on the edge of the cliff. "If we hadn't stopped we'd have hit that boulder or…"

"But you did stop and we didn't do either." He turned her to face him and brushed a strand of her silky blond hair back from her cheek. "Come on. Molly was making fresh bread. I haven't had fresh bread since…well, hell. I don't think I've ever had fresh bread. Mom wasn't much of a cook because she worked full-time."

He guided her back to the Jeep and settled her in the passenger seat. Then he took the wheel and eased away from the cliff and back onto the right side of the road. The rest of the trip was completed in silence, with Chance focusing all of his attention on what little he could see of the road in front of him.

Devil's shroud was an accurate description of the fog. But what had been the white aberration that had nearly caused them to fly off the edge of the cliff?

Chapter 5

Jillian had almost stopped shaking by the time they pulled into the parking area in front of the McGregor mansion Molly and her brother, Gabe, had converted into a bed-and-breakfast. The wide front porch and the lights glowing from inside warmed her and made her eager to get out of the Jeep and into the house.

She liked the mystery of the devil's shroud and respected the danger involved, but she'd never had something drop out of the fog in front of her when she'd been driving. Jillian knew that section of the road. If she had driven off the cliff, they would have died the instant they hit the rocks two hundred feet below. A shudder rippled through her, and she hugged the kitten closer. "Poor baby," she cooed softly, stroking the animal's fur.

Chance shifted the Jeep into Park, got out and opened her door for her before she could unwind the clingy kitten from her hand.

Jillian stepped out of the Jeep and stumbled.

Chance looped an arm around her waist and clutched her to him. "I gotcha."

She laid a hand on his chest, the kitten pressed between them in her other hand.

"Are you okay?" he asked.

Jillian looked up at him; the light from the porch reflected in his eyes made her knees weaker. "Yes. I guess I'm just a little tired."

He brushed his knuckles against her cheek. "You've had an interesting day."

His hand was warm on her skin, making tingles spread throughout her body. "I have. Thank you for all the help."

"My pleasure." He stared into her eyes, his arm tightening around her waist.

When he leaned toward her, Jillian thought he might kiss her again.

"I can stand on my own now," she whispered, then her gaze shifted to his mouth.

All coherent thought deserted her head. When his head lowered more, Jillian rose up on her toes, her lips drawn inescapably to his.

"There you are," Nova's voice called out. "Molly just sent me out to find you and bring you back before her clam chowder gets cold."

Chance stepped back, dropping his arms to his sides.

Jillian swayed toward him, then straightened, remembering where she was. She turned toward Nova with a strained smile. "Sorry we took so long. Since we got everything out of the trailer, I thought it best to return it to Mr. Runyan. Which meant taking the truck back to Dave."

"I'm not worried, but Molly might have a heart attack if we don't stick to the schedule."

"I will not." Molly emerged from the house and swatted Nova's arm. "I'm absolutely flexible…as long as everything is going according to plan."

Nova laughed and pulled his fiancée into his arms, planting a loud kiss on her lips. "Now that everyone is here, can we eat?"

"The truth comes out. He was coming to look for you because he was hungry, not because I sent him after you." Molly winked. "The table is set. I could use help bringing everything out."

Jillian loved the way Nova and Molly sparred, laughing and picking, with their love shining from their eyes. She envied that deep, everlasting emotion, wishing she could find someone who made her feel that complete. With a sigh, she held up the kitten. "I'll help. But first I need to find a place for this guy."

"Oh, sweet heaven. Where did you find him?" Molly descended the steps and took the gray tabby kitten.

"He was in the basement of Jillian's house," Chance said.

A shiver rippled down Jillian's back as she recalled the stairs, the kitten calling to her and the light going out. No matter how hard she tried, she couldn't remember anything else until she woke to find Chance leaning over her. Though she hadn't let on that it bothered her, it did. That wasn't the first time she'd passed out in a stressful situation.

"What?" Molly lifted the kitten up in the air. "How did you find your way into Jillian's basement? Come on, we'll find a soft towel, a box and a bowl of milk for this little one."

"How about a bowl of soup for me?" Nova said.

"You can help carry the food out to the dining table. The other guests have already eaten and gone to their rooms, so it'll only be the four of us."

Jillian followed Molly into the house, through the living room and into the kitchen.

Molly found a box and an old towel in the pantry. She carried the kitten into the downstairs bathroom, gave it a bowl of warm milk and then settled it in the box. "I'd leave it loose, but I'm afraid it might get lost in this big old house."

"The bathroom should be fine for now. I'll take him to my bedroom later," Jillian said.

When Molly straightened, she grinned and touched Jillian's arm. "So, what did you think of Chance? He's gorgeous, isn't he?"

Heat rushed up Jillian's neck into her cheeks. "I don't know. He was helpful unloading all my things into the house." She didn't add, *And he rescued me from the basement and kissed me*. She wasn't ready to admit to having passed out in her own home, and she couldn't come up with a good reason for the latch being locked on the basement door. Molly would have her brother, Gabe, out to investigate before the chowder got cold on the table.

"Helpful?" Molly shook her head. "Well, I think it's about time you started dating. Before you know it all the good ones will be taken."

"Molly, we've been over this before. I'm not in the market for a man in my life. I'm too busy with my business, your wedding, my house and now a kitten. I don't have time to cater to anyone else."

"I'm sorry, Jill. If the wedding is too much for you to

handle at this point, I can take care of the rest. You have far too much on your plate."

"And you don't?" Jillian took her friend's hand. "I love planning your wedding. I'm so happy for you, I'd do it all again." She hugged Molly. "You really do love him, don't you?"

"With all my heart," she said, her voice choked with emotion.

"Then we better get out there before he starves to death. Can't have the groom dying of hunger a few days before the wedding."

"No, we can't." Molly skipped out of the bathroom.

Jillian lingered on her haunches beside the box. The kitten had filled his belly with milk and now circled on the towel before curling into a furry ball.

Like every young woman, Jillian dreamed of falling in love and living happily ever after with the man of her dreams. Only that man hadn't come along yet. Here she was, twenty-six years old and still single. An image of Chance leaning close to her, his mouth nearly touching hers, came to mind. God, she wanted to kiss him again. Like Molly said, he was gorgeous with his dark hair, sexy eyes and those broad shoulders a woman could really lean on.

"He seems to be happy," a deep, resonant voice said behind Jillian.

She started and fell back, landing on her bottom.

"I'm sorry. I thought you heard me walk up."

"No, I didn't." Jillian couldn't admit she'd been thinking about him and when they'd kissed.

He reached down and lifted her to her feet as if she weighed nothing, pulling her up to stand in the circle of his arm, confirming the muscles weren't just for show.

"I'm not always this awkward," she said. "Sometimes I can stay on my feet for an entire day. You can let me go. I promise, I can stand on my own, thank you."

"Humor me." His arms tightened around her. "I'm beginning to think I jinxed you."

She tilted her head and stared up into his eyes. "You know, you could be right. It wasn't until you showed up that I started having all these problems."

"I'd offer to leave, but I was asked to be in the wedding of my dear friend."

"Then we just have to survive together for another few days."

"I suppose I should let go of you," Chance said.

"You should."

"Although…I have the crazy urge to…"

Jillian's pulse raced and her breath caught in her throat. Without realizing it, she leaned up on her toes.

Then Chance sighed and straightened. "We'd better get to the dining room before Molly and Nova come looking for us."

To hell with Molly and Nova!

Chance took her hand in his and drew her out of the bathroom, closing the door behind him. Then he led her back to the safety of the dining room, where Molly and Nova were wrapped in each other's arms, kissing.

Chance cleared his throat.

The happy couple broke apart, laughing.

"Sorry, we didn't hear you coming," Molly said, smoothing back her hair. "Shall we?" She motioned to the table. Homemade bread, a tossed salad and a big tureen of soup filled the table.

Nova held out a hand. "Pass me your bowls, I'll fill them."

After everyone had been served, Jillian started off the conversation with, "I double-checked with the photographer. He's still on for the wedding and will be here two hours early with his team to photograph and film the bride and groom preparing for the nuptials."

Molly laughed. "Two hours?" She reached for Nova's hand. "We should have eloped, like I suggested."

Nova lifted her hand to his lips. "I wouldn't miss this part for anything. My mother and sisters will be in seventh heaven helping you get dressed and do your hair."

Molly closed her eyes. "I don't know. You and I have been so busy, we haven't had time to visit your family. What if they don't like me?"

Nova kissed her fingers. "What's not to like? They will love you because you are strong, beautiful and an amazing cook. *And* because they will love whoever makes me happy. *Mi amor*, you make me very happy."

"They'll love you, Molly," Jillian said. "Everyone loves you."

"I love all of you, too." Her cheeks flushing pink, Molly pulled her hand from Nova's and dipped her spoon in her chowder. As she lifted her spoon to her lips, she said, "Nora came out to the B and B today to bring me samples of the cakes she'll be baking for the wedding." She poked the spoon in her mouth.

"And?" Jillian prodded. "Did you decide on a flavor?"

Molly nodded, swallowing. "I'm going with the almond flavoring in the wedding cake and the fudge chocolate for the groom's cake. They were both to die for."

"Good." Jillian broke a roll in half and slathered it with butter, the warm, rich smell of fresh bread making her mouth water. "I only have to double-check with the florist and the party rental company to make sure they show up on time, early the morning of the wedding."

"You're too good to me. I couldn't have done this whole wedding thing without your help."

"How is Nora?" Jillian asked. "Did she get over her cold?"

"Yes, she's much better." Molly stirred the chowder in her bowl. "She's a little worried about you, though."

"Me?" Jillian frowned. "Why me?"

"Seems the whole town is a little worried about you." Molly smiled. "You've made quite the impression in the two years you've been in Cape Churn."

Jillian forgot about the roll in her hand. "Why are they worried?"

"Because of the house you bought." Molly handed the basket of rolls to Chance. "Have another."

He accepted, selecting one and setting the basket back on the table.

"It's just a house," Jillian said, defending her new home. "And I don't believe in ghosts."

"Nora said there was some trouble at that house almost twenty years ago. Something about a missing little girl."

"I've heard the tale." Jillian set the buttered roll on the plate beside her bowl, having suddenly lost her appetite. "I suppose I'll spend some time in the library looking up the history of the house and the town to put the story to rest."

Molly sighed. "You know how people can be superstitious. And I wouldn't have believed in ghosts if I hadn't had that experience here in the B and B during our annual ghost tour last year. It was just too real to discount."

"Well, I don't believe in ghosts." Jillian laid her napkin beside her plate and pushed back from the table. "Molly, the meal was wonderful, but I'm wiped out. I guess all the moving wore me out." She stood. "If you'll excuse me, I think I'll call it a night."

Molly stood. "I'm sorry if I upset you, Jillian."

Jillian smiled at her friend. "No, you didn't. I've heard the same story at least a half dozen times since I bought the house. I'm not worried about stories. I love the house, and I don't regret buying it. It'll be beautiful when I'm finished remodeling."

Molly hugged Jillian. "I'm sure it will. You have a keen eye for tasteful design. Get some rest, sweetie."

"Thank you." Jillian hugged Molly, feeling lucky to have such a good friend in a town where sometimes she was still considered an outsider. She hadn't grown up here, therefore she was a transplant.

She left the dining room, collected the kitten, box and all, and climbed the stairs to the room Molly had offered to let her stay in for the next couple of days until she had running water and electricity in her haunted house.

"Haunted." She stared down at the kitten in the box, curled up in a ball, lifting his sleepy head as if questioning her. "Don't look at me like that. I know what I'm doing. The house can't be blamed for what happened in or around it. It's just a house. You and I will bring it back to life and make it a happy home to live in. Just wait and see."

Jillian settled the box next to the white iron bed decorated with a beautiful, old-fashioned quilt. Then she gathered toiletries, her nightgown and robe, and walked down the hall to one of the shared bathrooms. Not all of the rooms had a connected bathroom. But Jillian wasn't picky. Having no home to go to, she was glad for a room in the B and B, where she could be close to Molly.

In the bathroom, Jillian locked the door, stripped out of her dusty clothes and stepped into the claw-foot bathtub. She loved how Molly had decorated with care, going with early-twentieth-century furnishings. Each bedroom had a brass, white iron or rich mahogany four-poster bed. The electricity and plumbing had been brought up to code during her remodel, but she'd used old-fashioned tile and bathroom fixtures to give the guests a feeling of entering a bygone century.

Jillian hoped to recreate similar decor in her home. She'd choose each piece of furniture with care. But first, she had to get the house livable. After sitting empty for seventeen years, it had quirks, like the bird nests they'd found in the attic and the kitten in the basement.

Standing in the warm spray, Jillian let the stress of the day wash down the drain. The house would be fine. The kitten would be a welcome companion, and the man she'd nearly kissed downstairs would be gone once the wedding was over.

No use getting excited about a man who wouldn't be around in less than a week. Never mind his broad shoulders, dark good looks and those incredibly blue eyes a woman could fall into and never want to come out of.

Jillian rinsed shampoo out of her hair and turned off the water. A good night's sleep would help her put thoughts of ghosts and one hunky man out of her mind. Determined to get back on track with all she had to accomplish in the next week, she dried off, combed the tangles out of her hair and slipped into her nightgown and robe.

She wished she'd brought one of her less revealing

robes instead of the one that matched the baby-doll night-gown beneath. Too much of her legs showed beneath the short, diaphanous robe.

With a sigh, she gathered her things and carefully balanced them while managing to unlock the door. Pushing it open with her hip, she backed out of the bathroom and into a solid wall of naked muscular chest.

The items she'd been carrying exploded out of her arms and scattered across the floor. Flustered, she bent to collect them, but strong, warm hands reached for them first, bumping into hers, sending little shock waves through her body.

"I didn't mean to startle you." He handed her a brush and her toiletries bag, holding on to her discarded clothing with one hand. With the other hand, he helped her to her feet, cinching her to his warm body until she had her balance.

Holy hell. He felt so good and smelled of the outdoors, naked skin and 100 percent male. Jillian's brain synapses fired off in every direction, scrambling her wits. "I'm okay," she said, more to ground herself than for him. She had to remind herself to breathe in and out.

So what if she stood in her short nightgown and robe, her legs visible from just below her bottom to her toes painted with pretty pink polish? She was wearing more than anyone would see in a bathing suit. And Chance… Holy hell, he looked so big, strong and handsome with all that lovely tanned skin stretched tight over incredibly solid muscles.

Short of breath, Jillian managed to push words past her vocal cords. "I was just finishing up. You can lay those across the rest." She held out her arms, mortified when she realized he was carrying not only her jeans and shirt, but her lacy black bra perched on top of the pile, in plain sight.

"I'll carry them. Which room?" He turned, as if looking for the right door.

With a silent groan of resignation, Jillian said, "Second on the right." Then she followed, her gaze drinking in every inch of his bare back, marked with a few disturbing scars that only managed to make him even sexier.

"Next door to mine," he commented as he walked to the door and reached for the crystal doorknob. He pushed the door open and stepped inside, filling the room with his size and presence.

Jillian stopped in the doorway, her mouth dry. Her tongue darted out to wet her lips. Seeing him wearing nothing but blue jeans and standing beside her bed made her knees weak.

Chance set her clothes on the bed, his fingers lingering on the black bra. When he turned to her, his blue eyes were a steely shade of gray, his face dark and brooding. His gaze slipped for a brief moment to the deep V of her filmy robe. "I hope you sleep well." Before Jillian could respond, Chance brushed past her, closing the door behind him.

What did he mean by *I hope you sleep well*? She felt as though a heated whirlwind had blown past her, leaving her hot, dry and in need. Of what, she didn't know.

Actually, she did, but she wasn't ready to admit she needed him. With every red blood cell in her body. She needed that man to come back into her room, take her into his arms and kiss her to show he meant it. Then kiss her again. Hell, he could have had her with just a crook of his finger.

Jillian went through the motions of patting the kitten,

turning back the covers and crawling into the antique bed. But sleep was the farthest thing from her mind. Not with Chance standing naked in the shower a few short steps down the hallway.

She listened, though she couldn't hear the shower. Eventually, a door opened and closed, and the wooden floors creaked ever so slightly outside her room.

Jillian held her breath, straining to hear the footsteps, but realized he'd been barefoot, just like her. She didn't hear the floorboards creak for a few long seconds, and then they sounded again, the creaking moving away from her door and farther down the hallway. A door opened and closed.

As tired and achy as she was, she willed her body to relax. Sleep would help fix what hurt and hopefully give her a fresh start in the morning, free of wickedly sexy thoughts concerning a certain groomsman.

Staring at the clock for an entire hour, her eyes remained wide-open, with not a hint of the fatigue she'd felt earlier. No matter how hard she tried, she wasn't going to force herself to go to sleep. Jillian gave up. Perhaps a cup of hot cocoa would help to settle her nerves and make her drowsy.

She threw back the covers and shivered at the chill in the air. Wrapping the worthless but sexy robe around her, she draped a hand-crocheted throw over her shoulders like a shawl and headed down the stairs for the kitchen.

Strategically placed night-lights illuminated her way on the steps and through the great room. In the kitchen, she switched on the light and rummaged through the cabinets until she found a mug and a package of pre-mixed hot cocoa powder. A minute in the microwave and she had a steaming cup to wrap her fingers around.

She was halfway across the great room when she decided going back to her room wasn't an option. The room was too small for an armchair. She'd have to sit on the bed and risk spilling chocolate on the beautiful quilt. The great room was cozy with the embers of the dying fire giving off a welcoming warmth and glow. Though it was tempting, Jillian had been feeling claustrophobic since her trip to the basement of her derelict house.

In need of air, she opted to go outside and sit on the wide front porch. There she wouldn't be reminded that Chance was on the other side of her bedroom wall, possibly sleeping naked.

Barefoot, she stepped out the front door and walked across the cool boards, which were damp with the heavy fog cocooning the B and B in darkness.

A single porch lamp gave just enough light to dispel the creepy, horror-movie feeling of the devil's shroud and illuminated the swing on one end of the long porch. Holding the warm mug between her hands, she settled on the swing, tucked her legs beneath her and wrapped the throw around her entire body as best she could with one hand.

When she'd shored up the gaps allowing cold air to touch her skin, she burrowed into the warmth and sipped the sweet cocoa, swaying back and forth with little effort.

She had to remember to save enough money to add a porch swing to her house. This was heaven, and so relaxing she could fall asleep out in the fog.

With no one to bother her, she forced thoughts of ghosts and Chance out of her mind and concentrated on how good the cocoa felt going down, warming her insides. She licked sweet chocolate from her lips, wondering what it would be like to have a man like Chance do the job for her.

Jillian closed her eyes and groaned. There she went again, thinking about a man who wasn't for her. The slight squeak of a hinge made her open her eyes.

The man she'd been trying to erase from her mind stood on the porch, as if conjured by her imagination.

Swallowing a curse, Jillian bit down on her tongue to keep from blurting out something utterly stupid.

He wore nothing but a pair of jeans, his hands dug into the pockets. He walked to the rail and leaned against one of the posts, staring out into the fog.

That was when Jillian realized he hadn't noticed her sitting in the swing at the end of the porch. She sat very still, studying every curve and edge of the man, hoping he'd go back inside without seeing her.

Chapter 6

After an hour of tossing and turning, jumping at every sound and lying in the dark, staring at nothing but reliving everything, Chance gave up. He was afraid to go to sleep. Afraid of going back into the same dreams that plagued him every night.

What he feared most was what he might do when caught in the throes of his nightmare battle. Would he wake up before he caused damage to the place, or before he hurt someone? When he'd still been on active duty and stuck in a barracks before going home, he'd woken up slugging the hell out of the guy who'd been sleeping in the rack below his. It took four men to pull him off and shake him awake. The man he'd beaten had been taken to the hospital, suffering a broken nose, a concussion and a broken rib. And he'd been a friend.

Granted, the nightmares still came, but the violent

reactions had dissipated. He hadn't hit a man in over a year. He had punched a couple of walls and a multitude of pillows, which indicated he still wasn't fit to sleep with anyone else in his room.

Tonight he'd dared to think about taking a woman to bed. Hell, he'd had sex since he'd deployed, but he hadn't stayed the night, hadn't allowed himself to fall asleep beside a woman.

He couldn't risk what might happen if he got caught up in another violent dream. Chance couldn't forgive himself for hitting a woman, even if he did it in his sleep.

When he'd run into Jillian in the hallway, he'd nearly lost his grasp on reason. She'd worn that incredibly sexy nightgown, displaying long, beautiful legs, and the mysterious and sexy swell of her breasts. Chance had almost thrown caution out the window.

He'd barely been able to stop himself from taking her into his arms and kissing her not once, but several times that evening. Though he'd kissed her at her house, he couldn't let it happen again. He was afraid he wouldn't stop at just a kiss. Jillian deserved a man who'd treat her right. Someone who didn't have a crap load of drama going through his head 24/7.

Unwilling to let himself sleep while Jillian lay in the room next to him, Chance had gotten out of his bed, pulled on his jeans and left the house. Out on the porch, he stared out into the fog, unable to see a single star. If it weren't so dangerous, he'd have gotten into his rental and driven until he was so tired he wouldn't have a chance to dream. Then he remembered—the SUV he'd rented was parked in front of Jillian's dilapidated house.

Metal scraped on metal nearby. Chance spun toward

the sound, dropping into a fighting crouch, his fists bunched, ready to throw the first punch.

A shadowy lump swayed on what appeared to be a porch swing at the end of the porch.

"Who's there?" he demanded.

Silence met his question, and then a soft whisper drifted across to him. "Me. Jillian."

His heart squeezed in his chest and his groin tightened as if that one word wrapped around him and constricted. *Walk away*, he said to himself. *Go back to your room. Stay away from her.* No amount of self-coaching worked. He found himself crossing the porch to stand in front of Jillian, wrapped in a blanket, holding a mug in her small hands. Her blond hair had dried, the tresses curling softly around her shoulders.

"Couldn't sleep?" she asked.

He shook his head, torn between staying and leaving.

With her free hand, she patted the seat beside her. "Then you might as well swing."

He told himself he accepted her offer so that he didn't appear rude, but the truth was he couldn't refuse it. Being close to her was what he'd craved since he'd helped her off the floor of the basement. She was beautiful, optimistic and full of sunshine. She was everything he wasn't.

Chance sat beside her, the cool, damp slats pressing against his naked back, barely chilling his desire.

"Lean forward." Opening her blanket, she slipped it behind him, her arm sliding across his skin.

He flinched.

"I'm sorry," she said. "Did I hurt you?"

"No." He leaned back, his arms crossed over his chest to keep from touching her.

But the blanket wasn't quite big enough for both of them. Jillian slid closer, her arm pressing against his.

He sat for a long moment, the electricity initiated by her touch pinging around his insides like a ball trapped in a pinball machine. If he didn't get away, he'd do something stupid, like kiss her again.

Chance jerked to his feet, sending the swing rocketing backward. It came back to knock him in the back of his knees, almost making him fall back into the seat beside Jillian.

"What's wrong?" Jillian asked, unfolding a long, slender leg to place a foot on the ground and stop the wild swinging.

"Nothing." He stepped away from her and the swing and leaned his hands on the damp porch railing. If the stars were out to light his way, he'd go for a walk, a drive, anything but stay with Jillian. She was too beautiful to ignore, and sexy as hell in that nightgown the blanket did little to hide.

But he couldn't.

The porch boards creaked and a hand touched his shoulder. "What's wrong?"

How could he say that her hand on his shoulder made him want to turn and bury himself inside her, to have hot, naked sex with her until she screamed out his name? She'd call him a pervert, run screaming and tell Molly and Nova what a compete jerk he was. Or worse, she could love it as much as he knew he would and want more. From what he'd seen in her, she wasn't the type of woman who would go for a string-free one-night stand. She'd want commitment. Maybe even a ring to go with the sex.

"Don't touch me," he said through gritted teeth.

She snatched her hand away. "Why? Does it hurt?"

"No."

Again her hand rested on his arm. "Then tell me what's bothering you."

He spun to face her, stalking her like an animal ready to slice into her with razor-sharp teeth.

Jillian's eyes widened and she backed up a step. "If you'd tell me what's wrong, maybe I can help."

His lip curled back in a snarl. "You can't."

When he started to go around her, back into the house, she touched his arm again.

Wound so tight his control vanished, Chance grabbed her arms and pushed her up against the wall. "You can't help me unless you want me to handle you like this."

"I'm sure you have a r-reason," she said, her hands resting on his chest, her fingernails curling against his skin.

"No reason. No control, just gut instinct."

"Instinct to do what?" she asked, her voice a gravelly whisper.

"This." He lowered his head and claimed her in a harsh kiss, grinding his lips against her soft, pliant mouth.

She gasped. Her mistake.

Chance drove his tongue through the gap and dragged his along hers.

At first her body was rigid, stiff against his, probably frightened by his sudden attack. Then she softened, leaned into him, and her hands slipped upward, feathering into the hair at the nape of his neck.

He pressed his hips to hers, nudging her with the rock-hard erection straining behind the fly of his jeans, desperate to take her, there on the porch, dressed in nothing but the encroaching fog.

Her leg curled around the back of his calf and slid up to his thigh.

Chance dropped his hands from her arms to her waist and lower to cup her bottom. Then he lifted, wrapping her legs around his waist. She locked her ankles behind him, freeing his hands. He dug his fingers into her gorgeous hair and tugged, tilting her head back. His mouth moved from hers, crossing the line of her jaw. He nipped at her earlobe and trailed a line of kisses and nips to the base of her throat, where her pulse pounded wildly beneath her skin.

He was on a one-way trip to heaven with a final destination in hell. With nothing but the thin fabric of her gown between him and her breasts, he could feel the last of his control slipping. He couldn't. Let. This. Happen.

He tore his lips from her skin, dropped his hands to her arms and leaned his head back, breathing like a marathon runner. Then as quickly as it began, he untangled her legs from around his waist and set her at arm's length.

She stood in that damned short nightgown, with the pathetic yet sexy excuse for a robe, and trembled. Her lips were swollen from his harsh kisses, and her hair hung in beautiful disarray.

"Go to bed, Jillian."

Her chin lifted, her shoulders squared and she wrapped her arms around her middle. "Not until you tell me what just happened."

"Nothing. And it won't happen again." He turned his back to her so that he didn't have to see how the beaded tips of her breasts made twin tents of the filmy fabric of her nightgown. So that he didn't have to see the accusation in her eyes.

He'd kissed her, damn it. When he'd sworn he wouldn't do it again. Now all he wanted to do was to keep kissing her and take her up to his room, where he'd make love to her until the next morning. But he couldn't risk it.

"Okay. I'll go," she said. "But this isn't over."

"Yes. It. Is." Without looking, he could feel her disappointment, maybe even anger at his behavior. Chance balled his fists, refusing to let himself hold her again.

"I don't know what kind of struggle you're going through, and I don't really know how to handle it. So for now, I'll go." She touched his shoulder. "But I'm not much on leaving a battle until the war's won. So don't think this is done."

Before he could argue the point, the door to the B and B opened and closed behind him. When he turned, she was gone.

He was left on the porch with a deep ache that made him feel even more alone than before he'd arrived in Cape Churn.

On shaking legs, Jillian walked away from Chance, closing the door between them, feeling as if the closed door was more than physical. He'd made it clear he didn't want anything to do with her.

Then why had he kissed her the way he had, stirring in her a desire she couldn't turn off like the burner on a stove? Her core throbbed with need, and she turned around twice on the stairs, ready to march back down and confront Chance. How could he do this to her?

Anger and pride got her to her room, but she couldn't

lie down and sleep. Not when her pulse raced and her insides ached. She wanted him, even though he'd pushed her away.

Flopping down on the bed, she lay still, listening for his footsteps. Fifteen minutes passed, then thirty. Finally the floorboards creaked outside her door and down the hallway. She heard his door open and close and then nothing.

Jillian pounded her fists into the soft mattress. *Damn him.*

Rolling over, she hugged one of the two pillows to her chest, a poor substitute for flesh and blood, but all she had available. Chance could have had her, and she'd have gone willingly to his bed. Well, he'd missed his opportunity. Her best bet was to be gone before he rose in the morning. The less she saw of him before the wedding, the better.

With her plan firmly in mind, Jillian closed her eyes and willed herself to sleep. But sleep didn't come for another hour. When it did, it was filled with erotic dreams of lying naked with the man in the room next to hers.

Before the sun rose the next day, Jillian was up, dressed and on her way to her office in town, determined to get some work done before she swung by to check on the remodeling efforts. She took the kitten with her so that he wouldn't be under Molly's feet.

She'd acquired three new listings over the past couple of days and had yet to get them up on the Multiple Listing Service. She had taken the photos but needed to upload them and create the text describing each vacation cottage in detail. For the next two hours, she worked steadily, pausing only long enough to pet the kitten in her lap. The sun had been up for an hour when she got the call. She answered by hitting the speaker key so that she could keep her hands free to continue working on the computer.

"Miss Taylor?" said a male voice.

"This is she." She clicked a check box for fireplace and moved on to the field for garage and entered a two.

"This is Bob Greer. I'm at your house. We just got here and I…uh…think you need to come out before we get started."

Her gut clenched, but she refused to get excited by the tone of Bob's voice. With forced calm, Jillian picked up the receiver, her full attention on the caller. "Why? What's wrong?"

"There's been some vandalism at the work site."

"What kind of vandalism?"

"Mostly paint. Some of the supplies were disturbed, but mostly it's paint."

"I'm on my way. Don't touch anything until I get there." She hung up and dialed Gabe McGregor's cell number.

He answered immediately. "Hey, Jillian, what's up?"

"Are you on duty?"

"I am," he answered in his usual cheerful tone. "What can I do for you?"

"Could you meet me at my house?"

"Sure. Why?"

"Bob, my contractor, called to say there's been some vandalism."

"I'll be there in five."

"Me, too." She hung up, grabbed her purse, keys and the kitten, and headed out the office door. Who would vandalize a house that had been sitting vacant for seventeen years? It didn't make sense.

When she cleared the trees of the drive leading up to her house, her heart pinched. Bright red paint marred the exterior walls, windows and railing.

She climbed out of her Jeep and stood for a moment, breathing deeply, reining in the jolt of anger that fired up her blood. This was not a huge deal. The house had yet to be painted and the windows all needed to be replaced with energy-saving double-paned models.

But until those two things happened, the house would appear to be bleeding with one giant word sprayed in full view: *HAUNTED*.

Yes, she was angry, but the house wasn't finished and this wouldn't cost her more than a second coat of primer over the red paint. She could handle this setback.

"Miss Taylor, I'm glad you're here. I wasn't sure who else to call." Bob stepped down from the leaning porch and joined her on the front lawn.

"You called me and I called the police." Jillian shook the man's hand. "You did right."

"Yeah, well, I didn't recognize the vehicle sitting in the drive. I didn't think it was yours, but I didn't know who to call about it."

Jillian frowned and turned toward the SUV in the driveway at the side of the house. She'd forgotten Chance had ridden with her to drop off the trailer and truck the night before. Which meant his rental had been at the house overnight.

Once again, her heart dived into her belly as she crossed the grass to the rental, sitting in the shade of an evergreen. At first she didn't see the damage, but when she got closer she could see the bright red paint that graced the house was also sprayed in broad swirls over the hood, windows, doors and side panels.

She pulled out her cell phone and cursed. No reception. "How did you get a call out to me from here?"

Bob laughed. "I had to drive halfway to town before I got a signal."

Heading for her SUV, Jillian paused when she heard the sound of a vehicle crunching gravel along the drive into her secluded homesite.

A Cape Churn Police Department SUV pulled up beside her vehicle and stopped. Gabe McGregor got out, shaking his head. "Yeah, I'd say someone did a number on your house."

She sighed. "That can be fixed. I'm more worried about the damage to Chance's rental car. Can you radio in a call to him and let him know what's happened?" She held up her cell phone. "No reception."

"I can do that." He touched the key on the mic clipped to his shoulder and gave the dispatcher instructions to call Chance at the McGregor B and B. When he was done, he reached into his SUV and pulled out a camera. "Let's get started."

"Begin with the house. The sooner my contractor can get back to work, the better. I'm sure an adjuster will need to be called about the car."

Besides the paint on the walls inside and outside the house, a few more broken windows, and paint on the lumber that had been scattered across the yard, the house was intact. Jillian was glad she'd locked her belongings in the back room using one of the skeleton keys she'd found in the back of a drawer in the kitchen. Otherwise, her furniture might have fallen victim to the graffiti artist.

Gabe completed a thorough investigation of the premises and dusted for fingerprints on the doorknobs and the sill of the broken window on the first floor, the probable source of entry into the house. Since Bob's crew had been all over the house for the past few days, Gabe also took all their fingerprints so that he could rule them out. Once he finished his work on the house, he cleared the contractor to start working again.

Gabe had just started photographing the rental car when an SUV pulled up next to Gabe's vehicle.

Nova climbed out of the driver's side and let out a long low whistle. *"Madre de Dios."*

When Chance exited the passenger seat, Jillian's pulse quickened and heat rose up her chest into her cheeks.

He took one look at the house and then headed straight for her, pulling her into his arms.

Jillian melted against him. Something about him made her feel protected and unnerved all at once. Damn. He was already getting under her skin and she'd only known him a day. This had to stop.

Chapter 7

As they'd driven up to Jillian's house, Chance saw the paint first, dripping like blood on the faded and peeling white paint. As soon as he was out of Nova's truck, he went straight to Jillian and pulled her into his arms. She'd been gone when he'd woken that morning and he'd been thanking his lucky stars at the same time as he missed her presence. "Are you all right?"

She nodded, her fingers curling into his shirt. "I'm fine, but I'm afraid your rental car isn't."

He shook his head and glanced past her. "That's what insurance is for. I'm more concerned about you." He stared at the house.

A man in a police uniform who had been snapping photos of the damaged vehicle joined them. "Me, too." He held out his hand. "Gabe McGregor."

"Chance McCall."

Gabe grinned. "The best man?" His grin faded. "Sorry about your rental."

"It's just paint," Chance said and rested a hand against the small of Jillian's back. "I'm not worried about it." But he was worried about the owner of the house. His gut was talking to him, telling him the situation was more dangerous than he'd originally thought.

"This house has been empty for seventeen years. Why would someone choose to vandalize it now?" Jillian asked.

"Have you been through it thoroughly? Does it appear as if someone was living in it before you started the rehab?" Gabe asked.

"It was completely empty." Jillian pushed her hair back from her face. "No sign of inhabitants, except maybe mice."

"It doesn't make much sense." Gabe tucked the small camera into his front pocket. "I'll run a check on the fingerprints. My advice to you is install security cameras."

She shook her head. "I don't have the money in the budget for that."

"You know the staffing of the police department. We can't position an officer here 24/7."

"And I don't expect it." Jillian smiled at Gabe. "Thanks for coming out. Just find the bastard who did this."

"I'll do the best I can. In the meantime, I'll notify dispatch and the guys on the night shift to swing by periodically to check on things. But until we catch the culprit, it could happen again."

"Maybe they won't try anything once the house is occupied at night." Jillian chewed on her bottom lip, staring at the old structure. "I'll be moved in before they start painting the exterior."

"All the more reason to install a security system tied into the police department," Chance added to Gabe's argument.

Her lips twisted. "I'll look at what I can take off the renovation list. I might have to wait to remodel one of the bathrooms." Jillian sighed. "I thought Cape Churn was one of those places where you could leave your doors unlocked and not worry about it."

Gabe's jaw hardened. "Like most communities, we've had our share of pranks and a couple of real criminals. I don't recommend leaving your doors unlocked anywhere."

"Don't worry," Jillian said. "I don't. I lived in Portland long enough to make it a habit to lock up even when I'm home during the day."

"Good." Gabe glanced once more at the house. "I'm sorry about the damage. I'll do my best to find the one responsible."

"Thanks, Gabe," Jillian said. "Say hello to Kayla for me, will ya?"

"I will. We're looking forward to Molly's wedding. Let us know what we can do to help."

"Just be there with your tux on and Kayla in her bridesmaid dress. The rest should be taken care of." Jillian hugged the man.

Once again, Jillian's friendly hug sent a brief spike of anger through Chance. If he wasn't mistaken, that feeling was something akin to jealousy. Jillian was free to hug anyone she felt like. He had no say in the matter.

"I'll be fine," she was saying. "Go on. I'm sure you

have better things to do than chase after punks with cans of spray paint."

"This is serious, Jillian," Gabe said. "If they're targeting your house, who's to say they won't target you? Be aware at all times."

She nodded. "I will."

Gabe climbed into his SUV and drove off. Nova walked around the house, inspecting the damage, leaving Jillian alone with Chance.

She drew in a deep breath and let it out slowly. "I guess I'd better clean up what *can* be cleaned and live with the rest until the windows arrive and the painter does his magic on the exterior."

The electrician's truck arrived and Mitchell got out, giving a low whistle. "Damn. Someone either doesn't like you much or doesn't want you moving into this house."

Jillian's eyes narrowed and she stared at the house. "I can't remember making anybody mad enough to vandalize my house. Do you think someone doesn't want me to move in?"

"I don't know. I just wire houses." Mitchell opened a side panel on the back of the truck and pulled out a toolbox and a reel of electrical wire. "Speaking of wiring, if all goes well, I should have it done this afternoon. Is it possible to get paid for the job today?"

Jillian smiled. "Thank you, Mitchell. You just gave me one bright spot in an otherwise crappy start to the day. Yes, I can pay you this afternoon."

"Thanks. I have to pay my workers and it helps to have the funds." Mitchell entered the house.

"All I've been waiting on to move in is electricity and running water." Jillian glanced up at Chance. "Depending on the plumber, I could move in as soon as the day after tomorrow. Then maybe I can keep this kind of thing from happening again."

"I'm not sure a lone woman is going to scare off whoever did this to your house."

"How about a lone woman with an HK .40 caliber pistol and the skill to use it?"

Chance chuckled. "That might help if you post a sign on the exterior of your house stating it." He ran a hand through his hair and glanced at the house. "I think Gabe's right. You need a security system installed."

"Those are really expensive."

"Not if you do some of the work yourself."

She tapped a finger to her jaw. "Assuming I can get one and install it immediately. I'm serious. As soon as the water and electricity are on, I'm moving in. Besides, Molly has a pile of people coming in for the wedding. I don't want to tie up one of her rooms in the B and B through next week."

"Then get a room at one of the hotels in town," he suggested.

She shook her head. "And leave my poor house to these vandals? That's not happening."

"I take it your mind is made up." He shook his head. "You're a stubborn woman."

"Damn right, I am. It's one of my better qualities." She smiled. "Now, if you'll excuse me, I have some paint to scrape off." With those parting words, she marched into the house.

Chance stood where she'd left him, admiring the sway of her hips and the tilt of her chin. The woman was a fighter. Not much could get her down. He hoped whoever had done the paint job wasn't interested in harming the woman who owned the house.

He got in his ruined rental and drove to town, where he was able to get a cell phone signal. The first call he placed was to the car-rental company, advising them of the vandalism and assuring them the vehicle was drivable. They promised to send a representative out to trade vehicles and take the damaged one back for repairs. Chance told them not to bother for a couple of days. With the vandals still on the loose, it didn't bode well for a second rental car.

The next call he made was to Royce Fontaine, his boss.

"Chance, how's the wedding plans going?" Royce answered without a real greeting, which was his style.

"Fine, but we have a little bit of a problem with the wedding planner."

Royce chuckled. "Can't you stay out of her way until the wedding's over?"

He wished he could, but Chance was genuinely worried about Jillian more than she was worried for her own safety. Her lack of concern made him feel he needed to be concerned for her. "That's not an option." He explained the situation and asked, "Could you put Geek onto this and see what he can discover about that house and anything that might help us find who's responsible for the vandalism?"

"I'll do that, but have you considered that it could be local teenagers making a nuisance of themselves?" Royce offered.

"Yeah, but my gut is telling me there's more to this than meets the eye."

"I'll put Geek on it. He likes sleuthing, and things are a little slow around here right now."

"That's a good thing."

"Or it means something big is about to happen. We rarely have downtime."

"What is it you're always telling us? Don't borrow trouble, but be ready."

Royce laughed. "You've got that right. I'll have Geek do his magic and get back to you as soon as we have anything. Meanwhile, you're supposed to be resting and relaxing. I'll probably have something for you in a couple of weeks."

Chance ended the call.

Rest and relax. That was what he'd had in mind when he'd come to Cape Churn. Somehow that wasn't how it was playing out. He hoped the vandalism was nothing more than a teenage prank. But to make sure Jillian remained safe, he had other plans.

Thankfully, Jillian had an extra set of work clothes in her SUV. After changing from her skirt and blouse to jeans and a flannel shirt, she went to work on the inside of the house, scraping off old wallpaper. She liked performing the manual labor required to restore a house to a livable state. Not only did it burn off nervous energy, it had a positive result.

In this case, the red paint wasn't coming off. She applied several coats of primer to the walls that would be painted soon and peeled a couple of layers of wallpaper off the walls that needed to be stripped anyway. She'd planned on returning to her office to check messages but ended up staying at the house all day.

The workers banged, hammered and ripped out sections of drywall to get to the plumbing and electricity. A couple of men were removing the rotted railing and floorboards on the porch. Bob was in the basement with another worker studying the supports.

Things were moving along on her house. It wouldn't be long before she could move in.

Jillian wadded a long band of wallpaper under her arm and walked through the house with the intention of carrying it out to the huge bin Bob had positioned in front of the house for the refuse generated from the demolition. As she passed a window overlooking the backyard, she noticed one of the men emerging from the woods. She stopped, wondering why he'd chosen to relieve himself out there when Bob had provided a portable toilet for the men, as required by state law.

As the man got closer, she recognized him as Daryl Sims. Everyone in Cape Churn knew Daryl. He was a big guy with the mental capacity of a five-year-old. Those who had the work employed him to perform easy manual labor. Bob had hired him on a regular basis to help with the demolition and cleanup on construction sites.

Jillian smiled. He probably hadn't considered using one of the portable toilets. When he got close enough to the house she could see him more clearly. He appeared to be holding something in his hands. If Jillian wasn't mistaken, it was gray, furry and small, like...

She looked left and right. During the time she'd been cleaning, she'd forgotten about the kitten. Now, she hurried through the house, looking, but couldn't find the little guy. The men in the basement had been careful to keep the door closed to keep the kitten from going down there, but it was possible someone had left one of the main floor doors open while carrying pieces of dry-wall and lumber in and out.

When she couldn't find the kitten, Jillian stepped out-side.

Daryl had just reached the porch and, as she sus-pected, he carried the kitten in his hands. He'd admired the feline earlier when she'd carried it outside to do its business.

"Thank goodness you found him." Jillian held out her hands. "I hate to think of the little guy getting lost in the woods."

"He went for a walk." Daryl deposited the kitten in Jillian's hands. "I like kittens."

"Me, too."

"I have four."

"I bet they're as cute as this guy."

He nodded.

"Daryl!" Bob shouted from the other side of the house.

"I'm here!" Daryl shouted back.

"We need you up front!"

"Coming." Daryl patted the kitten again and smiled at Jillian. "You're pretty."

Jillian gave Daryl a gentle smile. "Thank you. You better go. They need you."

He shuffled off, looking back at Jillian and the kitten several times until he rounded the corner of the building.

Tucking the kitten into the crook of her arm, Jillian hurried back into the house. She'd been tearing wallpa-per out of the living room. She decided to stay out of the way of the workers on the main level and climbed the stairs to the first bedroom at the top of the landing.

She closed the door behind her and set the kitten on the floor. This room had wallpaper, much like many of others in the house. Something about the tiny rosebuds and ivy struck a chord with Jillian. She could imagine a little girl growing up in this room with frilly curtains rustling in the breeze of an open window. She almost hated tearing the paper from the wall, but it had yellowed with age and was peeling on the edges.

If she married and had a little girl, she'd paint the room in a soft pastel pink, and stencil roses and ivy in a lovely border pattern. With that promise in her mind, she went to work removing the brittle wallpaper from the wall.

Images of a little girl with blond hair and blue eyes like hers flashed in her mind. She'd love to have a little girl to hold and love. And a little boy with black hair and blue eyes.

She couldn't help thinking of Chance. He'd make beautiful babies. But Jillian wasn't in the market for a relationship. She drew in a deep breath and shook her head. She'd only known the man a day. The thought of making babies with him was silly and nonproductive. Nevertheless, her core heated and she couldn't get the bare-chested secret agent off her mind.

While she peeled wallpaper, the kitten played with the debris, swatting at curls of paper and dust balls. Fifteen minutes into stripping the rose room, as she had named it, a light tap on the door pulled her out of her musings. "Come in."

The man she'd been dreaming about appeared in the doorway, carrying a large box. "You've been busy." He stared at the walls, his gaze returning to her face. "And you have a smudge on your nose."

She stared cross-eyed at the tip of her nose.

Chance balanced the big box in one hand and brushed the smudge off her nose with his thumb. "There."

He tipped his head toward the box. "I found a security system at the hardware store. It's simple and not very expensive, but something is better than nothing where safety is concerned."

"You didn't have to do that." She rubbed her hands down the sides of her jeans and grabbed the kitten as it made a dash for the open door. "Let me pay you for it."

"I'd like to consider it a housewarming gift."

"I can't accept something like that from a stranger."

"I insist. It will give me peace of mind knowing you have something better than a kitten to guard you at night. Besides, we can't be considered strangers. We've kissed."

She hugged the kitten to her chest and stared at this man she'd only just met and smiled. "You confuse me."

"How's that?"

"You just do." She let out a long breath. "I'll see if Mitchell can fit this into his wiring schedule."

"I'll help with the installation. It will make it go faster and save you money."

She tilted her head. "So you're a secret agent and an electrician?"

"Let's just say I've done my share of wiring."

She stared at him hard. "I won't ask what you wired. I'm afraid of the answer."

"I promise I'll only wire the security system. Nothing else. And Mitchell can inspect my work."

"Okay." Jillian chuckled. "I guess I'll have that security system." She poked a finger at his chest. "But I still want to pay you for it."

"We'll talk later. Right now, I want to get a start before it gets too dark."

"I can help if you and Mitchell tell me what to do."

"You're on." He led the way down the stairs.

Jillian found Mitchell in the basement adding wire and fixtures that would eventually light the entire room. A large working light stood to the side, powered by the generator outside, giving him just enough light to see what he was doing.

Mitchell climbed down from the ladder he was working on and brushed the dust off his hands. "Oh, good. A security system is exactly what you need, especially if you're going to live here alone." He took the box from Chance and studied the writing on the side. "I have heavy-duty wire in my truck, but the electronics in this unit will work fine for now. You might want to upgrade eventually."

"So you'll do it?" Jillian asked.

Mitchell rubbed a hand through his hair. "I don't know. I need to finish this room, rewire the upstairs and install the recessed lighting in the kitchen." He looked around. "I'd hoped to turn on the main breaker this evening."

"I've done some wiring," Chance said. "I can help."

"With direction, I can help, too," Jillian offered.

"Fortunately, the drywall guys haven't repaired the walls where I rewired each room." He nodded. "I'd feel better knowing you had a security system installed. Okay. Let me get you started and you can run the wire. I'll install the controls."

Jillian and Chance worked side by side, running wire through the walls to the windows, doors and corners. When Mitchell finished the basement and kitchen, he installed the control panel, tapped into the wires for the new phone line and set up cameras in strategic corners inside and outside the house. They were able to complete the wiring and electronics installation. All they needed was for the electricity to be turned on and the phone lines to be connected by the telephone company.

All the time, Jillian couldn't help admiring how good Chance was with his hands. And how sexy those hands were. The more she worked with him, the more she wondered how those hands would feel on naked skin.

Holy hell. She had to get Chance and his sexy bare chest and capable hands out of her naughty thoughts.

"Did you say something?" Chance paused in his effort to thread the wire through a hole that had been drilled through a stud.

"No, no, I didn't." Her cheeks burning, Jillian bent her head and unrolled more of the wire from the spool.

Mitchell entered the room. "I'm ready to turn on the main breaker to test out the lights. We can finish the security system tomorrow. I need to get home to my wife."

"The timing is good. We need to make a dash into town before they roll up the sidewalks," Chance said.

"We do?" Jillian asked.

"Yes." Chance nodded to Mitchell. "Let's light up this place."

"On it." Mitchell left the room and headed for the pantry in the kitchen, where he'd updated and upgraded the breaker box, bringing it into the current century.

Jillian held her breath. The light from outside had faded, and they were working in near dusk conditions.

A loud click and then several more, and lights came on in some of the rooms.

Jillian clapped her hands, her spirits rising. "I feel like there really is a light at the end of the tunnel."

"Let's check all the rooms." Chance flipped the switch in the living room and the recessed lights gave it a soft glow.

Jillian ran to the dining room and flipped the switch. The few recessed lights came on. Mitchell would add a separate chandelier when the flooring and painting were done.

"How's it looking?" Mitchell called out from the kitchen.

"Great so far," Jillian responded. "We'll check the second story."

Chance started up the stairs. Jillian snatched up the kitten and followed. He went right, she went left. They met in the master bedroom.

Jillian couldn't tone down the smile on her face. "I'm that much closer to moving into my very own house. I can't tell you how great that will be." Sharing the moment with Chance seemed natural. When he opened his arms, she stepped into them.

Too bad he wasn't going to be around to see the house when it was completed. Her happiness dimmed. For a long moment, she remained in Chance's arms, soaking up his warmth. Then she moved away. "Mitchell will need to be going, and I need to pay him for all of the work he's done so far."

"I want to get to town before the local library closes." He followed her out of the bedroom. "You're welcome to come with me."

"Did you need to use a fax or copier machine? I have one of each in my office."

"No, I thought we'd see what we could find out about this house."

"That's right. I meant to do some homework and look up its history. I'd really like to put an end to the rumors that this house is haunted." As much as she liked to think she was open-minded about a lot of things, believing in ghosts wasn't one of them. And ghosts didn't use spray paint to vandalize buildings. "Let's go."

Chapter 8

Chance waited while Jillian wrote a check to Mitchell. The contractor and his crew locked the generator in the house, stacked the lumber neatly and four of the five men climbed into the truck's crew cab.

The contractor yelled, "Daryl, it's time to go!"

Jillian was standing with Mitchell, holding the kitten. She glanced around the yard.

The fifth man of the construction crew was nowhere to be seen.

"I don't know where he gets off to," Bob said, "but he's always disappearing."

"I'll check out back," she offered.

"I've got it." Chance hurried around the exterior of the big house, searching for the missing man. When he'd made it around the back and was starting for the other side, he still hadn't found Daryl. "Daryl!" he called out.

He and Jillian had made a final sweep of the house before Bob's crew locked the generator inside. Daryl hadn't been in the house.

Rustling in the woods behind the house alerted Chance's attention. A big man, wearing faded denim overalls and a blue flannel shirt, emerged from the woods.

"Are you Daryl?" Chance asked.

"Yup." Daryl carried a ball of fluff in his hand. "I found a kitten."

"Your boss is waiting for you. They're heading into town."

"I wanted to give Miss Jillian the kitten."

When Chance looked closer at the kitten, it appeared to be a replica of the one he'd found in the cellar of the house. "She's around front."

Daryl plodded along. A big man with a tiny kitten in his meaty fists. Not all men liked cats, but apparently, Daryl did.

A horn honked and Bob called out, "Daryl! Either you come now or you can walk back to town."

Chance stepped into the front yard. Mitchell had left and Jillian was taking the second kitten from Daryl. "Thank you, Daryl." She juggled the two squirming fur balls and shot a smile at her construction foreman. "Bob, I'll give Daryl a ride back to town."

"Okay. We'll pick him up at the café in the morning." Bob drove off with the other construction workers.

"Since we're going the same direction, we can ride together. If that's all right with you." Chance didn't like the idea of Jillian riding alone with Daryl. Not that the man had been anything but nice to her. Given the fact someone had locked her in the basement and vandals had desecrated the house with paint, Jillian couldn't be too careful.

"Are you sure?" She glanced across the furry creatures. "I don't want anything else to happen to your rental."

"I don't mind leaving it here. The damage is already done."

"I might need you to drive, since my hands appear to be quite full." She laughed. "I didn't know I'd inherited a family of kittens when I bought the house." A frown creased her brow. "I wonder if there are any more."

"Two. Only two," Daryl said. "Can I ride shotgun?"

"Sure." Jillian piled the kittens on top of each other, dug the keys out of her pocket and tossed them to Chance. "I'll just sit in the back and keep these two out of your way."

Dressed in dusty jeans and a red flannel shirt and with her hair pulled back in a messy bun, Jillian couldn't have been prettier. Gone was the sophisticated real estate agent and in her place was a real, flesh-and-blood girl next door with two gray tabby kittens snuggled beneath her chin.

Chance found himself wanting something he could never have—a home, a woman just like Jillian and a life filled with sunshine and rewarding work fixing up a house they both could love.

Unfortunately, that would never work for him. As long as he still had the nightmares, he couldn't be the kind of man a woman like Jillian needed.

Chance climbed into the driver's seat of Jillian's Jeep, adjusted it to fit his long legs and waited for Daryl to get in and buckle up.

"Where are we taking you, Daryl?" he asked.

"Mama picks me up at the café."

Chance shot a glance at Jillian's reflection in the rearview mirror.

"The Seaside Café." She smoothed a hand over a kitten. "You probably passed it on your way through town. Head into Cape Churn. I'll tell you where to turn."

The drive into town only took ten minutes, most of which was slow going on the bumpy gravel driveway. Once they reached the highway, it was smooth sailing all the way to the parking lot in front of the café. The sun angled toward the horizon, turning the sky and bay to fire.

Daryl got out at the Seaside Café and waved at Jillian in the backseat.

"Did you want to join me up front?" Chance asked.

"I'll just stay back here." Jillian pointed ahead. "The library is two blocks down on the right. It closes in twenty minutes, so we'd better hurry."

"Yes, ma'am." He winked and shifted into Drive. "What's the story on Daryl?"

"From what I know, he's mentally challenged. As far as I can tell, he's harmless. Most folks look out for him."

"That's good to know. Is this the place?" Chance slowed in front of an old brick building and parked.

"This is it." Jillian pulled the two kittens free of her shirt and placed them on the backseat.

Chance got out and held the door for her.

In the library they stopped at the front desk, where Rita Sims was stacking returned books on a cart. "We close in twenty minutes," she reminded them.

"We'll try to be quick," Jillian promised. "Could you point to the local newspaper archives?"

"Sure. What are you looking for?"

"I'm curious about my house," Jillian said. "I'd like to find the news articles from seventeen years ago."

Mrs. Sims frowned. "Reading through all of those will take longer than twenty minutes."

"We'd like to get a start, if you don't mind. We'll leave when it's time to lock up. Oh, and we gave Daryl a ride into town. He's waiting for you at the café."

She paused with a book in her hand. "Why didn't he ride with Bob?"

"Daryl was busy bringing me a kitten." Jillian smiled. "We didn't mind giving him a lift into town."

"Still, he needs structure." The lines on Mrs. Sims's forehead deepened in the grooves. "He forgets things when he doesn't stay in his routine, and he needs to keep this job."

"I'm sorry," Jillian said. "I didn't think it would matter who brought him to the café. I'll keep it in mind in the future."

"I should hope so." She pointed to the computers lining the walls. "The archives have been scanned and digitized. There are instructions next to the computers." Mrs. Sims pushed the cart away, muttering, "Kittens. That boy is always collecting things. I don't know where he keeps them."

Jillian led the way to the computer bay.

Chance followed. "Is she always that gruff?"

"I hadn't really noticed, but I guess she is somewhat abrupt." Jillian sat at one of the computers.

Chance sat next to her. It took a few valuable minutes to find the archives and the year they were looking for.

Chance clicked on January. "I'll take the first six months."

"I'll take July through December."

For the next ten minutes, they were silent, skimming through articles until Chance found a front-page article with the caption Search Continues for Missing Girl.

Chance's pulse kicked up a notch. "I think I've found something."

"I'm sorry, folks," Mrs. Sims called out. "I need to close the library and lock the doors."

"We're wrapping it up now," Jillian responded. To Chance, she said, "Print it out. We can take it with us and read it later."

"It requires change." He dug in his pocket and pulled out the right amount of coins, feeding them into the machine. Then he hit the print button and pushed back his chair. The pages printed out quickly. He grabbed them, hooked Jillian's arm and smiled at Mrs. Sims as they exited the library.

Once outside, Jillian took the pages from him. "You have the keys, you can drive."

"Back to the B and B?"

Jillian slid into the Jeep, settled the kittens in her lap and glanced at the clock on the dash. "No. I told Molly not to hold dinner for me since I was going to be working at the house. We can go to the Seaside Café and grab a bite while we read through this article."

Chance drove to the café and parked. Jillian settled the kittens on a towel in the backseat. They entered, finding Daryl seated at the counter on a stool.

"Jillian, how are the house renovations coming along?" A gray-haired woman wearing an apron and carrying a coffeepot stepped out from behind the counter.

"Hi, Nora." Jillian grinned. "The electricity is on."

"That's a step in the right direction." Nora held up the pot. "Coffee?"

"I'd love a cup," Chance said.

"Nora—" Jillian turned to Chance "—this is Chance McCall, Nova's best man. He got in yesterday for the wedding."

"Welcome to Cape Churn." Nora set two mugs on a table and poured coffee into them. "Are you staying in town or at the B and B?"

Chance held Jillian's chair for her and then sat. "I'm staying with Molly and Nova at the B and B."

"I hear there's going to be quite the crowd. I can't wait for the wedding. The last one we had was Gabe and Kayla's. They make such a good couple." Nora took a pad and pencil out of a pocket. "Are you two just having coffee or are you here for dinner?"

"Dinner." Jillian sat back in her seat. "I'll have the fresh catch of the day, blackened."

"I'll have the same. Could I get a salad and baked potato to go with it?"

Nora nodded. "Sour cream and chives?"

"Only butter."

"Got it." Nora left them with the fragrant brew.

About that time, Mrs. Sims poked her head through the door of the café. "Daryl."

Daryl swiveled on his seat and glanced behind him. "Coming." He climbed down from the seat and followed his mother out the door.

Chance lifted his mug and sipped his coffee. He watched Jillian's face as she read the first page of the article. She passed it to him and continued on to the next page. He read quickly and held out his hand for the next page. Jillian waited for him to finish.

Nora arrived with two bowls. "Here are your salads. Your dinners will be out in a few more minutes."

Setting the papers to the side, Jillian laid her napkin in her lap. "Thank you, Nora."

"Whatcha reading?" Nora asked. "Tell me it's none of my business if you don't want me to know. I'm just a busybody."

"Damn right she is." An older man walked up behind her and hugged her around the middle. "Is my wife interrupting your date?"

"We're not on a date," Jillian was quick to correct the man. She couldn't help the heat rising up in her cheeks. "Chance, this is Tom Taggart, Nora's husband and the chief of the Cape Churn Police Department." She explained Chance's connection to Nova and glanced at the papers. "We were researching the history of the house I bought."

"The old Thompson place?" he asked, his brows furrowing. "What did you want to know?"

"People say it's haunted," Jillian said.

"Nonsense. No one I know of died in the house. But I'll bet that's why it never sold. Rumors can be damned destructive."

"We did a little digging in the newspaper archives and found this article about a missing girl." Chance handed the pages to the chief. "Can you tell us anything about it?"

Taggart held the papers up, his frown deepening. "I was a patrolman back then. I remember helping in the search for that little girl. We had people from all over the state come in to search. Spent a week combing the woods on the path from the school to her house. We never found any sign of her. And it started raining before we could get the tracking dogs in."

Jillian pinched the bridge of her nose, feeling a headache coming on. She pushed past the pain. "The article said they thought someone might have snatched her."

"Had to have been. She was gone for over thirty days. We'd given up hope. Some of the local business owners donated money for a sizable reward for finding her. Her mother, Sarah, blamed herself for letting her daughter walk home from school. She never gave up. Then thirty days later, the little girl just showed up."

"Showed up?" Chance shook his head. "From where?"

The chief held up his hands, palms up. "We don't know."

Nora sighed. "Little Julia walked into her house and collapsed in her mother's arms. Sarah brought her to the Cape Churn Hospital."

Tom continued. "Other than being dehydrated and a little thinner than she'd been when she went missing, she appeared to be physically fine."

Nora lowered her voice. "They did one of those rape kits on her, but she didn't show any sign of sexual abuse."

"Where had she been?" Jillian asked.

"That's just it." Tom shook his head. "When she woke up, she couldn't remember anything about what had happened to her. No amount of questioning by the social workers or psychologists could unlock the story from her mind. They said she had some kind of amnesia."

"Poor kid." Jillian stared at the pages, her eyes glistening. "Who would abduct a child like that and hold her hostage for thirty days?"

"We might never know," Nora said. "It was kind of scary. Everyone with children kept them on short leashes after that. Whoever took her had to have been someone from Cape Churn."

Nora shook her head. "Sarah Thompson couldn't stand the thought of the abductor still walking free. She was so afraid he'd come back for Julia, she packed her things and left with her daughter. Some say they moved to Portland. But I looked, hoping to send them a Christmas card and ask how the little one was. I never found Sarah Thompson in Portland. It's as though she disappeared."

"I can't blame her," Tom said, his fists bunching at his sides. "I don't know what I would have done if that had been my daughter."

Nora glanced toward the kitchen. "I bet your dinner is ready. Enough talk of the past. Don't let that old story dampen your enthusiasm for your house. I always hoped someone would show it some tender loving care. It's not the house's fault those things happened. And there's no reason for a ghost to haunt it. No one died." Nora left for the kitchen.

"Gabe told me what happened this morning," Tom said. "I was on another call, or I would have come myself. After we ruled out your prints and the construction crew's, we ran the remaining fingerprints through the AFIS database and didn't come up with a match. Gabe checked at the hardware store. No one has purchased red spray paint since the beginning of summer, and his records indicate that was someone from Seattle, probably here on vacation. I'm sorry we don't have more information for you. We'll keep our eyes open, but we don't have much to go on."

Jillian touched the chief's arm. "Thank you."

Tom turned away, stepped behind the counter and helped himself to a cup of coffee.

Nora came out with two plates laden with blackened walleye, asparagus and baked potatoes.

Jillian dug in, having worked up a healthy appetite working in the house. Chance ate everything on his plate as well, finishing a little before Jillian.

She was so intent on her food, she didn't look up until she ate the last bite of potato on her fork. When she noticed Chance staring at her, she frowned. "What?"

Chance leaned back. "I'm used to women picking at their food and wasting half of it."

"I only ask for what I can eat. I hate to waste, as well. But I worked hard today." She lifted her chin. "I earned every calorie."

Chance raised his hands. "I didn't say you didn't earn them. It's refreshing to see a woman enjoying her meal."

She tapped her lips with her napkin and tipped her head toward his plate. "You can't go wrong with anything on the menu here."

"I believe it." He took another sip from his coffee mug and set it on the table. "If you're ready to go, I am, too."

She nodded. "I need to get the kittens back to the B and B and feed them. I'm sure the little bit of cheese I gave them at noon has long since worn off."

"Let's get the little guys home." He stood and held her chair while she rose.

Jillian could get used to a guy who opened doors and held chairs for his woman. Shaking the thought out of her mind, she shifted to neutral ground. "One of them is a girl and the other is a boy." She pushed to her feet. "And they need names."

"Don't look at me." Chance smiled.

Jillian's heart flipped and butterflies erupted in her tummy. Chance's face changed with the smile, making him even more handsome. She swallowed hard to tamp down the desire rising rapidly in the presence of this man. "How about Tweedledee and Tweedledum?"

"Dee and Dum for short?" Chance shook his head. "Dee is all right, but do you think Dum might get a complex?"

"Try again?" She liked this playful Chance. He was making it really hard not to like him. Too bad he would be leaving in a week. "How about Jack and Jill?"

"That works." He pulled out of the parking lot, driving slowly through Cape Churn. Darkness blanketed the town, and fog had crept in. If anything, the fog was more ghostly than what Jillian had seen at the house, blurring the streetlights and making it hard to see more than ten feet in front of them.

The kittens had settled in Jillian's lap, quickly falling to sleep. She kept a hand on each to keep them from rolling out of her lap. While Chance had his attention on the murky road ahead, Jillian studied him.

"You were in the army with Nova?"

"Yes." His fingers gripped the wheel, his knuckles turning white with the effort.

"Deployed?"

In the light from the dash, Jillian could see his jaw tighten. "Yes." His answer was abrupt, discouraging further questioning.

She continued to stare at him, wondering what he'd gone through that just the mention of the army and deployment made him tense. Rather than dig deeper, she said softly, "Thank you for your service. It must have been hard."

He sat rigid for a long moment and finally his hands loosened on the steering wheel. "It's past." He shot her a glance and then he returned his attention to the road ahead.

Jillian wanted to ask so many more questions, but she'd obviously hit a sore spot for him. She'd just turned to face the road as well when movement in the corner of her right eye caught her attention.

Her hands tightened on the kittens, but before she could open her mouth to scream, something plowed into her side of the vehicle, crushing it inward.

Jillian was flung to the left and then jerked back to the right, hitting her head on the passenger window. Pain shot through her skull, blinding her for a split second. Then she fought the fog curling around her vision. Her fingers gripped the two kittens even as she slipped into darkness, the fuzzy streetlights and the illuminated dash blinking out as if someone had turned them off.

Chapter 9

Chance held onto the steering wheel as the Jeep skidded sideways. He hadn't seen the truck coming out of the side street until it hit the passenger side of the Jeep. It all happened so fast, but he could swear the truck's headlights had not been on when it plowed into them.

When the Jeep stopped turning sideways, Chance pulled to a halt and shifted into Park with the intent of getting out, a string of curses at the ready on his lips. Who the hell would drive like an idiot when the streets were shrouded in fog? One glance at Jillian made him change his mind. He took one hand off the steering wheel. "Jillian." Movement beyond Jillian's slumped body made him glance past her.

The truck backed up.

Before Chance could react, the truck spun tires and raced toward them, slamming into the side of the Jeep again.

Chance pushed the gearshift into Drive and hit the accelerator. He had to get away from the maniac using the truck as a battering ram. The Jeep's tires spun for a second on the damp road, found traction and jettisoned them out of range of the attacking truck.

Chance shifted his gaze between the foggy road ahead and the rearview mirror. When the truck didn't appear to be following, he turned onto a side road and circled back. He used a different route to head toward Cape Churn Hospital. Since they'd been hit the first time, Jillian hadn't spoken a word, and the way she was bent over, Chance suspected she was out cold.

He thought about digging out his cell phone and calling 911, but he was afraid to take his hands off the wheel long enough to make the connection. His best bet was to get Jillian to the hospital and then notify the police of the attack. What had just happened had been no accident. One hit might have been unintended, but when the driver had backed up and hit them again, the game changed.

Turning to connect with the main street running through Cape Churn, Chance sped through town.

The lights of a patrol car lit up behind him and its siren wailed. Chance hit the hazard lights, refusing to stop for anyone until he got to the hospital with Jillian.

The building suddenly loomed ahead and to the right of him. With the fog so thick, he almost missed the turn into the emergency entrance. Jamming his foot on the brake, he skidded sideways into the drive-through drop-off area and brought the vehicle to a more sedate halt.

He jumped out of the Jeep and rounded to the passenger door. It was so mangled he couldn't get it open.

"McCall? Is that you?" Tom Taggart stepped out of his patrol SUV. "What happened?"

"Someone broadsided us. Hit-and-run." Chance yanked at the door handle. "Jillian's hurt. She's unconscious and I need to get her out."

"I'll be right back." The chief ran for the entrance of the ER, talking into the mic on his shoulder. "I'm at the hospital with a victim of a hit-and-run. Call the fire department. We might need help getting her out of the vehicle." As he cleared the inner doors, he shouted. "We need some help out here! Bring a gurney!"

Chance rounded the Jeep to the driver's side and knelt in the seat, reaching across to Jillian, afraid to move her in case she'd suffered a spinal injury with the force of the collision.

Another siren wailed nearby and a fire truck appeared at the same time as Chief Taggart emerged from the hospital.

"Let the emergency medical technicians handle this. They'll know best how to get her out."

Chance stood back as the firefighters and the EMTs took over. Within minutes, they had the Jeep door open and Jillian out on the gurney. She opened her eyes and blinked at the lights overhead. "Chance?"

He stepped up beside her and took her hand. "I'm here."

"Where are the kittens?"

He chuckled, appalled at the hint of hysteria in the sound. He'd never been anything but calm and cool in a battle. But seeing Jillian lying on a gurney, her face pale and bloody, he couldn't help it. And then for her to ask about the kittens seemed over-the-top ridiculous.

"Looking for these?" A firefighter raised the two kittens in his hand. "Were there only two?"

"Only two." Jillian looked up at Chance. "They haven't had anything to eat."

"Darlin', they'll be all right until after we take care of you." Chance walked alongside her as they entered the hospital.

She squeezed his hand. "Please."

"We'll take her from here," a nurse said and tried to nudge Chance out of the way.

"I'll take care of Jack and Jill." He bent and pressed a kiss to her cheek, noting the knot on her right temple and a drying track of blood leading from it down the side of her face. His gut clenched. Reluctantly, he released her hand.

The hospital staff wheeled her into the back. The door marked Authorized Personnel Only closed behind them.

His gut twisting, Chance marched back outside. The Jeep had been moved to the parking lot. The chief stood beside it, taking photographs of the damage. Gabe Mc-Gregor, dressed in jeans and a black leather jacket, had joined him. The firefighters were just finishing stowing their equipment.

"Will you be taking these?" One of the first responders held out Jack and Jill.

Chance took the kittens. He would have reached to shake the man's hand, but he had a tough enough time holding onto the two squirming felines. "Thank you for rescuing Jillian. She'll be really happy the kittens are okay."

"Just doing our job." The man grinned and then left with his crew.

The chief and Gabe stood beside the Jeep.

"What happened?" Gabe asked as Chance approached.

"We were on the way back to the B and B when a

truck barreled out of a side street and hit us broadside." Chance's throat tightened. "I was driving. Jillian took the brunt of the collision. She must have hit her head on the window."

"Can you describe the truck?" the chief asked.

Chance shook his head. "It didn't have the headlights on, and it was so foggy I didn't see what was coming until it hit. When it backed up, I caught a vague glimpse of the front. The grille looked like an older model. That's about all I could see. It hit us twice. Otherwise I would have assumed it was an accident. I didn't wait around to see if the driver would go for three."

The chief stepped away from Gabe and Chance and spoke into his radio mic. "Tell the units to be on the lookout for an older truck with a smashed front end. I'll be at the hospital until further notice."

Chance glanced toward the ER door. "If you're done with me, I'd like to check on Jillian."

Gabe waved a hand toward the door. "We want to check on her, too."

"Any idea who would want to hurt Jillian?" Chance asked as he walked toward the hospital entrance. "An attack as blatant as that had to be deliberate."

Gabe shook his head. "It doesn't make sense. Everyone in town loves Jillian. She may be new to Cape Churn, but she fit right into the community." Gabe led the way to the reception desk. "Let us know when we can go back to see Miss Taylor."

The woman behind the counter smiled up at Gabe and promised she would.

Chief Taggart entered as Gabe rejoined Chance.

"Bailey found the truck a couple blocks from where the attack occurred."

Chance's pulse quickened. "Whose is it? Did they find the driver?"

The chief scratched his head. "Belongs to Olie Olander, the owner of the marina. I called him and he didn't even know his truck had been taken. He and his wife were just sitting down to a late dinner at the marina. Knowing Olie, he probably left the truck unlocked with the keys in it. I mean, it's old and beat-up. Who'd want to steal it?"

"Someone who wanted to crash into Jillian's Jeep." Chance paced a few steps away and turned back to the two police officers. "First the locked basement door, then the vandalism at the house and now this. Makes me think the rock that dropped down in front of us on the highway last night might not have been so accidental either."

"What rock?" Gabe and Chief Taggart said as one.

"On the way to the B and B from Jillian's house last night, a boulder the size of a medicine ball fell from a cliff onto the highway and nearly hit us. If Jillian hadn't swerved and hit the brakes, it would have. We almost went over the side of the road."

"The curve in the road with the bluff on one side?" Gabe asked.

Chance nodded.

Gabe exchanged a glance with Taggart. "There's a pullout drive up to a scenic overlook at that point. Anyone could have driven up there and dislodged one of the many boulders hanging by a thread."

"Excuse me, Chief Taggart," the woman at the reception desk called out. "You can see Miss Taylor, now." She hit a button behind the counter and the door beside her desk opened. As Chance walked by, she held out her hands. "I'll take those while you're back there."

Chance handed over the kittens.

Chief Taggart led the way, and Gabe and Chance followed. The on-call doctor met them outside the exam room. "Miss Taylor is doing fine. She hit the window pretty hard, but so far she's not showing any signs of concussion and can leave the hospital. Someone will need to keep an eye on her and wake her every four hours to check on her. If she has a headache, dizziness, vomiting or confusion, call 911 and have them bring her back to the hospital."

After the doctor left, a nurse came out of the room and nodded. "Gabe, Chief Taggart, she's ready for questioning." The woman turned to Chance with a grin. "You must be Chance. Jillian told me about you." She stuck out her hand. "I'm Emma Jenkins, her nurse and friend. You can talk to her for a few minutes, but she's getting cranky."

"I heard that," Jillian called out from inside the room.

Emma winked. "She wants to go home."

Letting the chief and Gabe go in first, Chance followed and stood near the door, reluctant to crowd Jillian. He was fortunate the doctor and nurses let him come in at all when he really had no right to be in the room. He wasn't part of the police force, and he wasn't her fiancé or husband.

For a moment, he wondered what it would be like to be married or engaged to Jillian. Would his nightmares stop? Would he feel confident that in sleeping with her, he wouldn't wake up with his hands around her throat, caught in a terrible dream?

Jillian lay on the bed wearing a faded hospital gown, her pretty blond hair tangled and matted where blood had congealed. She had dark shadows beneath her eyes and her face was pale.

Chance wanted to kick everyone else out of the room so that he could hold her and tell her everything would be all right. But the police needed to know if she'd seen anything different, something that could lead them to the driver of the truck.

The chief asked her the same questions he and Gabe had asked Chance. Jillian didn't have any more definitive answers.

"It was foggy. I didn't see it coming." She touched a finger to her sore temple and winced. "I just want to go home to bed. I'm tired and need a shower."

"I can give you a ride there, since your Jeep is out of commission," Gabe offered.

"Thanks." She glanced past the chief and Gabe, her gaze on Chance. "Are you all right?"

"I'm fine. Just worried about you." He walked up to the side of the bed and took her hand. "I should have seen it coming."

"You couldn't have. I was there, I didn't see it until it hit. I'm glad you're okay." She bit down on her lip. "What about Jack and Jill?"

"Jack and Jill?" Emma laughed in the doorway.

Jillian gave the nurse a slight smile and winced. "Kittens."

Chance squeezed her hand lightly. "They're fine. The receptionist is holding on to them for now."

"Oh, good." She dragged in a deep breath and let it out slowly. "Can we go now? I need to get back and feed them. They have to be starving."

"All right. Everyone out," Emma said, shooing the

men toward the door. "The sooner she's in her clothes, the sooner I can discharge her."

The three men left the exam room and Emma closed the door.

"I'll bring my vehicle around to the door," Gabe offered and left.

"I'm worried about Jillian." The chief rocked back on his heels, staring at the closed door to the exam room.

"Me, too," Chance agreed.

"Based on all you've said, she could be in a lot more danger than she knows."

"You know her better than I do, but I'd venture to guess she wouldn't let any of this curtail her activities. She's a beautiful but stubborn woman."

The chief chuckled. "I don't know too many women who aren't stubborn, my wife included. I don't have enough staff to assign an officer to watch out for her. Since you're here for the wedding, could you keep an eye on Jillian?"

Chance nodded. "I'll stay with her as much as she'll let me."

"Thank you," the chief said. "I like the girl, and I don't want anything bad to happen to her."

The door opened and Nurse Emma wheeled Jillian out in a wheelchair.

Jillian wore a frown, her arms crossed over her chest. "I could have walked on my own," she grumbled.

"You'll have your opportunity to prove it when we get you outside the door," Emma said with a smile.

The two sets of automatic doors opened as the nurse wheeled Jillian through.

Once outside, the chief touched Jillian on the arm.

"Keep someone with you at all times. Until we figure out who's doing this, you might not be safe."

"Oh, for heaven's sake," Jillian exclaimed. "I don't want to be afraid of my own shadow."

"And we don't want to lose you." Chief Taggart bent down and pressed a gentle kiss to her forehead. The uninjured part. "Nora would never forgive me if something were to happen to you."

Jillian huffed but followed with a soft, teasing snort. "I'm fine. Everyone is making far too much out of a little bump on the head."

"Darlin'—" Chance extended a hand to her "—you were out for a couple minutes. You can't be too careful at this point."

Her cheeks flushed a pretty pink. She took his hand and let him pull her to her feet and into his arms.

Chance had wanted to hold her since she'd been knocked unconscious. Seeing her slumped over in her seat had brought back so many memories of men injured in battle, unable to get themselves out of the situation. Chance had carried his share of buddies from danger only to find they were dead. Their faces haunted his dreams. That hopeless, helpless feeling that he could do nothing to help them threatened to overwhelm him, even now.

Some of those feelings bled over into this situation. He hadn't been able to take care of Jillian immediately and, when he'd gotten to a safe location, he'd been unable to get her out of the vehicle without the help of the firefighters. Frustrated and helpless. Not something he ever liked being.

For a long moment he held Jillian pressed against him,

smelling the lingering scent of shampoo in her hair and feeling her warmth and the softness of her body.

Gabe cleared his throat loudly. "If you plan on getting home anytime soon, you need to get in the vehicle."

Chance eased Jillian to arm's length. "Okay?"

She nodded. "Yes, thank you."

"Front or backseat?" he asked.

"I'll take the back. I might want to lie down."

Chance caught Gabe's gaze.

Gabe nodded. "You should ride in the back with her. To keep an eye on her."

Glad Gabe understood, Chance helped Jillian into the backseat, then ran around to the other side and slid in beside her. He rested his arm behind her on the seat. "If you need to, you can lean on my shoulder or use me as a pillow."

She smiled. "Thanks, but I don't want to be a bother."

As they left the hospital in the back of Gabe's SUV, Jillian sat up straight without touching Chance. By the time they reached the edge of town, her shoulders sagged.

"Come here." Chance pulled her against him, holding her in the circle of his arm. "You've had a rough day."

She laughed softly. "Tell me about it." But she didn't pull away. Instead, she nestled against him and closed her eyes.

If he wasn't mistaken, she fell asleep halfway to the B and B.

"Is this where the rock hit?" Gabe asked softly, slowing at the curve against the cliff.

Chance leaned his head toward the window. "Yes."

"I'll have someone get up there and check it out."

"Thanks."

As Gabe pulled into the yard in front of the bed-and-breakfast, Molly and Nova descended the steps and hurried forward.

Gabe shifted into Park. Chance was reluctant to move and wake Jillian.

Nova reached the SUV first. "Emma called to let us know you'd be coming. How's Jillian?"

"I'm fine." Jillian sat up and blinked. "Just a bump on the head."

"I've got towels warming in the bathroom," Molly said. "I can help you with a shower."

Chance got out, rounded the SUV and held out his hands. "I'll get Jillian, if someone can take the kittens."

Jillian held out the two kittens.

Chance took them.

"Kittens? You have more than one now?" Molly laughed. "Are they like cells and they multiply?"

"You would think so." Chance handed off the kittens to Molly and then held out a hand to Jillian.

Jillian stared at Chance, her brows wrinkling. "I don't need help. I'm really okay." To prove it, once Chance pulled her to her feet, she stepped away from him. Immediately she swayed and her face turned white. "Well, maybe not—"

Chance scooped her up in his arms and carried her toward the bed-and-breakfast.

Nova hurried up the steps ahead of him and opened the door.

"Put me down," Jillian said. "I'm just tired. My legs work fine."

He didn't let go, but continued up the stairs. "I'm only helping you inside."

Jillian crossed her arms over her chest. "Helping is

offering an arm to lean on, not throwing me over your shoulder and carrying me like a caveman."

"I didn't throw you over my shoulder, and I'm not a caveman, although the idea has its appeal." He winked. "Just shut up and let me act macho. It's good for my ego."

She frowned. "Pumping up your ego is completely unnecessary and not my responsibility. It's already enormous."

He glanced down at her. "That hurt. And here I was, trying to be nice."

Her frown deepened. "Really? Or are you just pulling my leg?"

"Now, I can't quite pull your leg if my hands are full of the rest of you, can I?"

Nova chuckled. "Playing with fire there, McCall."

Maybe he was, but Chance liked sparring with Jillian. When she sighed and let him carry her inside, his chest filled with something he'd never felt before. A warmth that permeated his entire body and made him hungry for more.

Once inside, Jillian wiggled. "You can put me down."

"Sorry. That's not happening." He wasn't ready to let go of her and he wasn't willing to let her try the stairs on her own, fall and make her injuries worse. Besides, she was light. Her body pressed against his was doing crazy things to his insides and, well, after all that had happened, he couldn't let go. Not yet. Not anytime soon, for that matter. "This trip lasts all the way to the destination."

Chapter 10

Jillian held on as Chance carried her up the sweeping staircase without breaking a sweat or breathing hard. Based on the hardness of his muscular arms beneath her knees and behind her back, and the solid wall of his chest pressed to her side, he worked out and stayed in shape. Why was she arguing with him? If the man wanted to carry her, she should shut up and enjoy the ride.

Maybe she was afraid. Not of being dropped or of being too heavy for Chance to handle, but afraid of getting used to how he was being nice to her. Afraid she'd mistake nice for him falling in love with her, a relative stranger.

Chance didn't stop at the top of the stairs. When he started for her bedroom, she shook her head. "I'm far too dirty to get right into bed. I'd rather get a shower first."

Before she could tell him she could walk the few short

steps down the hallway, he'd carried her into the bathroom and set her on the closed toilet lid.

She put up a hand. "I draw the line here. I can undress myself and take a shower without your help."

"Are you sure?"

"If I wasn't able to do it on my own, I'd have Molly help."

"Did I hear my name?" Molly popped her head in the doorway. "Need a hand?"

Jillian shook her head. "No, thanks. Unless it's to convince this man I don't need him to help me into the shower."

Molly grinned. "Sounds like fun to me."

Jillian glared, heat climbing into her cheeks. She'd been thinking the same thing, only she would never have said it out loud.

"I guess you're not in the mood with that bump on your head." Molly clucked her tongue, letting her gaze sweep over Chance. "That's a shame, because he's hot."

Jillian gasped. "Molly! You're almost a married woman."

"Married. Not dead." Molly touched Chance's shoulder. "Don't mind me. I tend to speak my mind. Sometimes it gets me into trouble."

He grinned. "No offense taken. But I would feel better if she had someone with her to make sure she doesn't get dizzy and fall."

"Fine." Jillian wasn't going to convince the man otherwise. "Molly will stay with me."

Chance backed out of the room and closed the door.

As soon as the door was closed, Jillian let her guard down and sagged a little.

"Oh, baby, you aren't feeling so fine, are you?" Molly

turned on the water and adjusted the temperature. "Bath or shower?"

"Shower. I want to get in, get out and get to bed. I'm really tired from stripping wallpaper all day."

"I assigned Nova to kitten duty, so no need to worry about them. They're being fed as we speak."

Jillian unbuttoned her flannel shirt and pulled it off. "I'm sorry. I didn't mean to bring more work for you here at the B and B."

"Two kittens aren't work."

Jillian laughed. "Give them time to get used to the place. I'll bet you won't be saying they aren't work, then."

"Maybe not."

Jillian slipped out of her shoes and jeans and stood in her underwear. Molly turned her back while Jillian finished stripping and stepped into the shower. "I'm not in the least dizzy, if you want to leave."

"Are you sure?" Molly asked.

"I am. I won't be in here long."

"Then I'll leave you to it. Promise you won't fall and crack your injured head on something? Chance won't forgive me if you do."

"Why he should care, I don't know."

"Well, it's obvious he does. And I don't want him to be mad at me."

"I promise not to fall." Jillian squirted shampoo into her hand and rubbed it into her scalp. "Go on. I know you have better things to do than babysit a grown woman."

"Okay. I'll bring you a cup of hot cocoa." The door opened and closed.

Jillian tipped her head back and scrubbed her hair, careful not to touch the bandage and bump on her temple. She rinsed the suds out of her hair and then washed all the old house dust from her skin. She used a citrus-scented soap and felt the tension and soreness dissipating, going down the drain with the dirt.

When she'd finished, she applied conditioner to her hair and was rinsing when the door opened. "Molly?"

"Not Molly," a deep male voice said. "It's me, Chance. Just making sure you're okay. You've been in here a long time."

With conditioner streaming down her face, Jillian couldn't open her eyes. "I'm fine, and almost done." She finished rinsing her hair, her body burning hotter than the water. Chance was in the bathroom, on the other side of the shower curtain. And she was naked. All she had to do was pull back the curtain and invite him to join her.

She reached for the edge of the curtain before she realized what she was doing and snatched her hand back. Instead, she listened for the sounds of Chance leaving and the door closing behind him.

No sounds came to her in the bathroom. "Too bad he left. It might have been fun to share the shower." She turned off the water and gripped the edge of the curtain.

A towel flew over the top of the curtain rod and draped down to within Jillian's reach. She squealed and almost slipped on the slick floor of the tub. "Chance?"

He chuckled. "Still here."

She pressed a hand to her naked chest. "Damn. Don't you ever give up?"

"Not easily."

Jillian bit her bottom lip, grabbed the towel and wrapped it around her body. "Tell me you didn't hear my last remark."

"I didn't hear your last remark," he said.

Jillian let go of the breath she'd been holding. Thank

God. She wouldn't have been able to face him if he'd heard what she'd said.

"I'll be in the hall if you need anything." He opened the door. "And for what it's worth, all you had to do was ask. I'd have said yes to sharing a shower."

"Jerk!" She picked up the bar of scented soap and flung it over the curtain toward his head.

The door to the bathroom closed before the soap hit it and fell to the floor.

With the towel firmly anchored around all the important parts, Jillian slid back the curtain and stepped onto the floor mat. Chance was gone, but she could still feel his presence. Her anger was short-lived and by the time she dried herself, she was smiling at his casual flirting.

And he *had* been flirting. Why else would he admit to wanting to share a shower with her?

Wrapping another towel around her hair, Jillian looked for her clothes. The pile she'd left on the bathroom floor was gone. Molly had probably taken them down to be laundered. She couldn't ask for a better friend.

Covered sufficiently with the towel, Jillian pressed her ear to the door. She didn't hear anything. Perhaps Chance had gone to his room to gather his toiletries for his shower. Which would give Jillian time to make a dash for her bedroom, thus avoiding coming face-to-face with the man who now knew she wanted to shower with him.

She flung open the door and hurried into the hallway and almost tripped over Chance leaning against the wall.

He gripped her arms, pulling her against his chest to steady her. "I thought you said you weren't dizzy."

"I'm not." She glanced down at his feet. "Your big feet were sticking out. I tripped."

He pushed her to arm's length and stared down at her. "My apologies."

Jillian took a step back, out of his reach, her arms tingling where he'd touched her skin. If she didn't get away from him soon, she might ask if she could join *him* in the shower. And what would that get her? She'd shrivel up like a prune and be heartbroken when he left.

No. She was better off steering clear of entanglements. Straightening her shoulders, she said, "I survived in the shower by myself. I think I can make it to my bedroom."

He nodded. "Then I'll leave you alone. Have a good night."

Jillian stood for a moment. That was it? He wasn't going to insist on walking her to her door, or carrying her to her bed? Jillian's core heated at the thought of Chance carrying her when all she wore was a towel that could easily slip open…

Hiding her disappointment, Jillian tilted her chin and moved past him. If she put a little sway in her hips, so be it. The man needed to know what he was missing by giving up too soon.

She made it all the way to her door, and he hadn't said one word.

Fine. What was she trying to accomplish anyway? She turned the knob and was about to enter when his voice stopped her.

"Jillian?"

She turned slowly, her heart in her throat. Would he tell her he wanted her?

"Leave the connecting door between our rooms unlocked. I'll check on you in the night like the doc advised." He held up his hands. "It's either me or Molly, but I'd rather you didn't leave your door to the hallway unlocked."

Jillian stared at him, her mind taking in what he'd just said. Leave the door unlocked between them? Her thoughts sprinted ahead of her, the possibilities endless and titillating.

"Don't worry," he said, his mouth quirking upward at one corner. "I won't take advantage of you. I made a promise to the chief to look out for you."

"Okay." Jillian entered her room and closed the door, leaning against it, her pulse pounding. How was she supposed to sleep when Chance could be entering her room at any time during the night?

She let the towel drop to the floor and crossed the room to the lock on the connecting door. With a quick flick, she unlocked her side. He'd have to unlock his before he could enter. Standing in front of the door naked, Jillian closed her eyes and willed Chance to twist his lock and check on her now.

After a few moments, Jillian realized how silly and pathetic she must look. He said he wouldn't take advantage of her. Yeah, he said he'd have taken a shower with her, but he might have been kidding.

Jillian turned away, unwound the towel from her head and reached for panties and a nightgown, opting for her best and sexiest.

Just in case.

Once she was dressed, she sat on the cushioned stool in front of the dresser mirror and combed the tangles out of her damp hair. Still, Chance hadn't unlocked his side.

With a sigh, she reminded herself that she wasn't interested in a really short relationship with a man destined to leave when the wedding was over. With that thought firmly planted in her head, she climbed into the bed and pulled the quilt up to her chin, feeling a little sad.

A soft tap on her hallway door made her abandon the bed and hurry to answer.

Molly stood on the other side, carrying two mugs of steaming, sweet-smelling liquid. "I thought I could sit with you long enough to share a cup of cocoa."

"I would love that." She turned back to the bed and climbed in, pulling the blanket up around her. Then she patted the bed beside her. "Have a seat."

Molly sat beside her, kicked off her shoes and crossed her legs. "Nova made a bed for Jack and Jill in the laundry room. They both ate and are now fast asleep on a fleece blanket. That will give you a night of uninterrupted sleep."

"Thank you for all you've done."

"Me? You're the one managing my wedding. I wouldn't have had a clue what to do. How do you know all this wedding stuff?"

Jillian grinned. "The internet."

"You are such a good friend." Molly touched her knee. "I feel like we've known each other forever and it's only been two years."

"Yeah, me, too."

"The chief filled me in on what happened today. I wish I knew who was doing all this. I'd take them out," Molly said, her tone fierce, her eyes flashing. "You're one of the nicest people I know. You don't deserve to be terrorized."

"I can't figure out why. I don't recall making anyone mad enough to hurt me. I've been here two years, doing the same thing—selling real estate. What's different?"

Molly stared down into her mug. "Seems like it all started when you bought the house."

"Oh, please. Don't tell me you think a ghost crashed Olie Olander's truck into my Jeep."

"No, of course not. But do you think someone is trying to scare you away from it?"

Jillian sipped her cocoa. "It's been empty for seventeen years."

"Maybe it's hiding secrets. Have you looked for any hidden panels or doors? Are there any loose boards in the floor?"

Jillian snorted. "There are loose boards everywhere and half the walls are exposed to the beams. We've ripped out cabinets, torn up old flooring and peeled wallpaper. Short of bringing in a bulldozer and knocking it down, I don't know what else to do."

Molly lifted her brows.

"I'm not bulldozing that house. It's my home and no one is going to scare me away from it or from Cape Churn."

"I don't blame you, but I also don't want my best friend and wedding planner hurt."

"Don't worry, Molls," Jillian said. "I'm going to see you through your wedding, come hell, high water or ghosts."

Molly smiled and took Jillian's empty mug from her. "I'd better let you sleep now. Surely everything will be brighter in the morning."

When Jillian started to rise, Molly held up her hand. "I'll lock up on the way out. You just lie down and get some sleep."

"Yes, Mother." Jillian winked. "Thank you for taking care of me."

"I love you like a sister. And tomorrow, if you go back out to your house, you can leave the kittens here. That would be one less thing to keep an eye on."

"Thank you. I'm sure they'll be safer here than among all the construction."

Molly twisted the lock on the doorknob, let herself out and closed the door behind her.

Suddenly more tired than she could remember being, Jillian stretched out on the bed and pulled the blankets up around her chin.

If Chance had plans to ravage her body, he'd have to wait now. She was too tired to participate. Maybe in four hours when he checked on her, she'd be up to seducing the man.

She yawned once, her eyelids so heavy she had to close them. Moments later she drifted to sleep.

Chance stripped down to his boxers and would have climbed into the bed, but he couldn't. Wound up from the attack and what it meant, he couldn't settle his thoughts. Instead, he paced the room on the other side of the wall from Jillian. Several times he stopped short of throwing open the connecting door and marching in to see how she was. Each time, he forced himself to wait. He needed sleep, but to sleep meant to dream.

Minutes before, he'd heard the click of the door lock on Jillian's side, which meant she'd chosen to leave their adjoining door unlocked.

A warm glow spread through him. She trusted him to keep her safe.

All the more reason for him to stay awake. He couldn't risk falling to sleep. What if his nightmares took him into Jillian's room and he tried to kill her, thinking she was the enemy? He couldn't forgive himself. Just in case he did drift off, he set his timer for four hours. He'd wake Jillian and check on her. Then he'd have her lock the door behind him so he could sleep without worrying that he'd hurt her.

Chance continued to pace, knowing he had to fight exhaustion for the next four hours. An hour into his vigil, he sat in the chair by the window and opened a magazine about the Oregon coastline. Somewhere in the middle of the stories about pirates and pioneers, and the tenth photo of a lighthouse, he slipped into a troubled sleep.

Their squad had infiltrated the Afghan village shortly after midnight, slipping through the dirty streets like shadows. Intelligence reports indicated the village was harboring a Taliban leader responsible for the raid on a US Army outpost that ended in twenty-three Americans and six British soldiers dead, and thirty wounded.

Chance knew one of the men who'd died in that raid. He left behind a wife and two little girls.

Taking out the leader responsible for his death wouldn't bring him back. But it would keep the bastard from making more widows and orphans.

The village had been too quiet. Their unit had expected resistance from the get-go. So far it was too easy. Where were the guards? It felt like a setup, a potential ambush situation. Going from building to building, they'd found only civilians, women and children. Where were the men? Where were the Taliban fighters?

An explosion rocked the village, shouts sounded and gunfire erupted. Chance raced toward the sound, his weapon ready.

Another explosion went off in front of him, the force knocking him flat on his back. For a moment he couldn't get his breath. His ears rang and sounds came to him as if from down a long tunnel. He pushed to his feet and swayed. He staggered toward the corner of a building. His buddy who'd just turned that corner ahead of him lay on the ground, his body mangled and his eyes staring up at the sky. A Taliban fighter stood over him, an AK-47 rifle pointing at the soldier's chest.

Rage ripped through Chance. He jerked his rifle up and fired a burst of bullets, nailing the bastard. Another enemy fighter appeared from a side street, shouting and firing his AK-47 at Chance.

Adrenaline running high, Chance unloaded his magazine at the fighter and the one behind him. He dropped the empty magazine and shoved another from his vest into his weapon and ran in the direction from which the three Taliban fighters had come.

He came across an enemy fighter with a knife positioned at the neck of a fallen American soldier. Chance pulled the trigger and nothing happened. He shouted to keep the enemy fighter from plunging his knife into the soldier.

The man looked up, dropped the knife and reached for the weapons slung over his shoulder.

Chance slammed his hand on the magazine and pulled the trigger again. Nothing happened. He flung the weapon aside and charged the Taliban fighter, hitting him in the middle before he could get his weapon up. The man fell backward, landing hard on his back.

Chance pounced on the man and grabbed him by the throat, squeezing with all his strength.

A beeping sound pierced his concentration, pulling him back, out of the fight, out of the village and out of Afghanistan. He opened his eyes and stared around an unfamiliar room, filled with antiques and a four-poster bed.

He was drenched in sweat and his hands were curled around the armrests, his fingers digging into the cushion. The beeping continued until he located its source—the watch on his wrist. He let go of the armrests and touched the button on the side of the watch. The sound ceased immediately, leaving him surrounded in an eerie silence.

For several long moments he sat still in the chair, the lingering effects of the nightmare still fresh in his mind. As his thoughts cleared, he shook his head to banish the remainder of the dream, his thoughts turning to the watch alarm and why he'd set it.

Everything that had happened the previous day came back to him in a rush and he pushed to his feet. Crossing the floor in three long steps, he reached for the knob of the connecting door to Jillian's room.

A sound came to him through the thick panel of the old door. Was it a whimper, a high-pitched cry of a kitten, or had he imagined it? Pressing his ear to the door, he heard it again, only louder. This time he could tell it was a sob, followed by another and the quiet cry, "Please, let me go."

Chance twisted the knob and yanked on the door, but it didn't budge. It took him a precious second to remember he hadn't unlocked his side. After twisting the lock, he yanked open the door and rushed in.

Expecting to see someone hurting Jillian, he was surprised to see her asleep in the bed, her eyes squeezed tightly shut, her fingers tangled in the sheets, tears streaming down her face.

She rocked and thrashed her legs. "I want to go home,"

she murmured. More tears fell and she sobbed. "Please. It's so—" she sniffed "—dark...and cold."

The anguish in her cries tore at Chance's heart. He switched on the lamp on the nightstand, sat on the bed beside her and gathered her in his arms.

Jillian struggled against him, her hands flailing, her tears soaking his chest.

"Jillian, darlin', wake up," he said softly, stroking the blond hair out of her face. "Jillian, it's okay. Everything will be okay."

Chapter 11

"No. It's not. I want to go home." She wrapped her arms around his neck and pressed her body against him.

"You'll go home soon. I promise. Just wake up now."

"No. Want to sleep. So tired. So dark." She had yet to open her eyes and her tears were Chance's undoing.

"Please, Jillian. Open your eyes. You'll see. It's a dream. You're okay."

"Not a dream. Dark," she whispered. "Dark and cold."

He kissed her forehead, his heart aching with her pain. "Baby, wake up. I promise, everything will be okay." He rocked her, holding her close and knowing how real dreams could feel. He had lived through so many of his own nightmares.

"Don't want...to wake." Jillian snuggled closer. "Don't know where home is," she finished on a whisper.

His chest tightened and he pressed his cheek to her

hair. She was lost in a dream, not knowing where she was or which way was home. All the trauma of the day before must have left her feeling more insecure than she let on. "Open your eyes, Jillian, and you'll see. It's a dream." He kissed the top of her head and tipped her face up. Then he touched his lips to one of her eyelids, then the other. "Wake up, sweetheart. It's just a dream."

Her lashes fluttered. She opened her eyes and stared at him. Then she shot a glance left, then right and back to Chance.

He could see recognition dawn in her eyes, and she smiled. "Has it been four hours?"

Chance nodded.

She closed her eyes again and rested her cheek on his chest. "This is nice."

"Yes, it is." It beat the hell out of the horrible nightmare she'd been having. He tightened his hold and stayed where he was.

Jillian's breathing grew deeper.

Though he wanted to lie down next to her and hold her for the rest of the night, he didn't dare. Only minutes before, he'd had the dream that had plagued him since Afghanistan. He'd dreamed he was choking the enemy. Chance smoothed a stray hair back behind Jillian's ear. He couldn't risk it. He had his demons to fight. Apparently, Jillian had some of her own. But he wasn't her knight in shining armor come to slay hers.

When he started to turn away and slip out from beneath her, she draped an arm around his middle and opened her eyes. "Please stay."

With her blue eyes staring up at him, he froze.

The tears hadn't dried on her cheeks.

He couldn't risk falling asleep with her in his arms. It

was too dangerous. Could he stay awake? He squeezed his eyes shut and sighed. "Okay."

Her eyes drifted closed and the corners of her lips tilted upward. "Thanks."

When Chance leaned toward the light to turn it off, Jillian's fingers dug into his skin. "Don't." A tremor shook her body. "Leave it on."

If he'd had doubts about staying with her, Chance didn't anymore.

"Just curious…" she said. The blanket slipped down to her waist, exposing a filmy blue nightgown that did little to hide what was beneath it.

"Yeah?" he said, his voice tight, his groin tighter.

"Why are you in my bed?" Her hand flattened on his abdomen. "Not that I'm complaining."

"You were having a bad dream. I did the only thing a gentleman could do. I held you until you woke."

"Oh." She looked up at him again. "Did I snore?"

"No. Actually, you were crying."

Her brow puckered. "I was?"

"Do you remember what you were dreaming about?"

She lay still against him, her breasts pressed against his side, the sheer, filmy fabric tickling him. "No."

"You were moaning and you said something about it being dark."

She shook, her fingers digging into him again. "Dark?" she said, her voice shrinking to a whisper.

"Hey. Let it go. I'm sorry I brought it up."

Her entire body shook. "It was cold and dark. I didn't know where I was. I just wanted to go home, but I…"

"Didn't know where home was," he finished for her. He slid down in the bed and gathered her in his arms, smoothing his hand over her hair. "Now that you're awake, you know it was all a bad dream."

"Yes. Of course." She didn't sound completely convinced.

"Home is here in Cape Churn. You have your friends, Molly, Gabe and Nova." *And me*, he wanted to add, but he couldn't. He wasn't going to be around for long.

"And Nora and Tom, Emma and Dave," she said. "My friends are all the family I have."

"They can be enough. They all know you and love you. That's what counts. This is your home."

"And I'll soon have a house to live in." Her body relaxed against his. "Thank you for saving me."

"From what?"

"The dark."

"Glad to be of assistance." He lay for a long time, trying to hold back the rising sensations generated by her body nestled against his and her arm riding low on his belly, close to the elastic waistband of his boxers. God, this was the worst kind of torture.

When she slid a slim naked leg over his, he came so close to losing it, he groaned.

"Are you okay?" she asked, her voice soft and husky from sleep.

"No." He shifted. "I need to go back to my room."

"Why?"

The smoky tone of Jillian's voice sent raw heat south to Chance's groin. "Lying here with you is making me crazy. If I don't go now, I might do something I'll regret."

Her hand slid lower, bumping against the hard evidence of his rising passion beneath the fabric of his boxers. "*I* won't regret it."

"Sweetheart, that bump on your head is making you delirious."

"My thoughts are clear. I'm not dizzy, and I've never wanted anything more than I want you." She closed her hand around his arousal. "Right now."

"You're playing with fire, Jillian."

"Then warm me up." She raised her leg over his thigh, rubbing her sex against him. He could feel the hot moisture on her panties and he couldn't take it anymore.

In a second, he rolled over, pushing her onto her back, and leaned over her, planting his hands on either side of her head. "You're a very attractive woman, and you're quickly pushing me to the edge."

Her lips curled in a slow, sexy smile. "Good. What do I have to do to send you over?"

"This." He bent to claim her lips in a hard kiss, his erection pressing into her warm, soft belly. "And this," he said, his words mingling with her breath. With his tongue, he traced the seam of her lips until she opened and let him in. Quickly advancing, he thrust his tongue into her mouth, caressing hers in a primal mating dance.

After thoroughly tasting what she had to offer, he rose for air. "There's something you need to know."

She smiled, her eyelids lowering to half-mast. She leaned up and kissed his chin, his neck and his collarbone before responding, "Go on."

Everywhere she touched him lit up like the Fourth of July. Chance sucked in a deep breath and let it out. "I'm not fit for long-term relationships." There. It was out in the open. She could end it or live with it, but at least she knew the stakes.

Jillian raised her hand and cupped his cheek. "Was I asking for one?"

"No, but you need to stop me now, if that's what you want."

"I don't. I want what is here and now. Tomorrow is another day."

"If you don't stop me now, there may be no going back."

Jillian dragged her fingernails lightly down his back and beneath the waistband of his shorts to slide over the curve of his buttocks. "Trust me, there was no going back from the day I met you. Please," she said, her fingers digging into his flesh. "Don't stop. I know what I'm getting into. Only one thing…"

He sucked in a breath, so close to shooting over the top, he didn't think he'd last ten seconds in her hands. "What?"

"Protection."

Protection. His mind spun for a full second before he pictured the condoms he's stashed in his wallet several months ago, on the off chance he ever had time to date and just maybe get lucky.

"Hold that thought." He shot out of the bed, dashed to his room, riffled through his wallet and let go of the breath he'd held when he found the two foil packets stashed in one of the little pockets. He was back in less than a minute, slowing as he neared the bed, realizing he hadn't been gone long but possibly long enough for Jillian to change her mind.

She was sitting up in the bed, her hair spilling around her shoulders, the blanket pulled up over her chest.

"Change your mind?" he asked, sending a silent prayer heavenward. He'd have to take a really long, cold shower if she decided to back out at the last minute.

Jillian shook her head slowly and lowered the blanket.

Hallelujah echoed through Chance's head.

Oh, she was ready, all right. She'd removed the frothy blue nightgown and her full, perfectly formed breasts reflected a golden radiance from the soft glow of the nightstand lamp. "I believe you're overdressed. Do you need help stripping?" She tilted her head toward his boxers.

"I've got this." He winked and shed his shorts. Standing in front of her, he let his gaze travel over her lightly tanned face, neck, shoulders and breasts. "You're beautiful, Jillian."

Her gaze traveled from his head to his knees. "You're pretty hot yourself." Then she tossed the blanket to the side.

Chance let out a low whistle.

She lay against crisp white sheets, completely naked. With slow deliberation, she pulled her legs up, bending her knees and then letting them fall to each side.

That was all the invitation Chance needed. He crawled onto the bed between her knees and kissed her with all the emotion and passion he'd accumulated since he'd awakened her. When he'd fully conquered her mouth, he trailed kisses along her jaw and down the long, graceful length of her neck, pausing to tongue the wildly beating pulse at the base of her throat.

Continuing lower, he found the distended tip of one of her nipples and sucked it between his teeth, rolling it around and around.

Jillian gasped. She wrapped one of her hands against the back of his head and held him there while he laved the tip of her nipple until it tightened into a firm bead. This was where he wanted to be. Where he needed to be. If he died after this day, he'd die a happier man than he'd been in a very long time. But he wasn't dead and every cell in his body was alive and well, ready to take this woman all the way.

Jillian's breath hitched in her throat as Chance lavished his attention on first one, then the other of her breasts, sucking, nipping and tonguing them until the sensations pulled her core so tight she thought she might come apart if he stopped.

He trailed his mouth down her torso, kissing his way south toward the triangular tuft of hair covering her sex.

The path he traveled left her in tense anticipation of him reaching the goal. Curling her fingers into his hair, she struggled between wanting him to stop and dying for him to take it all the way there.

Chance paused, parted her folds and blew a warm stream of air over her heated skin.

Breathing became difficult and shaky. "Please," she whimpered.

He thumbed the center strip of flesh packed with hundreds of tiny nerve endings, each firing messages to her brain, screaming for more. He swept his tongue down the middle of her folds, sending electrical shocks speeding through her body.

Jillian pulled her knees closer and braced her heels against the mattress. Despite her determination to let him do what he would, she couldn't stop her hips from rising with every thrust of his tongue. Like the musician strumming the chords of an instrument, Chance drew the best music from her, lighting her entire world in a radiant glow.

When she thought she couldn't take such exquisite

pleasure one second longer, she rocketed over the edge, catapulting to the heavens.

As her hips rocked and her insides quaked in spasms, Jillian threw back her head and emitted an exultant cry. She tensed, drawing out the pleasure of her release until she drifted back to earth.

As satisfied as she was, she knew it could be even better with Chance buried deep inside. She laced her hands in his hair and tugged gently.

"Hey." He chuckled, climbing up her body. "That hair is attached."

"I want you."

"I'm all yours."

She shoved him to the side.

He dropped to the bed and rolled onto his back. "Pushy little thing, aren't you?"

"I don't want to lose what I have before you get there with me."

He grinned. "I like the way you think."

"Yeah, then you'll like this even better." She straddled his legs and wrapped her hands around his shaft. Slowly, she raised and lowered her fingers, squeezing gently, settling into a rhythm. Soon she increased the tempo.

Chance closed his eyes, his jaw taut. He thrust upward, matching her pace, his shaft sliding through her hands. Faster and faster until he froze and gripped her arms. "I can't hold out much longer."

"Protection," she said and held out her hand. Chance grabbed one of the packets he'd left on the nightstand and placed it in her hands.

Jillian tore it open, removed the condom and rolled it down over his engorged shaft.

Then he sat up, rolled her off him and pinned her beneath him. "I can't go slowly."

"Don't," she said, her voice shaky. Delicious anticipation made it hard to breathe.

"I don't want to hurt you."

"You won't unless you stop. Enough talk." She spread her legs, bringing her knees up.

Chance pressed the tip of his erection against her entrance, dipped in and drew it out. His face was strained, his breathing ragged.

Anxious, yearning and past her ability to be patient, Jillian grabbed his buttocks and slammed him into her.

He glided into her drenched channel, filling her with his length and girth, stretching her wonderfully.

Jillian wrapped her legs around his waist and pressed her heels into his backside, urging him go deeper, to take more.

He pulled out and thrust hard.

Startled and thrilled, Jillian exclaimed, "Yes!"

Apparently encouraged, Chance slammed into her again and again, taking her long and hard.

Squeezing her thighs and calves, Jillian matched his rhythm and then dropped her heels to the bed, pushing up to meet him, their bodies coming together in an explosion of sensations.

Tingling started at her core and flared through her, spreading so fast she thought for certain it would burst out of the tips of her fingers and toes.

Chance drove in one more time, going deep. He held, his body tight, his jaw rigid and his eyes closed, his shaft throbbing against the walls of Jillian's channel. Finally he drew in a deep breath and lowered himself, twisting sideways to lie beside Jillian, taking her with him, never breaking their intimate connection.

She snuggled into him, pressing her cheek to his chest, feeling complete with him still inside her. Jillian lay awake for a long time, counting his heartbeats, her hand pressed to his chest.

Having only known this man for such a short time, she shouldn't have such deep feelings for him. So many questions flowed through her mind, questions only time and getting to know him would answer.

Did he have family somewhere? What was he like growing up? Was he mischievous? Did he get into trouble? Could he ride a bicycle? Were his parents still alive? What was his favorite color? Could he ever consider living in Cape Churn? Did he want children? Did he believe in love? For all Jillian knew, the man was a confirmed bachelor, willing to sleep with a woman but never settle down.

Her heart squeezed hard in her chest. Just because she had made love with this gorgeous man didn't mean they would be together forever. She couldn't expect him to declare his undying love based on such short acquaintance and sex. Hadn't he said he wasn't staying?

Closing her eyes, she lay still, willing herself to go back to sleep. Whatever the next day brought, at least she had that night and the connection they'd shared. She wouldn't ask for more. But if he were willing to give more…she'd consider it.

Chapter 12

Light pushed through the seams of Chance's closed eyes, nudging him from the deepest sleep he'd had in a very long time. He blinked and stared up at an antique light fixture. He lay still, trying to remember where he was.

A warm, soft hand slipped across his belly and lower to where his rock-hard erection tented the blanket.

He jerked awake and stared down at Jillian, her blond hair spread on the pillow beside him, her cheeks rosy, her lips swollen from kissing the night before.

Holy hell, after he'd discarded the condom, he'd been too tired and too comfortable to move. Telling himself he'd only be there for a few more minutes, he'd fallen to sleep, holding Jillian in his arms.

What a mistake—a huge mistake.

His heart raced and his pulse pounded against his

ears. He could have had another one of his nightmares. Damn. He could have hurt or killed this woman who was coming to mean more to him than he ever wanted or expected. What had he been thinking?

That was it, he hadn't been thinking. Making love to Jillian had wiped all other thoughts or precautions from his mind. When his body was sated, he'd fallen asleep with her in his arms.

God. I could have hurt her.

As much as he wanted to stay, wrapped in the warm cocoon of her body and the blankets, he couldn't lead her on. He'd never intended to sleep with Jillian. She wasn't the kind of woman who would appreciate a one-night stand, and he wasn't the kind of man who would take advantage of her. Yet he had. The trouble was, he couldn't be anything more to her than a one-night stand. Sleeping with her on a regular basis would put her at too much risk.

Convinced she would be better off without him, Chance shifted his body in an attempt to leave the bed without waking her.

As soon as he moved, her hand pressed against his abdomen and she curved a leg over his, rubbing her naked sex on his thigh.

Chance swallowed a groan. This woman was sweet, sweet torture.

Jillian moved against him, her breasts nudging his side, her hand dropping lower, slender fingers wrapping around his jutting shaft.

He couldn't move now if the house was on fire. While his mind told him to leave, his body would have none of it. This was what he wanted. But he couldn't let her think he was in it for the long haul. That wasn't a possibility. At least not until the dreams went away. Who knew when that would happen?

Come to think of it, he hadn't dreamed at all with Jillian in his arms. One night of sleep wasn't enough to call it a cure. It had to have been a fluke.

"Jillian, what we're doing…" he started.

"Mmm?" Her eyes were still closed and she moved slowly as if still half-asleep.

"I can't make any promises."

Her hand slid the length of his erection. "Not asking for any," she said, her breath warm against his naked chest.

"I leave after the wedding."

"I know." She shifted and rose up to kiss his mouth, her eyes open. "I'm not asking for anything other than this morning."

"I don't want to hurt you."

"Who says I won't hurt you?" She winked.

"Sweetheart, I believe you could." He thrust upward in the circle of her fingers. "But I can't imagine you doing it intentionally."

She moved her hand up and down, the warmth and friction bringing him quickly to the peak.

Placing a hand over hers, he stopped her. "It doesn't take much to send me over the edge in the morning."

"Good." She reached for the last foil packet on the nightstand, tore it open and rolled it down over him. Then she straddled him, positioning her entrance over him.

The chill air made her nipples taut.

Chance covered her breasts with his hands as she lowered herself, taking him into her. Her chest rose as she drew in a deep breath and closed her eyes. "Oh, yes. I remember this from last night."

He slipped his hands from her breasts to her hips. "You feel amazing."

"I was going to say that." She rose up and lowered herself again, her eyes opening, her hands resting on his chest. "Do you want me to go faster?" She rose up again.

"Yes." She felt so good, he could hardly breathe. Her tight channel encased him like a hot, slick glove, squeezing gently around him. He tightened his hands on her hips and brought her down, guiding the pace, making it faster, harder.

The bedsprings squeaked with the force of their coupling, making it even sexier.

Chance thrust hard and held Jillian down over him, his shaft locked inside her as he shuddered and throbbed to the end.

Jillian smiled and lay down on him, a slight shiver shaking her body.

"Are you cold?" he said, pulling at the covers, dragging them up over both of them.

"A little, but this feels too good to move," she said, her lips finding one of his hard brown nipples and kissing him there.

For a long time, they lay entwined, the sun peeking through the curtains. Chance had no desire to move, and every desire to remain with Jillian for a very long time.

Jillian could have stayed burrowed in the bed with Chance forever. She'd never felt more protected, cared for and—

A knock on the door jerked her out of her euphoric cocoon.

"Jillian?" Molly's voice said through the wood panel. "Will you be coming down for breakfast? I'm about to put everything away and want to make sure you don't go hungry."

Jillian clutched the quilt to her bare breasts, as if Molly might see through the door and catch her in bed with Chance. "I'm...uh...not hungry, but thank you."

"I could save a plate for you in the refrigerator, if you change your mind," Molly persisted.

"Oh, okay."

Chance swept his hand along her side at her most ticklish spot, making Jillian giggle. "Stop," she whispered.

"Are you feeling okay?" Molly asked.

"I'm fine." Chance tickled her again. Jillian swallowed hard on a full-on laugh.

"I could bring your breakfast up to you, if you like."

Choking now on her laughter, Jillian could barely get out, "No...no... I'll be down soon." She swatted Chance and leaned over to kiss him on the mouth. "You're a menace."

"I'll take that as a compliment." He kissed her and hugged her close.

Molly's footsteps could be heard moving down the hallway.

A knock on the next door made Jillian lose it and laugh out loud.

"Chance?"

In a voice loud enough to be heard through the door and down the hall, Chance said, "Save me a plate, too. I'll be down with Jillian, and I'm starving."

From the hallway, Molly said, "Oh. Well, then. I'll save two plates. Take your time." Her footsteps faded away.

Jillian frowned up at Chance. "Now you've done it. Molly will be beside herself until we go downstairs."

"Molly's a grown woman with a wedding less than a week away. I'll bet she doesn't have time to worry about all of her houseguests."

Jillian rolled her eyes and sat up, letting the sheet drop to her waist. Hell, he'd seen all of her, having left the light on all night. Being in bed naked with Chance made her feel more sensual than she'd ever felt in her life. But Molly was waiting and Jillian had a ton of things to do that day. "Get up."

Chance crossed his arms behind his head. "I'm on vacation. I think I'll spend today in bed. Care to join me?"

"I would, but Molly is expecting Nova's family today, and I should clear out so she can make room for them."

A frown formed on his brow, making him even sexier in a brooding way. Jillian couldn't stop herself from kissing the lines forming on his forehead. "Stop frowning. If all goes well and on schedule, I should have running water in my house today. Which means I can move in." She swung her legs over the side of the bed with the intention of getting up.

An arm around her middle pulled her back against Chance and he fondled a breast. "If you're worried about clearing a room, you can move next door with me. Or vice versa. I could sleep on one of the chairs."

Chair, hell. Tempted to take the offer, Jillian chewed on her bottom lip. She came back to the fact she could get too used to this man in her bed, all too quickly. And then what? He'd be gone. "Much as I appreciate the sacrifice, I want to get used to living in my own house as soon as possible. It's the first house I've ever owned. I want it to be home. Besides, my staying here would only add to the burden of the B and B. One more mouth to feed." Jillian hugged him again and tried again to leave the bed.

Chance sat up and gripped her arms. "You can't stay in that house alone. It's too dangerous."

She stiffened. "It's my house. I will be living there alone for a very long time. The sooner I get used to it, the better." She cupped his cheek. "Thank you for worrying about me, but I've lived alone for a long time. I can take care of myself."

"In all the time you lived on your own, how many times has someone physically attacked you or vandalized your place?"

Damn. The man had a point. "I do own a gun. I'll keep it in the nightstand." She looked him square in the eye. "I'll be okay."

Chance let go of her arms and she got out of bed. She grabbed a robe and slipped it over her shoulders before she turned to face him. "I want you to know, last night was great, but you're under no obligation to keep me entertained."

"I don't expect to entertain you." He rose and stood in front of her, naked and…wow…magnificent.

Jillian swallowed hard and tried to make herself clear. "I mean you're not responsible for me or my happiness. I won't make any demands of you. I know you're leaving when the wedding's over." Jillian realized she was babbling and she didn't know how to stop. "I just wanted you to know last night was fun, but I'm a big girl and don't expect what happened last night to mean anything."

He crossed the room, parted the robe and circled her naked waist with his big, warm hands, making her knees weak. "Shh."

"I know what I got myself into."

He kissed her lips. "You're not staying in your house by yourself. At least not while I'm here."

She frowned. "I don't need a babysitter."

"Darlin', I think of you in a lot of ways, but baby isn't one of them." He bent, hooked the back of her thighs in his arms and lifted, wrapping her legs around his waist. "Do you think Molly would mind if we were a little longer going down for breakfast?" he said, nudging her entrance with his hardened erection, still encased in a condom.

Jillian captured his cheeks between her hands and pressed her lips to his. "Molly who?"

An hour later, after making love again, a shower together and dressing in work clothes, Jillian led the way down the stairs to the kitchen.

"About time you two showed up. Nova's parents, aunt and uncle called from the airport. They're on their way and I have a ton of things to do to get ready." Molly studied Jillian's temple and gave her a sly smile. "I take it the bump on your head didn't slow you down."

Heat rose up Jillian's neck and into her cheeks. "Never felt better."

Molly's grin spread wide. "Glad to hear it. Your breakfast is in the refrigerator. You can help yourselves."

"Thank you," Jillian said. "Don't let us get in your way. I packed my things and stripped the sheets. I expect my electricity and water to be on today."

Molly frowned. "And if they aren't?"

Jillian shrugged. "I'll make other arrangements. You need the room for your in-laws."

Molly touched Jillian's arm. "I don't like the idea of

you living in that house with someone trying to hurt you or vandalizing the place."

"I'll be okay. I have a handgun."

"And I'll be staying with her." Chance slid an arm around Jillian's waist and pulled her back against him. "Until we find out who's behind the attacks, I don't think she should be alone," he said, his warm breath stirring her hair.

Jillian leaned into him for a moment, loving the way he made her feel safe and protected. Though he wasn't going to be around forever, dare she enjoy him for now?

Molly's brows rose. "Are you sure? I hate to reassign your room if you're going to need it. Nova's sister decided to come after all, and I wasn't sure where we'd put her."

"Let her have my room," Chance insisted. "I can camp out with Jillian."

"Okay." Molly beamed. "I'm glad you two are getting along so well. Hopefully this ugly business with the attacks will clear up before the end of the week."

Jillian hugged her friend. "Don't you worry about me. You have a wedding to enjoy. This week is all about you and Nova. Which reminds me, I need to stop by the florist and the party rental places for a final verification. I'll do that on my way through town."

"You should run by your insurance adjuster and report the hit-and-run," Molly advised. "Oh, Nova brought your Jeep to the B and B, though it's pretty banged up. If you like, you can use my SUV."

"Was the Jeep drivable?"

"Yes, but getting in and out of the passenger side is difficult."

"Comes with having to pry you out with the Jaws

of Life." Chance frowned, remembering how helpless he'd felt.

"We can take the Jeep for now, and switch with Chance's rental at the house," Jillian said. "I'll take the kittens off your hands when I get settled in."

"Don't worry about Jack and Jill. Nova likes playing with them, and you have too many workers traipsing in and out during the day. I'll keep them until the wedding."

"Great." No wonder she loved Molly so much. The woman would do anything for a friend.

Molly left the kitchen, headed for the upstairs bedrooms to prepare them for the influx of Nova's family.

Jillian removed the two plates from the fridge and popped one in the microwave. She and Chance sat across the kitchen table, eating fluffy scrambled eggs, sausage and biscuits like a couple, the silence between them comfortable.

Though the atmosphere and company were perfect, Jillian couldn't help thinking this was all a very bad idea. At this rate, she could fall in love with this guy. And where would that leave her in a week's time?

Heartbroken and lonely.

Chance chewed on a bit of biscuit slathered in apple butter and swallowed. "I've been thinking."

"Mmm." Jillian had just taken a bite of her biscuit.

"If your troubles didn't begin until you bought the house, I'm willing to bet someone has a secret relating to that house. A secret they don't want you or anyone else to discover."

She swallowed and stared across the table with her incredibly blue eyes. "What secret?"

"We didn't find any articles about murders or deaths

associated with the house. But then, we didn't have time to look back before little Julia disappeared."

"Do you think Julia Thompson's disappearance might be the reason someone is trying to scare me away?"

"Maybe. I have my boss checking on the missing girl and the case surrounding her disappearance. I'll give him a call when we get back in cell phone coverage in Cape Churn."

Jillian smiled. "It's one of the perks and one of the difficulties of living out of town. Cell phones are useless and landlines are not obsolete."

Chance finished the last bite of biscuit and dusted the crumbs from his fingers. "I'm ready when you are."

"Are you sure you want to follow me around? It won't be much fun for a guy on vacation."

"As long as I don't have someone shooting at me or trying to blow me up, it'll be a great vacation," he said, and meant it.

"I'll grab my bag and meet you at my banged-up Jeep." She frowned. "My poor Jeep. Another thing to add to my list—stop by my insurance agent's office in town. I hope they cover hit-and-runs."

Though Jillian made light of the previous night's attack, Chance wasn't letting his guard down. Someone wanted Jillian out of the way completely, or so scared that she'd leave Cape Churn.

Why?

Jillian drove into town in the damaged Jeep. Chance managed to pry the passenger door open enough to get in and out, but it didn't close well and the glass was broken.

Once in town, Jillian headed for the florist. While she was inside checking on the flowers for the wedding, Chance placed a call to Royce at SOS headquarters.

"Chance," Royce answered on the first ring. "Glad you called. I have a little information on the missing-girl case."

"Good. Things are heating up around here."

"Tell me about it."

Chance filled in Royce on the attacks.

"I'm not sure the missing girl has anything to do with it, but there were a couple of suspects questioned. You might see if they're still around."

"Shoot," Royce said.

"You can start with Sarah's ex-husband, Alan Thompson. Another name came up, George Williams, a man who'd been stalking Sarah since her divorce. If you could find them, you might get more information out of them than the news articles and police records indicated."

"Thanks." Royce paused for a moment and then added, "Anything else? Any older cases involving the house itself? Cold cases? Murders, deaths?"

"Nothing. The house was originally built by a banker for his family, Sarah's great-grandfather, and was passed down to members of the same family. Sarah inherited it from her father. And she sold it and moved away after her daughter's disappearance."

"I'd move, too, if my daughter disappeared for thirty days and turned up like Julia," Royce said. "I can imagine how frightening it might have been for the mother to know whoever held her daughter hostage wasn't captured and put away."

"Did you find anything on where Julia and Sarah disappeared to?"

"Geek's checking with the Social Security database to see if Sarah officially changed their names and requested new Social Security numbers."

"He has access to that database?" Chance never ceased to be amazed at what Geek was able to hack into.

"Let's just say he's tiptoeing through cyberspace to find information." Royce paused. "What about Jillian? You said she's only been in Cape Churn for two years. Is she running from something? Hiding from her past? Could it be someone finally caught up with her?"

Chance hadn't looked at the situation from that direction. "You can't tell me you didn't research her on the off chance she has a troubled past."

Royce chuckled. "We did, but didn't find much. She's from Portland and she's involved in real estate. Before that she graduated from Oregon State University with a degree in marketing. Her mother and stepfather, Robert and Sandra Taylor, raised her. We did find where Robert Taylor adopted Jillian. Sandra and Jillian's prior last name was Warren. No mention of her biological father or where he might be."

"No Mr. Warren? Did you find a birth certificate?" Chance wondered if Jillian would be angry with him for digging into her past. His lips pressed together in a tight line. If digging kept her safe, he would risk her anger.

"No. That's the strange thing. We have no birth record of Jillian Warren."

"Maybe she was born in another state?" Chance offered.

"That's possible. We'll run a check against her Social Security card when we do the lookup on Sarah and Julia Thompson. When applying for a Social Security number, the parent has to submit a birth certificate for verification of citizenship. There should be a digital copy of that certificate or a number associated. Either way, we should be able to track down her birth certificate."

Jillian exited the florist shop, sniffing a white rose-bud, a smile on her lips.

"Let me know what you find," Chance said. "I'm out here." He ended the call with Royce and waited for Jillian to get into the Jeep.

"Who were you talking to?" Jillian asked as she slipped into the driver's seat.

"My boss."

She stilled with one hand on the steering wheel, the other on the key in the ignition. "Are you going back to work before the wedding?"

He took the rose from her, and dragged the velvety white petals against her cheek. "No, I'm here to make sure Nova lives up to his promise." Chance winked and leaned across the console to kiss her.

"Good." Jillian twisted the key in the ignition. "If he doesn't want you back at work, what *did* he want?"

"He has access to certain information." Chance chose his words carefully. So much of what they did with Stealth Operations Specialists was classified top secret. "I was hoping he could find information about the house and the people who lived there."

"And?" She shifted into Reverse, pulled out of the parking lot and drove toward the party rental store.

"He gave me the names of two of the suspects in Julia Thompson's disappearance. George Williams and Alan Thompson."

Jillian shot a glance his way as she pulled into the parking area of the party rental store. "Alan Thompson?"

Chance nodded. "As in Julia's father—Sarah's ex-husband. Julia's father might still be alive."

Jillian shifted into Park.

"George Williams." Jillian tapped a finger to her chin.

"Seems there's a George Williams on the construction team. What are the chances he's the same George we need to talk to?"

"As small as Cape Churn is, it's likely they are one and the same."

"We can question him when we go out to the house. And I need to check on the status of the plumbing. If it's done today, I'm moving in."

"While we're at the house, we can switch vehicles. My rental might not look great, but the doors open and close without a crowbar."

Chance kept a close watch out for vehicles coming out of nowhere to ram into them. He doubted it would happen in the daylight, but it didn't hurt to be aware at all times.

Three trucks stood in the yard of Jillian's house when they pulled in.

Bob came around the side of the house as Jillian and Chance got out of the Jeep. His eyes rounded. "What happened to your Jeep?"

"Someone didn't yield to the right of way." Jillian smiled at the older man. "How's it going?"

Chance hid a grin. Though she had been attacked, she kept a good sense of humor. Another reason to like the woman.

"The paint should be dry in the upstairs bedroom you wanted us to finish first. We were able to salvage the original hardwood flooring. It just needed sanding and a finish. You can move in as soon as the plumber has your water turned on."

Jillian beamed. "Thanks, Bob." She touched his arm. "You and your crew are doing a great job. Speaking of your crew—" she glanced around "—George Williams is one of your guys, isn't he?"

"Yes, ma'am."

"Is he here today?"

"He sure is. I have him stacking lumber and cleaning up in the back of the house, since Daryl didn't show up at the café this morning."

"He didn't?" Chance frowned. "Was he sick?"

"I called his house, and his mother answered. She said he wasn't going to help on my crew today." Bob shrugged. "I can't decide whether or not I'm disappointed. He wanders off too many times."

"That's a shame. I hope he's feeling okay."

"I like helping out, but I need people I can count on." Bob tilted his head. "George is out back."

"Thanks." Chance hooked Jillian's arm and led her around the house.

A man tossed a board onto a stack, muttering as he turned to lift another. "He could hire a monkey to do this work. I'm a damned trim carpenter, not a janitor."

Jillian cleared her throat. "George?"

The man spun, frowning. "Yeah?"

Chance stuck out his hand. "I'm Chance McCall. Nice to meet you."

George stared at the hand for a moment, his eyes narrowing. Then he glanced up without shaking. "What do you want?" The man's tone was defensive and belligerent.

"To ask you a few questions." Chance dropped his hand and straightened to his full height, a couple inches taller than Williams.

Jillian started, "Mr. Williams, do you remember the former owner of this house, Sarah Thompson?"

George stared at Jillian, as if looking right through her. His face softened and the frown disappeared. "Yeah. I remember Sarah."

"We understand you were questioned in the disappearance of her daughter."

His jaw tightened and he pushed past Jillian and Chance. "I didn't have anything to do with her daughter's disappearance. I was interested in Sarah, not Julia. I'm not a pervert."

"We're not saying you were." Jillian hurried after the man as he entered the house.

"Why are you bringing it all up again? That was almost twenty years ago. The girl showed up, they moved, end of story." He lifted a flooring slat and flung it onto a pile of similar boards and continued into the kitchen.

"George," Bob called out from the front door. "Did you bring those cans of paint down from the upstairs bedroom?"

"Gettin' it," he yelled. George glared at Chance. "I got work to do." Again, he veered around Jillian and Chance and started up the stairs.

"Mr. Williams, is there any reason someone wouldn't want me to move into this house?" Jillian placed a hand on the banister, one foot on the step, preparing to follow Williams.

Chance stood behind her, adding, "Perhaps a reason that has something to do with Julia's disappearance?"

George stopped at the top of the stairs and leaned over the railing. "I didn't take Julia. I told the Cape Churn police, the state police, the sheriff and anyone else who would listen. I loved Sarah. I wouldn't have done anything to hurt her or her daughter."

"Do you know anyone who might have done it? Or who might want Miss Taylor to stay away from here?"

George stood straight, his face red, his eyes narrowed and angry. "I don't know now, any more than I did then. If I knew who took the kid, I'd have killed him myself." George leaned on the railing again. "The accusations, the suspicion ruined my life. You think I wouldn't have turned over the guy who did it to save my own stinkin' life?" He slammed his hand on the rail. "I'd have done it in a heartbeat—"

A loud crack sounded and Williams lurched, his arms flying out to his sides. The railing in front of him fell, crashing to the hardwood floor. Williams followed.

Jillian screamed.

Chance darted toward the man but couldn't get there in time to break his fall.

Williams hit the floor, landing on the pile of broken spindles, and lay still.

Chapter 13

Her heart lodged in her throat, Jillian rushed to George's side and bent to feel for a pulse. After several heart-stopping moments, she could feel the steady thump of his heartbeat, pushing blood through his veins. She released the breath she'd held. The man was unconscious but alive. For now. "I'm not moving him in case he's had a spinal injury. We need an ambulance. Now."

"On it." Chance ran out of the house. "Bob!"

The contractor rushed into the house, took one look at George and said, "I'll have to drive to the nearest house and use their phone or into town before I can get any cell phone reception."

"Go," Chance said. "I'll stay with Jillian and Mr. Williams."

Bob left the house and a moment later, Jillian heard an engine rev and the crunch of gravel as the contractor's truck raced out of the yard.

"I have a blanket in the back of my Jeep." Jillian said. "He'll need it if he goes into shock."

Chance didn't say a word, just ran for the Jeep and returned a minute later with the blanket. He spread it over George and squatted down on his haunches, shifting the railing spindles away from the man lying as still as death.

"We shouldn't have pushed him." Jillian chewed her lip, staring down at Williams. "He might not have slammed the railing."

"All he had to do was lean on it a little and it would have broken anyway."

"Was the wood that rotted?"

"No." Chance held up spindle and pointed at one end. "Several of these were sawed over halfway through at the base. Anyone leaning against it would have fallen over."

Jillian sucked in a deep breath and let it out slowly. "I'm supposed to move in tonight. If Mr. Williams hadn't been so angry, I would have been the one to lean on that rail."

Chance shifted closer and slid an arm around her. "We'll do a special walk-through to check for any other signs of sabotage."

"Someone really doesn't want me here." She shook her head, tears clouding her vision. "Why? What did I do?"

"You bought an empty house that someone wanted to remain empty. It's not you. I think anyone who bought this house would have the same issues."

Jillian blinked, refusing to feel sorry for herself when a man lay in front of her, possibly paralyzed or fighting for his life. All because she insisted on living in this house. The house that had seemed like the perfect home now seemed to be a terrible nightmare. "Maybe I should give up on the house."

"This is your house." Chance turned her toward him and brushed a tear from her cheek. "No one has the right to frighten you away."

"I don't want anyone else to get hurt."

"You'll be here at night. With me. We can stop the vandals from doing damage just by being here."

"What about when you leave?"

"Hopefully by then, we'll have caught them."

"And if we haven't?"

Chance gave her a tight smile and sat cross-legged on the floor. "Don't borrow trouble, darlin'." He kissed her lips and pulled her across his lap, into his arms.

Two of the other workers entered the house and stared down at George.

Brandon Quinn looked from George to the landing above and shook his head. "Too many accidents happening."

"My wife says I need to quit and find another job that's less dangerous." Eli Severs took off his cap and ran a hand through his shaggy hair. "Never had this much trouble on a job site."

"It's this house," Brandon whispered. "Folks in town swore it was haunted."

"Never believed in ghosts, but this house has some seriously bad mojo."

Jillian pushed out of Chance's lap. "Ghosts don't spray paint all over houses." She lifted one of the cut spindles and held it up. "And they don't saw off spindles from banisters." She tossed the spindle to the ground. "*People* do those kinds of things. How would you feel if this was your home and someone was booby-trapping it?"

Brandon snorted. "No one would want my house. It's a two-bedroom dump."

"My wife would scare the sainthood out of an angel. No one's gonna mess with my house." Eli chuckled. "You should hire her as your security guard."

"I just need you two to keep working until this house is done."

"Nothing's gonna get done if we all fall over railings or are run over by a truck."

A siren's wail could be heard in the distance.

Brandon grabbed Eli and backed toward the door. "If it's all the same to you, we'll wait outside for the ambulance, so as not to crowd the emergency personnel."

"Well, don't go too far. The police will likely want to question you about that railing," Chance said. "Someone had to have cut it."

Eli's brows lowered. "You saying we did it?" His fists clenched.

"No," Chance said. "But they'll want to know if you saw anything or know what they could have used to cut the wood."

"Had to have happened last night when everyone was out," Brandon said.

Eli climbed the stairs, testing each step along the way. When he arrived at the top, he called out, "There's a saw up here in the pink room."

"Don't touch it. There might be fingerprints on it," Chance called out.

Eli appeared at the top of the staircase. "I know that. I watch the *CSI* shows on television."

Jillian would have laughed, but the unconscious man in front of her stole the humor from the situation.

The sirens moved closer until the paramedics' truck arrived in the front yard.

Jillian watched through the open door as they unloaded what appeared to be a toolbox and a stretcher and ran for the house.

Thankful for someone who knew what to do with a man who'd fallen ten feet, Jillian stood and moved out of the way.

The paramedics shot out questions about what had happened.

Chance answered in a calm, deep voice. He came to stand beside Jillian, an arm slipping around her waist.

She leaned into him, glad he was there. As he had advised, she shouldn't borrow trouble. Yes, he would leave after the wedding. Until then, Jillian was thankful for strong shoulders and arms to hold her when things seemed to be falling apart.

Within fifteen minutes, they had George loaded onto a backboard and a gurney and wheeled him out to the waiting ambulance.

While the paramedics did their magic to safeguard the patient, Jillian and Chance fielded the barrage of questions from Gabe, the policeman on duty, who'd responded to the emergency call. When he'd been informed of what had happened and had taken pictures of the sawed-off rails, Gabe pocketed his pad and camera and planted his hands on his hips. "The next question is…are you all right, Jillian?"

She laughed shakily. "I'm fine. I wasn't the one who fell ten feet onto a hardwood floor."

"Yeah, but knowing the railing was cut in your home and that you could have been the one to fall is enough to push someone over the edge."

"I'm not easily destroyed."

"You might want to stay at the B and B until this is all sorted out," Gabe said.

She smiled. "Can't. I gave up my room for some of Nova's relatives."

Gabe's gaze shifted to Chance. "What about you?"

"I gave up mine, as well. Seems all of Nova's family and extended family are coming in for the wedding." He pulled Jillian against him. "I'm staying here for the time being."

"Good." Gabe stared from Chance to Jillian. "Wouldn't be a bad idea to keep a gun or some pepper spray in case someone tries to break in."

"Got it covered." Jillian crossed her arms over her chest. "I have a small handgun and a can of wasp spray with a ten-foot stream."

Gabe grinned and shook his head. "Never thought of using wasp spray, but it's a great idea." His smile faded. "Main thing is to stay safe."

"We will." Chance tightened his hold around Jillian's middle.

"You sure you're up to taking care of this house and Molly's wedding?" Gabe shook his head. "You've got a lot going on. I can have Nora Taggart step in and relieve some of the burden."

"I'm fine. Most of the planning was done months ago. I'm just tying loose ends."

Gabe nodded. "When is the phone going to be installed?"

"I have it on order. It should have been installed by now, but they said they have a pretty big backlog."

"The sooner the better. It's not good you being out here alone and no way to dial 911."

"I know."

Gabe left shortly after, giving Jillian a hug before climbing into his patrol vehicle and leaving.

Jillian headed for the Jeep. "As far as I'm concerned, George is off my list of suspects."

"Agreed." Chance followed. "If he was the one sabotaging the house, he would have known not to lean on the railing."

"Right." Jillian stopped at the driver's side of her Jeep. "Do you mind following me to the body shop?"

He smiled. "I'll be right behind you."

The trip to town was accomplished without any further incidents. Jillian drove the Jeep straight to the body shop and handed her key over to the owner. "I'll let the insurance agent know you have it."

The owner glanced at Chance and the vandalized rental. "Wanna put that one in the shop, too? I have a special on paint jobs."

Jillian smiled. "Sorry, it's a rental." She climbed into the passenger seat of Chance's SUV and pulled out her cell phone.

"Where to?" Chance asked.

"The Seaside Café." She glanced across at him. "Nora might know where we can find Alan Thompson." While Chance drove, Jillian reported the damage to her Jeep to her insurance agent.

By the time she'd given all the details, they were pulling into the parking lot of the Seaside Café.

Nora met them at the door, her brow furrowed. "Tom told me what happened to you last night. And now George…" She hugged Jillian. "I'm sorry all this is happening to you. Please, come in. Can I get you some coffee?"

"I'll take a cup." Jillian slid onto a stool at the counter.

"Me, too." Chance settled on the stool to her right.

Nora served up two cups of steaming brew and set the

pot back on the burner. "I swear, someone is determined to keep you from moving into your house."

Jillian sipped the coffee. "Seems to be the case."

"Mrs. Taggart, do you know where we can find Alan Thompson?" Chance asked.

Jillian wrapped her hands around the coffee mug, letting the warmth seep into her.

"I can't say that I know. I haven't seen him in Cape Churn in years."

"Would anyone else know where we could find him?"

Nora's eyes narrowed and she tilted her head. "He used to play cards with Frank Mortimer back when he was still around. They were good friends. He might have kept in touch."

"When did he leave Cape Churn?" Jillian asked.

"About the time Sarah Thompson took her little girl and moved away. Been so long, I really don't know. But Frank might." She smiled and looked from Chance to Jillian and back. "Are you two thinking of paying Mr. Mortimer a visit?"

"Yes," Jillian said.

"He lives on the highway between the lighthouse where Gabe and Kayla live and the Stratford mansion. And wait…" Nora turned and disappeared into the kitchen.

Jillian shot a glance at Chance. Before she could say anything, Nora was back with a package wrapped in white butcher paper.

"Take this with you." She gave it to Jillian.

"What is it?" Jillian asked.

"Steak."

"Are we supposed to bribe Mr. Mortimer for information?"

Nora waved a hand. "Oh, heavens, no. But he has a dog that's half-wolf and more than a little intimidating."

"We're supposed to give the dog the steak?" Jillian held out the wrapped steak to Nora. "We'll just give Mr. Mortimer a call before we go. He can put the dog up while we're there."

Nora was shaking her head before Jillian finished talking. "You don't understand. Frank doesn't have a landline. And he keeps his wolf dog outside to ward off strangers and salesmen." She pushed the steak back toward Jillian. "Trust me. The steak might buy you enough time to make it to his front porch."

Jillian's gut clenched. "That doesn't sound very safe."

"It's not. Mr. Mortimer is an old recluse who doesn't like visitors. He spends his days writing—about what, I don't know—but he doesn't like to be disturbed. That's why he has the dog. Not many people venture past the wolf's snarling canines."

"Sounds like a nice guy." Chance finished his coffee.

"If that's what you call a grumpy old man." Nora wiped the counter with a clean washcloth.

"Ready to go?" Chance stood, dug out a few dollars and left them beside the mug.

Jillian took one more sip and handed the mug to Nora. "Thanks for the help and the great coffee."

Nora gave them both a serious look. "If that wolf dog comes at you, stay in the vehicle or get back in it, quickly."

Jillian shivered at the intensity of Nora's warning. "We will." She clutched the package of meat in her hand and left the café, wondering if finding Alan Thompson was worth the trouble of braving Mortimer's wolf.

* * *

Chance headed for the rental car and opened the passenger door for Jillian. But she wasn't right behind him, like he'd thought. She was still standing on the sidewalk in front of the café, staring at something down the street.

When he looked that direction, Chance spotted Daryl Sims, walking along, calling out something and ducking in and out of buildings.

"Are we going?" Chance asked.

Jillian continued to stare at the man headed their way. "I think Daryl's in trouble." She headed toward the man and met him in front of the hardware store.

Chance closed the car door and followed.

"What's wrong?" Jillian was asking Daryl.

The man's eyes were filled with tears and he'd been crying. "I can't find JT." He wrung his hands and glanced around. "I've looked everywhere."

Jillian hugged Daryl. "Sweetie, who is JT?"

"My dog." He lowered his hand toward the ground. "She's this big, white with spots and has black ears."

"How long has she been missing?" Chance asked.

"She was in the fence last night. Now she's gone. She never runs away. I think something terrible happened to her."

Though he wanted to get moving on finding Alan Thompson, Chance couldn't leave Daryl when the guy was so obviously upset by the loss of his beloved pet. And Jillian wasn't going anywhere until she helped.

"Have you called the local veterinarians?" Jillian asked.

"I stopped at Dr. Pierce's and he said he hasn't seen JT."

"What about the animal shelter?" Chance suggested.

Daryl shook his head. "I haven't made it that far yet."

"Hop in. We'll take you there," Chance said.

Jillian gave him a thankful smile and ushered Daryl into the backseat.

"JT is my only friend. I don't know what I'd do without her."

"Daryl, you have lots of friends."

"Mama says I don't. I'm not supposed to talk to anyone. I'm supposed to go to work and go home. That's what she said."

"Why?"

"She doesn't want bullies to hurt me."

Jillian turned and stared at the man in the backseat. "Not everyone is a bully, Daryl."

"I know. But Mama says I can't always tell who is nice and who isn't. It's best to keep my mouth shut and go straight home." He sniffed. "JT is my only friend. I can tell her anything."

Jillian gave Chance the directions. In minutes, they were turning into the concrete block building that was the Cape Churn animal shelter.

They entered the building and found a young man behind the counter, wearing a T-shirt that read Save a Life, Adopt From a Shelter.

Jillian smiled at the young man, leaning close to read his name tag. "Hi, Stewart. We're looking for Daryl's lost dog. Have you had any brought in during the past twenty-four hours?"

Stewart nodded. "Normally we only get one or two a week, but we had a rash of them last night. Must have been the fog. The new ones are in the pens on the right side near the rear of the building. You're welcome to look. And if you find one you like, today would be a good day to adopt," the clerk said, his face hopeful.

Jillian and Chance followed Daryl into the building, passing by cages holding pathetic pooches that had been turned in or captured as strays. The dogs all barked as one, the noise deafening.

With each cage passed, Daryl's shoulders sank more. He stopped several times and stuck his fingers through the wire to scratch a dog's chin. "I wish I could take all of you home," he whispered.

Chance knew how he felt. When he was a child, his father hadn't let him have a dog. They moved too often and not every place allowed dogs. When Chance brought home a stray, his father had promptly taken it to the shelter, claiming someone with more time and a big yard would give the animal a better home.

Chance stopped in front of a cage with a short-haired yellow mutt. In Afghanistan, Chance and some of his buddies had adopted a lone puppy that had wandered into the camp. Each one of them had wanted to take the dog back to the States, but they didn't know how. When the time came to redeploy Stateside, they came up with a plan to smuggle the dog on board the C-130 aircraft scheduled to transport them home. The plans were made and all they had to do was wait until the designated departure date.

A shiver slipped down Chance's spine. A member of the Taliban had lured the dog outside the wire, strapped explosives to it and sent it back inside the compound. The Taliban fighter waited until he was certain the dog was well within range of troops and then detonated.

Chance had seen the dog coming. Others had, too. The soldier nearest to the dog had known he didn't stand a chance and sat down to hug Ruger, using his body to block the shrapnel when the bomb went off.

Staring down at his hands, Chance expected to see the red stain of blood. In his mind, he could still see the aftermath of the explosion and smell the dry air, sand and the coppery scent of blood.

He didn't realize he'd stopped in the middle of the building, in front of a dog that looked so similar to Ruger, until a hand on his arm brought him back to the shelter. "What's wrong?" Jillian stared up into his eyes. "Chance?"

He shook himself. "Nothing. I'm fine."

"No, you're not. Your face turned as white as a sheet."

"It's nothing." He glanced over her shoulder.

Daryl dropped to his knees and stuck his fingers through the last cage. "JT! Oh, JT, how did you get out of the fence?"

"I think Daryl found JT," Chance said, hoping to divert Jillian's attention from him and back to the reason they'd come to the shelter in the first place.

Jillian turned and smiled, the entire depressing building lighting up with the sparkle in her eyes.

"Thank goodness." Jillian glanced back at Chance. "I still want to know what you were thinking, but it can wait until later."

"I'll get the attendant." Chance hurried to the front of the building and found Stewart, thus saving him from explaining what it felt like to have your friend splattered all over your body. All because of a dog that only wanted to be loved.

Chapter 14

Part of Jillian was jubilant because Daryl had found his pet. The other part of her worried about what she'd seen in Chance's face as he stood among the barking dogs.

She'd never seen such a desolate, heart-wrenching expression on anyone's face before. From the way he'd hurried away, he probably didn't want to talk about it. But she wanted to know.

The man had taken the time to help a guy find his lost pet, proving, once again, that Chance had a soft spot for animals and people in need. This was a must in Jillian's book.

She loved animals and had had pets when she'd been growing up. Her mother and stepfather allowed her to have a German shepherd in the house. They'd carefully chosen the animal and had it trained to protect her. Jillian didn't care about all the training. She was just glad to have a friend to greet her when she came home and sleep with her at night. He'd helped to keep her dreams at bay, nudging her awake when she cried out in the night.

Jillian stared at the cage near where Chance had been standing when he'd zoned out. A short-haired yellow puppy with a dark nose and wiggling tail stared up at her with big brown eyes.

Jillian's heart melted. If she could have, she'd have taken the dog home with her. But the house wasn't ready for her, much less a dog and two kittens. Steeling herself to walk away, she hurried toward Daryl and JT.

Stewart came to release the dog from the kennel. He slipped a lead around the dog's neck and led him to the front.

Chance had paid the fee. All they had to do was take Daryl and JT home and they could be on their way to find Alan Thompson.

"Daryl, where do you live?"

"In the trailer park by the elementary school."

Jillian was familiar with the area on the southern tip of town, closest to the road leading out to her house. She gave Chance the directions and looked over the seat at Daryl hugging JT.

"What does JT stand for?" Chance asked.

"I don't know," Daryl said. "I just call her JT."

Chance smiled into the rearview mirror and drove into the trailer park.

Daryl pointed to a small trailer with skirting that had seen better days and a small deck in front of a narrow metal door. "Mama will be mad if she sees me coming home with anyone."

"Why?"

"She likes to pick me up at the café." He ducked his head. "Let me out. She's not home."

Before Chance stopped the vehicle completely, Daryl flung the door open and jumped out. JT followed, racing toward the little trailer.

Daryl waved. "Thanks!" Then he turned and hurried toward his home, rounding the trailer to the back.

Jillian smiled. "Thank you."

"For what?"

"For helping Daryl find JT." She faced him, her smile fading. "Now it's our turn to find Alan Thompson. I'm ready to figure out what's going on. I can't live looking over my shoulder all the time."

Chance turned at the road in front of Daryl's trailer and pulled away from the trailer park. He glanced in the rearview mirror. "Is that Mrs. Sims?" he asked.

Jillian swiveled in her seat and glanced out the back window. "Looks like her getting out of her car."

Chance slowed at a stop sign.

The woman looked angry, pointing at Daryl and then JT. Jillian's heart sank. "Damn. Looks like she's yelling at Daryl."

"Want me to go back?" Chance asked.

"No." Jillian sighed, watching until Mrs. Sims and Daryl entered the trailer. "She might not appreciate us butting in." She settled in the seat and stared out the front windshield. Daryl had his challenges, but Mrs. Sims did, too. Jillian hoped the older woman let Daryl keep his dog. It seemed to mean a lot to him.

The drive to Frank Mortimer's was a short distance, but the road followed the coastline and was very curvy, forcing Chance to take it slow.

Jillian pointed to the lighthouse sitting on a point, overlooking the water. "There's the lighthouse where Gabe and Kayla live with their two children. We need to watch for the turnoff to Mortimer's place. I've driven between the lighthouse and the Stratford mansion many times, but I can't remember seeing the road for Mortimer's place. So it has to be well hidden."

Chance slowed to a crawl.

"There!" Jillian pointed to an overgrown driveway where the trees and bushes barely parted for a vehicle to slide between. Chance turned onto the road and bumped along the gravel until they reached a weathered gray cabin with a rickety front porch.

"Do you see the wolf dog?" Jillian asked, tension building.

"No. Maybe we'll get lucky and Mortimer will keep him inside."

Palming the packaged steak in her hand, Jillian reached for the door handle.

Chance touched her arm. "Maybe it would be better for you to stay here while I question Mortimer."

"No way. If Mortimer lets his wolf loose, I have the steak." Besides, she refused to stand by while Chance was ripped apart. She smiled at him. "I'm sure Nora was exaggerating. Let's get this over with."

"Please, give me the steak." He held out his hand. "I don't want you to be hurt."

"I can take care of myself."

"Yes, I know you can. Humor me, please."

Jillian held onto the package for a moment longer, but Chance wasn't getting out until she relinquished the dog's bribe. With a sigh, she handed over the butcher paper–wrapped steak. "I think there's safety in numbers."

"If I'm worrying about you, I'll lose focus on the reason for being here."

He had a point. She didn't like it, but he had a point.

His hand on the door handle, he stared across at her. "You'll stay?"

Crossing her arms over her chest, she nodded. If she pouted a little, so be it. "Yes."

Chance got out of the vehicle and walked toward the house.

A flash of silvery gray burst through the front door and charged at Chance.

Jillian stifled a scream and was halfway out of the vehicle when the dog pounced on Chance.

The beast of a dog planted his big paws in the middle of the man's chest and knocked him flat on his back.

Chance didn't move except to hold up the package of steak. "Hungry? How about a steak?" he wheezed.

The dog didn't glance in the direction of the meat. His lips curled back in a wicked snarl, and he growled deep in his throat.

Jillian rushed toward the pair, her heart hammering in her chest. "Shoo!" She waved her hands and stopped when the animal's growls became more vicious.

"Jillian," Chance whispered. "Get. In. The. Car."

She stood still, torn between doing exactly as Chance requested and throwing herself in front of the dog before he ripped into Chance's exposed throat. "But he'll kill you," she said.

"That dog's not gonna kill anyone," a gruff voice called out. "Unless I tell him to."

Jillian shot a glance to the porch, where a scruffy older man stood. Dressed in worn jeans and a plaid flannel shirt, he carried a shotgun in his hands.

"Mr. Mortimer?" she asked.

He snorted. "Who wants to know?"

"I'm Jillian Taylor and this—" she tipped her head toward Chance, trapped beneath the wolf dog "—is Chance McCall. We need to ask you a few questions."

"You're trespassing."

"Please, Mr. Mortimer," Jillian said, her voice shaking. "Call off your dog. We're not here to hurt you."

The shaggy man crossed his arms. "Ever stop to think before you come barging onto a man's property that he might not want visitors?"

"Yes." Jillian straightened, her chin lifting. She refused to let this man bully her or Chance. She reasoned that if the dog wasn't going to attack unless Mortimer told him to, they shouldn't have to worry. Surely he wouldn't tell the dog to kill Chance or her. That would be murder. "Sir, you're the only person we know of who might be able to tell us where to find Alan Thompson."

Mortimer's eyes narrowed. "Who told you that?"

"Nora Taggart."

"Damned busybody."

"Excuse me, Mr. Mortimer. She's a nice woman who only cares about the people of her community. You could take a page from her book." Jillian took a step forward. "We need to find Alan Thompson."

"Is that the only question you have for me?"

"Yes." Jillian stared at the man. "And we'd appreciate it if you'd call off your dog."

Mortimer stared at the package in Chance's hand. "Is that one of Nora's steaks?"

"Huh?" Caught off guard, Jillian glanced in the direction Mortimer was looking, at the untouched package in Chance's hand. "Er, yes, it is."

"I'll tell you where to find Thompson if you get that package to me without Loki eating it first." Mortimer chuckled, the sound as scruffy and gravelly as the man.

Chance tried to sit up, but the wolf dog snapped at his face and snarled angrily.

"Just stay still," Jillian said. "I'll get it."

"Don't do it, Jillian," Chance said. "You don't know what the dog will do."

"I'm not worried. Mr. Mortimer wouldn't let his dog rip my arm off for a steak." She shot a glance at the man, praying she was right. Jillian inched toward the animal and Chance's hand held out to the side.

The wolf dog growled, his gaze shifting to Jillian, though his paws remained firmly on Chance's chest. Apparently, he considered Chance more of a threat than she was.

"Please, Jillian, I'd feel a whole lot better if you just got back in the car," Chance said.

"You'd feel a whole lot better without a one hundred and fifty–pound animal on your chest." She reached out, her direct gaze never leaving the animal's, trusting her peripheral vision to guide her to the package.

When she was close enough, she spoke to the dog, "Nice wolf. I'm sure you'll be getting some of this. Your master wouldn't deprive a big old boy like you, would he?" She took the package amid a new chorus of growls and snarls. Then she backed away and held up the package. "If you want this, you'll have to call off the wolf."

"That's not the deal."

"Take it or leave it."

Mortimer's eyes narrowed and he glared at her. Then he finally clicked his tongue and called out, "Heel, Loki!"

The animal gave another low-pitched growl and stared

down at Chance, as if warning the man not to make any sudden moves. Then he stepped off his chest, trotted back to the porch and sat next to Mortimer like a trained pet.

Chance stood and dusted the dirt from his backside.

"I'll take that steak," Mortimer said.

"You can have it. But we still need to know where to find Alan Thompson."

"Why do you need to know?"

"Miss Taylor purchased the old Thompson place and someone has been trying to warn her away. We want to know why and were hoping Mr. Thompson could give us information about the place."

"That house didn't even belong to Thompson. It was his wife's house. He hated that house."

"Why?"

"Because he couldn't provide a house for her. The man lost his job just before Sarah's parents died in a wreck. When he finally got another, it was for chump change. If her father hadn't left her that house and a small annuity, they'd have been out in the cold. It was good timing, if you ask me. Alan didn't see it that way."

"So where is Mr. Thompson now?"

"Last time I saw him, he lived in the next county, thirty minutes from here. In a cabin he built himself. Never did get over losing Sarah and Julia."

"Could you be more specific about his address?"

Mortimer gave them an address, rattling it off so fast Jillian almost missed it. "Now, I'll take that steak and you two can get off my property."

Chance took the steak from Jillian and carried it to the porch.

Loki came up on all fours, his lips curling back in a wicked snarl.

Chance ignored the dog and handed the package to Mortimer. "Thank you, sir."

Mortimer snorted, turned and walked into the house, holding the door for the dog. "Come." The wolf dog growled once more at Chance and trotted into the house, and the door snapped shut.

"Are you all right?" Jillian asked, brushing dirt off Chance's back.

"I'm fine," he said, his tone surly.

Jillian couldn't help the smile tugging at her lips. "Don't like being bested by a dog, do you?"

He glared at her, hooked her arm and hurried her to the vehicle. Once she was inside, he rounded the car, got in and faced her. "I told you to stay in the car. How can I protect you if you don't do as I ask?"

Her smile widened. "I don't know how you could have protected me, lying beneath the dog. Oh, come on." She punched his shoulder lightly. "He didn't kill you. For that I can't help but be happy." She leaned across the seat and kissed his lips. "And you handled it beautifully."

He frowned, backed the vehicle around and then shifted into Drive. "I don't know how you could say that."

"You did the only thing you could. That wolf could easily have ripped into you. We would have spent the night in the hospital, and we wouldn't have gotten what we came for. As it is, you're fine, we have Thompson's address and we know a little more about Sarah and Alan's relationship. It could be Alan sabotaging the house to keep anyone from moving in. Maybe he still harbors resentment for the place."

"Sounds too easy."

"At the very least, maybe Thompson can shed some light on the situation." Jillian sat back in the seat. "I'm just glad we came out of our encounter with Mortimer relatively unscathed."

"You can say that. You didn't have a wolf pin you to the ground."

"Okay, I take that back. The only casualty from our Mortimer encounter was your pride."

Chance shot a glance at Jillian. That damned smile still played at her pretty pink lips and he found it difficult to stay mad at the woman. So, his pride had taken a hit. He'd get over it. And she was right—the dog could have ripped into his throat and left him to bleed out. He was lucky. It could have been worse.

But he didn't think facing Alan Thompson would be any less dangerous if the man was responsible for the vandalism to the house and crashing into Jillian's Jeep. If the man was that determined to keep people from living in his ex-wife's house, they could be up against a lunatic.

He turned south on the coastal highway and drove for the next fifteen minutes in silence.

"What happened back at the shelter?" Jillian asked out of the blue.

Chance lifted his foot from the accelerator. He'd been so buried in all the scenarios that could play out between them and Alan Thompson, he hadn't expected Jillian to bring up the trance he'd been in at the shelter. That seemed like hours ago. "Nothing."

How could he tell her of all the thoughts that had blown through his head in that moment he remembered Ruger? She couldn't begin to understand what it did to a man to watch your friend get blown apart hugging an animal that had done nothing to be a part of the war but be born in the wrong place.

Jillian sat for a while without saying anything.

Chance thought she'd given up questioning him.

"Do you have dreams about your time in the military?" Her voice was barely above a whisper, but he heard it like a shout. Every other sound faded into the background, amplifying her words.

His heart hammered even harder than when Loki had had him pinned, and the blood thundered against his ears. Sweat beaded on his lip and he started to reach for the button to lower the automatic window and let cool air in. When he realized what was happening, he remembered what the therapist had said when he'd processed out of the military. Anxiety was natural for a soldier attempting to reintegrate back into society. The hardest thing was to recognize what was happening. Once he did, he could deal with it.

Inhaling deeply, Chance willed his heart to slow and his fingers to loosen their death grip on the steering wheel.

Jillian reached out and touched his arm. Though her hand was light on him, he still flinched.

"It's okay. I have nightmares, too," she said.

He nodded. Her admission to the dreams seemed to give them something in common. Although he doubted her dreams were from watching buddies die, being shot at, bombed and constantly looking over your shoulder for the enemy. "You had one last night," he said, preferring to deflect attention to her.

She nodded. "I haven't had one in a very long time,

until last night. I used to get them a lot when I was a child."

"Did you have a traumatic event that triggered them?"

Jillian shook her head. "None that I remember."

"What do you mean, you don't remember?"

She shrugged. "I only have memories back to the fifth grade. Anything before that is a blank." Jillian fiddled with the hem of her blouse. "Do you remember back when you were a kid?"

Chance nodded. "Not all the way back, but I can still remember my first grade teacher letting me erase the board. I thought it was an honor to be chosen." Mrs. Talbot had been so kind and caring to every student in his class. "But I don't remember my other teachers until my seventh-grade math teacher."

"So it's not unusual to forget so much," she said, more of a statement than a question.

"I do remember wanting a puppy for Christmas, but my parents wouldn't let us have an animal. My father didn't want the bother, and my mother agreed with anything my father said."

"Did your brothers and sisters ever ask for a puppy?"

Chance gave her a crooked smile. "I have a brother I never see, and parents I see even less. My parents didn't let us have pets."

"I'm an only child. But my mother allowed me to have a dog. Daisy was always there when I came home. She was my friend when I didn't have any."

"What kind of dog was Daisy?"

"A German shepherd."

Chance laughed out loud. "And her name was Daisy?"

Jillian smiled. "I know. She looked like a badass

guard dog, but she was all mush where I was concerned. I loved that dog so much."

"What happened to her?"

Jillian glanced out the window, her smile fading. "She crossed the rainbow bridge the same year my mother and stepfather died in an airplane crash."

"When was that?"

"The year before I moved to Cape Churn. I was ready for a change. Everything about Portland reminded me of what I'd lost. I needed to get away."

"Why Cape Churn?"

"I saw an ad for a beach cottage rental when I was at my lowest and decided it was time for a change. I came to visit and moved here three months later."

"And you haven't regretted it?" He glanced her way. "Until now?"

"Even with all that's happened, I still don't regret it. This town, that house—they make me feel more at home than my apartment in Portland. With my mother and stepfather gone, I had nothing holding me back." She turned toward him. "Have you ever had a place call to you?"

He shook his head. "Can't say that I have. Other than the US in general. When I was fighting in the war, I wanted to come home to America. But no place in particular." Until now. Cape Churn was wrapping around his heart the longer he stayed. Could it be a trick to his senses, or a desire to belong somewhere? His gaze drifted back to Jillian. Or was it this woman? Though her house had been vandalized and she'd been attacked, she still believed in Cape Churn as her home.

If he could help her discover the root of the attacks

and lay them to rest, he'd feel a lot better about leaving after the wedding.

Chance faced the road, his fingers tightening around the steering wheel. Hell, who was he trying to kid? Cape Churn, his friend Nova, Molly, Gabe and most of all being with Jillian gave him purpose. Her spirit was infectious and her dogged determination to make that old house her home made him want to fight alongside her to ensure it happened.

Chapter 15

"Mr. Mortimer said we should be looking for a mailbox with an old tire attached to it." Jillian shook her head and chuckled. "That shouldn't be hard to see."

Chance slowed as they neared the area Mortimer had indicated. They'd climbed a rocky hillside, and the road clung to the edge of a cliff. At the top, the road wove inward amid tall stands of trees. Between bunches of bushes and trees, they could see the rocky shoreline.

"There!" Jillian pointed to a mailbox with an old rubber tire.

Chance pulled into the gravel driveway and drove through a stand of ragged bushes and old evergreens to a rustic cabin of cedar and stone, perched on the edge of a cliff. An old truck was parked to the side.

"Let me take this one," Chance said.

"Mr. Mortimer didn't say anything about Thompson owning a dog."

"He didn't say anything about Thompson owning a gun either."

Jillian sighed. "Okay. I'll stay until you give me the all-clear sign."

Chance started to get out, but a hand on his arm stopped him.

"By the way, what is the all-clear sign?" She grinned.

"Thumbs-up." Chance left her in the vehicle, a smile tugging at the corners of his lips. Jillian was like sunshine on a foggy day.

He climbed the porch steps, carefully scanning for any sign of vicious dogs or a gun pointing out of a window. Nothing made his hackles rise, so he knocked on the door.

For a moment, nothing happened and no sound came from inside.

Chance knocked again, louder this time. "Hello! Anyone home?"

Footsteps sounded from the side of the house. A man wearing painter's pants and a flannel shirt and carrying a paintbrush rounded the corner of the wraparound porch and stopped, a frown lowering his brows. "I'm not interested in buying anything, if that's why you're here."

"We're not selling anything," Chance said. "You don't have a big dog, do you?"

The man's frown deepened. "No."

"And you don't have a gun in your pocket?" Chance continued.

"No. Why?" He glanced from Chance to the car. "Should I have a gun? If you're here to rob me, you're going to come up on the short end of that stick. I don't have much to steal. Just this house and some old clothes."

"Are you Alan Thompson?"

The man nodded. "I am."

Chance gave Jillian a thumbs-up and then held out his hand. "I'm Chance McCall."

Alan shook Chance's hand, his brow wrinkling. "Nice to meet you. But why are you here?"

"We hope you can answer some questions for us." He nodded toward Jillian, who'd climbed out of the vehicle and crossed the yard to the house. "Mr. Thompson," Chance said, "this is Jillian Taylor."

Alan's gaze fixed on Jillian as she walked up the stairs. Something like recognition flashed in the man's eyes for a moment. Then he glanced toward the road leading out of his property.

Jillian stuck out her hand. "Thank you for seeing us with no notice."

Thompson was forced to look at Jillian, and he took her hand, his own wrapping around her fingers for longer than was necessary. "Miss Taylor. Do I know you?"

She tilted her head. "Perhaps you've seen me in Cape Churn?"

He shook his head. "I never go there."

"Never?" She raised her brows. "From here, isn't it the closest town to purchase groceries and gas?"

"Yes, it is." Thompson pulled his hand free of hers and tucked it in his pocket. "I prefer to go farther south."

"Why?"

"Too many bad memories in Cape Churn."

"Memories of your wife and daughter?" Jillian asked softly.

"Ex-wife." Again, Thompson stared at Jillian, his gaze combing over her face and her hair. "Are you sure I don't know you?"

"I'm pretty sure. I grew up in Portland and moved

to Cape Churn two years ago. Perhaps you met me in Portland?"

Thompson shook his head. "Haven't been there in fifteen years."

"Mr. Thompson, we'd like to know a little more about the house Miss Taylor purchased in Cape Churn. It used to belong to Sarah Thompson."

Thompson's jaw tightened. "I wish that house had burned down a long time ago. Nothing but bad memories for me there."

"Why?" Jillian asked. "Because of what happened to your daughter?"

"That house was nothing but a stick in my craw from the day we moved in." Thompson turned away, shoving a hand through his shaggy gray hair. "Hell, it wasn't really the house's fault. To be honest, everything that went wrong in that house was my fault."

"Even the disappearance of your daughter, Julia?" Chance asked, holding his breath, wondering if he'd get a confession out of Julia's father.

"Yes, damn it." Thompson turned back to Chance, his face haggard, his eyes glassy with unshed tears. "If I'd been a better husband…if I'd been there for Julia… maybe none of that would have happened. And I wouldn't have lost Sarah." He pushed past Chance and Jillian and dropped to sit on the porch steps, burying his face in his hands. "It was all my fault."

Jillian glanced at Chance and then sat on the step beside Thompson. She laid a hand on his shoulder. "Mr. Thompson, that was a long time ago."

"It's like yesterday. I lost everything."

"What happened?" Jillian persisted.

"We had a good life, Sarah, Julia and I. We had a

nice little place on the beach in Cape Churn. Julia was a beautiful little girl. She looked like her mother, all shiny blond hair, but she had my eyes." He lifted his head and stared at the driveway as if seeing the past, not the vehicles parked there.

"Then I was laid off at the bank. Hell, the bank closed down. That was about the time the bubble burst in the stock market. I lost my job, and Sarah lost her parents in a terrible car wreck." He shook his head. "I tried to be there for her, but I didn't know where my next paycheck was going to come from. We had a mortgage on the house, and I couldn't pay the note. We lost the place on the beach."

"And you moved into the house Sarah grew up in," Jillian stated.

Thompson glanced up at her, as if seeing her for the first time. "I should have been thankful, but I was so bitter. I was a failure to the woman I loved and the child I wanted to look up to me. I started working as a bartender in a bar on the edge of town. Sarah went back to teaching. It seemed that for every drink I served, I served one up for myself. I came home drunk more often than sober. Sarah, bless her heart, tried to understand, but she didn't want Julia growing up around an alcoholic, and she told me to shape up or ship out."

Jillian rubbed her hand on the man's arm. "So you moved out."

"Sarah gave me six months to get myself together. I was buried too deep in the alcohol. I couldn't see to get straight until the divorce papers arrived at my apartment. I signed them, knowing Sarah and Julia were better off without me. Then Julia disappeared on her way home from school." Tears slid down Thompson's cheeks.

Chance's chest tightened. Nothing in the man's demeanor indicated he had anything to do with the child's disappearance. From the look on his face, he had been devastated by the loss of his daughter.

His voice turned to wet gravel. "I was so drunk when the chief of police came to tell me, I couldn't lift my head off my couch. It wasn't until the next morning that it sank in. By then, every able-bodied man and woman in Cape Churn had been searching all night for my little girl." He stared at Jillian. "And I'd been passed out, too drunk to care."

Jillian fished in her jacket pocket and pulled out a clean tissue, handing it to Thompson. "But you did care."

He nodded and blew his nose. "I haven't touched a drop of alcohol since. But it was too late. Julia was gone and Sarah hated me for not being there when Julia needed a father to look out of her."

Chance slipped by Jillian and descended the stairs to stand in front of Thompson. "They questioned you about your daughter's disappearance."

Thompson looked up at Chance. "I would never have taken Julia away from Sarah. Those two were so close, and I was a terrible excuse for a father." His fists clenched. "But if I ever find out who took her for that thirty days, I'll kill him. No child should have to go through that kind of trauma."

"Did you see Julia when she came back?" Jillian asked.

He nodded. "Sarah asked me to come speak to Julia when she couldn't get her to open up about what had happened to her while she'd been gone. She thought maybe I could get her to talk." Thompson snorted. "That poor kid had been through so much, she had some kind of amnesia. Julia couldn't remember anything. I don't think she remembered me." His tears started again and he looked into Jillian's face, his own ravaged with his memories. "My own daughter couldn't remember me. She barely remembered Sarah, but she remembered enough to come back to the house when she finally got free of the bastard who was holding her."

Chance nodded. "I've seen soldiers with posttraumatic stress disorder have a kind of situational memory loss. I think they call it dissociative amnesia. The soldier who has been exposed to a traumatic event can't remember that event and sometimes even everything prior to that time. The trauma was so severe that the soldier's brain shuts off access to that memory. It's a defense mechanism."

Thompson turned to Chance. "My daughter couldn't remember anything before her disappearance. She was in a state of shock, and I couldn't do anything to help."

Jillian slipped an arm around the man's shoulders. "No one could. She probably had to have time to get over it."

"We still had no idea who took her." Thompson shrugged off Jillian's arm, pushed to his feet and paced the length of the porch. "Sarah lived in fear that whoever took Julia was still out there. I felt the same. She didn't know it, but I slept on the front porch in a sleeping bag. She took Julia to school and picked her up after. She even slept with Julia, afraid to let her out of her sight."

"Who could blame her?" Jillian still sat on the porch step, her face drawn and sad. "She got her baby back. She wasn't going to lose her again."

Thompson nodded. "Exactly. And the police had nothing to go on. No description. No location. Julia just appeared out of nowhere in the rain. Her tracks were washed clean, and dogs couldn't trace them back to where she'd been. With no lead on Julia's abductor, Sarah couldn't live in the house, knowing someone was still out there. She found me on the porch one morning and told me she was going to take Julia away, change their names and start over."

"Why didn't you go with them?"

Thompson shook his head. "Sarah and I were divorced. They had a better chance of starting over without me." He leaned his hands on the porch rails. "I let them go. I didn't hear from them again until I received legal documents from an attorney in Portland asking me to relinquish all rights to my daughter so that she could be adopted by her stepfather." The man's voice faded off and he drew in a deep breath. "I still didn't have a real job. I wasn't fit to be a father after being an alcoholic. My wife and daughter deserved the happiness I couldn't give them. I signed."

"I'm sorry for your loss," Jillian said, her eyes swimming in tears as she pushed to her feet.

"Yeah. Me, too," Thompson said.

Chance climbed the steps and wrapped an arm around her waist, pulling her against him. The woman had so much empathy for others. She probably felt Thompson's pain as acutely as he did. It made Chance want to hold and comfort her.

Thompson straightened, looking old and tired. "That's my sob story, and why I think nothing good ever came from that house."

Jillian's arm slipped around Chance. "But like you said, it's not the house's fault."

"It was my fault for failing my family."

"It was Julia's abductor who made it worse," Chance pointed out.

"It kills me to know he's still out there." Thompson's hands clenched. "Not a day goes by that I'm not racking my brain trying to figure out who took her."

"Any thoughts on who might have done it?"

"The police questioned a lot of people in town but kept coming back to me and George Williams. George had been panting after Sarah since high school. As soon as he knew we were divorced, he came calling." Thompson's lips turned up on the corners. "Sarah wouldn't have anything to do with him. I'd bet he had something to do with it, but he had an airtight alibi."

"We ruled him out when he fell victim to one of the attempts to get me to leave," Jillian said.

Thompson's brows rose.

Chance told the other man what had happened and went on to tell him about the wreck and the graffiti.

"Wow. Someone really wants you out of that house." Thompson touched Jillian's arm. "I'm glad to see you're okay. If it were me, I'd burn the house down. But then, that house only reminded me of what I couldn't provide for Sarah."

"I love the house," Jillian said. "It just needs the right person to care enough to make it a home again."

Thompson gave her a sad smile. "That's what Sarah said. I guess I wasn't the right person, or I didn't care enough to make it a home." Again, he stared out at the driveway. "If I had it all to do over again, I'd have done it right. Sarah and Julia were worth the effort. I just couldn't see past my own problems to know that. I'd give anything to beg their forgiveness. Even after all these years, I still love them."

"Mr. Thompson, I have to ask," Chance started. "Where were you last night around eight o'clock?"

Thompson nodded. "I understand. I'd be asking the same question in your shoes. I was at my Alcoholics Anonymous meeting. I've been going for the past seventeen years. Funny thing is, now I'm leading it." He pulled his wallet out of his back pocket and handed Chance a card. "Call my assistant, he can verify."

"Thank you." Chance pocketed the card and stuck out his hand. "And thank you for filling in some of the gaps."

Jillian hugged Thompson. "I'm sure if you had the chance to see Sarah and Julia again, they'd forgive you."

"It's the one thing keeping me holding on. I hope to find them one day. I don't expect to reestablish a relationship, but I will never have closure until I say I'm sorry."

Chance led Jillian back to the rental SUV. Once they were back on the highway headed for Cape Churn, he turned to Jillian. "I'll check his reference and have my boss do a background check on him."

"I don't think he's responsible for any of what's happening at my house. I think it has something to do with Julia's abductor."

Chance agreed, but it didn't hurt to check references. When it came to Jillian's life and well-being, he couldn't be too careful.

Jillian sat beside Chance on the way back to Cape Churn, her heart hurting for Alan Thompson, who had made poor decisions that cost him his family and home. The man obviously still suffered.

Deep down, Jillian knew he wasn't the one who'd abducted Julia, nor was he the one who was terrorizing her now.

"We're trying to solve a case the police weren't able to solve seventeen years ago," she muttered.

"So it seems." Chance shot a glance toward her. "Having second thoughts about the house?"

"Hell, no." She balled her fists. "It only makes me that much more determined to get to the bottom of this." She stared straight ahead. "One of the last people who saw Julia before she disappeared had to be at her school. From what Nora said, Julia walked home every day. Her mother was working as a teacher at another school and would have been home shortly after her. Maybe someone at the school saw something—anything that could have been a clue."

"Let's check with Chief Taggart. He would know who was questioned. He might even be able to check the cold case file."

Jillian couldn't wait to get to town. The more she learned about Julia's disappearance, the more she wanted to find the one responsible. That child had to have been through hell, and whoever the abductor was had gotten away with it. Hell, he could do it again. A shiver rippled down her spine.

As they entered cell phone coverage, Chance placed a call to follow up with Alan Thompson's alibi for the previous night. He placed another call to his boss, asking him to see if he could find any further information on Thompson. Chance was direct, to the point and didn't mince words. The man knew what to ask for, and his boss was obviously used to straight talk.

Jillian wondered what exactly Chance did as a supersecret agent and how dangerous it was. If he were to stick around Cape Churn to be with her, how often would he be called away to perform missions? How would she feel about his being gone all the time?

Like Molly, Jillian had established herself as an independent woman, capable of functioning without a man in her life. But Molly readily accepted that Nova would go on missions and was willing to take whatever time he could give to her. Could Jillian be as receptive to that kind of arrangement?

She almost laughed out loud. It wasn't as if Chance had asked her on a date, much less to marry her.

By the time Chance ended the short call to his boss, they were pulling into the police station. As soon as Chance parked, Jillian was out of the vehicle.

"What's the hurry?" he asked.

"I have questions that need answers." Jillian didn't wait for Chance. Instead, she plowed through the front door of the station.

Behind her Chance chuckled. "You're like a dog with a bone, and you're not letting go."

"Damn right. That's my house, and I'm not letting anyone scare me out of it." She stopped at the reception counter.

The receptionist smiled. "Hi, Jillian. Thanks again for helping me find my beach bungalow. I love waking up to the sound of the waves on the shore."

"I'm glad you're happy with it, Suzanna. It was a great buy." Jillian glanced over the receptionist's shoulder. "I need to see Chief Taggart."

"Let me see if he's in." She punched a button on her phone and leaned forward. "Chief Taggart—"

"Jillian, I thought I heard your voice." Chief Taggart stepped through a doorway and engulfed Jillian in a bear hug. "We were able to lift prints off the saw we found at the house."

Jillian's heart leaped.

"I'm sorry, but we didn't find a match in the AFIS database. Whoever cut those spindles doesn't have a prior criminal record."

Her hopes were temporarily dashed, but Jillian wasn't done yet. "Chief, do you have a list of the people you talked to at the school Julia attended? Are any of them still in Cape Churn?"

"Most of the teachers are still there. Except maybe two. Julia's teacher is now the principal at the same elementary school."

Jillian glanced at the clock on the wall. School would have been out for a couple hours. "Do you know where we could find her?"

"Are you talking about Principal Tillman?" Suzanna asked. "My niece goes to that elementary school. I know where Rebecca Tillman lives. Let me look up her actual address." The receptionist typed on her keyboard for a minute and then got up and walked to a printer located behind her. She came back with a sheet of paper with a map of the streets of Cape Churn with a red dot and an address listed. "Hope that helps."

"Do you want me to go with you?" Chief Taggart asked.

"No, we can manage," Jillian said. "I'd appreciate any other names of people who were questioned who lived around the school or on the path Julia would have taken home."

"The school is on the edge of town. There weren't many houses past it then or even now. Most of the community growth has been closer to the water and the beaches in the lower-lying areas. But I'll get a list of the people we questioned on the case. Stop by tomorrow and I'll have it for you."

"Thanks, Chief." Jillian held out her hand to shake the chief's but he pulled her into his arms.

"I'm sorry you're having troubles. When will you have that phone installed? I don't like that you have no reception out there."

She smiled up at the man who'd come to mean a lot to her in the two years she'd lived in Cape Churn. "I'm hoping before the wedding."

"You're staying at the McGregor B and B?"

"Not tonight, if I have running water by the time I get home."

The chief frowned. "You're not staying out there all by yourself, are you?"

Jillian's cheeks heated.

"No, sir." Chance stepped up beside her and slipped an arm around her waist. "I'll be there."

The frown eased from the chief's forehead. "Good. I'm glad she won't be alone. Until we find out who's up to no good, it's not safe for her to be alone in that house."

Chance nodded. "Agreed."

"I refuse to be scared away from my own home." Jillian stood with her arms crossed over her chest.

"Better scared and safe than dead," Chief Taggart said.

Jillian refused to be ruled by fear. She left the police station, determined to find answers. But as she got into the vandalized rental car, she couldn't hold back the shiver of apprehension slithering down the back of her neck.

Chapter 16

Chance pulled up at the address Suzanna had given them. The house was a neat little Cape Cod bungalow with a picket fence and mailbox in the shape of an open-mouthed fish.

He parked next to the curb and met Jillian at the gate.

Dusk was settling in and lights shone through the window into the dining room, where a man and a woman sat at their dinner table.

Though he didn't like disturbing people at dinner, Chance rang the doorbell and waited.

Jillian curled her fingers around his arm and leaned against him. "I feel bad for disturbing them."

Chance loved that they were on the same wavelength. It made him warm in the chilly evening air.

A man opened the door and stared out at them on the stoop. "Can I help you?"

"Sir, I'm Chance McCall and this is Jillian Taylor."

"I know Jillian—you helped us with a house for my mother-in-law. We were eating dinner. Can't it wait until we're done?"

"Sir, we'd like to speak to your wife about a student of hers from seventeen years ago."

The man snorted. "My wife has had a lot of students over the past seventeen years. You can't expect her to remember all of them."

"Mr. Tillman, I think she'll remember this one," Jillian said. "Julia Thompson. The child who went missing."

Tillman's lips thinned. "Jillian, why do you want to know about what happened before you even came to Cape Churn?"

Jillian's lips twisted. "I bought the old Thompson house from the bank. And ever since I started remodeling efforts, it seems someone is trying to stop me."

"Steve, let them in," a soft voice said behind the man.

For a moment Tillman stood, blocking their entry into his home. Then he sighed. "Come in." He held the door as Jillian and then Chance passed.

Rebecca Tillman greeted Jillian with a hug. "Don't let Steve scare you away. He's just trying to protect me. We had a journalist come around a couple years ago asking about the Julia Thompson case. He wasn't very nice and he refused to take no for an answer." She waved her hand to the front living room. "Please have a seat."

"We wouldn't bother you, but Jillian has had a couple attempts on her life."

Mrs. Tillman gasped. "Oh, dear. I'm so sorry. If there's anything I can do to help, I will. I just don't know what I can tell you that I didn't tell the police at the time they were searching for little Julia and her abductor."

"Do you know who was the last person to see Julia before she disappeared?"

Mrs. Tillman pressed her hand to her chest. "As far as I know, it was me. Julia always stayed late after school to help clean the boards. Her mother was a teacher at the middle school and didn't get home right away, so Julia would help me until I left. Then she would walk home."

"Which way did she go?" Chance asked.

"She took the road leading from the school toward her house a mile or so away."

"Were there other people who lived on that route?"

"Not at the time."

"Did other people travel that route on a regular basis?"

Mrs. Tillman shook her head. "Not that I know of. Her house was the only one at the end of that road. Some say there was another house a long time ago, but it burned to the ground before I was born. The historians think it belonged to a famous pirate who gave up his pirating ways to settle in Cape Churn and raise a family. I never put much stock in that story. Without a house or records, it was all just old wives' tales passed down from former residents."

"What was Julia's frame of mind when she left your classroom that day? Was she feeling well? Was she lucid?"

Mrs. Tillman's eyes clouded with tears. "She was so very happy. Because she was such a wonderful helper, I gave her a gift to show my appreciation for all she did to help me."

"What kind of gift?"

"It was a Russian music box I picked up when I backpacked through Europe and into Russia between my junior and senior years of college." The woman inhaled and let out a long slow breath. Then she smiled, tears welling in her eyes. "She was over the moon, thrilled. She couldn't wait to get home and show her mother."

"Which way did she go when she left the school?"

"Across the school yard and met up with the road leading toward her house." Rebecca stared out the window of her living room. "I remember watching her until she rounded the curve and moved out of sight. I always felt it was my fault she was abducted. I should have walked her home."

Her husband sat beside her on the sofa. "You can't walk all of your students home."

"I know. But I could have walked Julia home that day. She probably wasn't aware of anything but the music box. She was staring down at it all the way across the school yard, holding it out in front of her like she was afraid she'd break it."

"Mrs. Tillman, you couldn't have known what was going to happen," Chance said.

"I spoke with her mother in the weeks that followed. She said Julia sometimes cut through the woods to get home quicker." Mrs. Tillman bowed her head. "I should have offered to take her home, since she had to carry the music box."

Her husband laid his hand on her shoulder. "Hindsight doesn't change the past."

She raised her hand to cover his and gave a weak, shaky smile. "I was so relieved when she finally came home. Too many children gone that long are never found." Her brows furrowed. "I had her back in my class for a couple weeks before her mother pulled her out and moved away. I haven't seen or heard from them since. But not a day goes by that I don't think about them and wonder how Julia is now. She was a bright and happy child. As pretty as her mother."

"Had there been anyone lurking around the school during that time frame?" Chance asked.

Mrs. Tillman shook her head. "If there was, I was too busy working and straightening my classroom to notice. I believe the police asked the same question of every one of the school staff, and none of us had seen anyone suspicious."

"What about homes or businesses in the vicinity of the school?" Chance asked.

"The school sits a little bit back off the road." Mrs. Tillman shook her head. "It was built where it is on purpose. Only those people who had a need to be at the school come down the road. The closest buildings are the trailer park and the auto body shop, and they are a good quarter of a mile away."

"Were you the last one to leave the school?" Chance asked.

"No. I left at the same time as Melanie Bateman. We went to an exercise class together." She closed her eyes. "I remember being in the break room the next day. Every teacher was questioned, the admin staff and old Mr. Locke, the janitor, although he'd been home sick the previous afternoon. His wife took him to the doctor. Everyone had an alibi. Not that I could see any of the staff abducting a child. We love all of our students."

Jillian nodded. "Thank you for answering our questions. I know it's a long shot trying to figure out who held Julia captive. But with the attempts on my life and the damage to my house, I have to try. I can't think of anything else that might cause someone to feel threatened by my buying the house."

"I hope you figure it out." Mrs. Tillman squeezed her husband's hand. "For the past seventeen years, the parents and teachers in this town have lived in fear of a repeat abduction. Some have become complacent over time."

"Not you. Right, Rebecca?" her husband said. "I think she cried every night for months. And the nightmares…" He shook his head. "She still has them."

Chance rose and held out his hand to Steve Tillman. "Mr. Tillman." He shook hands with the man and turned to Rebecca and held out his hand, helping her to her feet. "Mrs. Tillman, thank you for answering our questions."

"I wish I could be of more help. If we had caught the one responsible for holding Julia hostage for a month, perhaps she and her mother wouldn't have left Cape Churn. Julia was such a pleasure to have in class and her mother was always kind. She worked at the middle school across town. We ran into each other at workshops."

Jillian left the house first. Chance followed, opened the door to the SUV and waited for her to get in. Once she was settled, he rounded to the other side and climbed in. "Did you get anything out of that session?"

Jillian sat silent for a moment, staring at her hands in her lap. "Julia wasn't paying attention. She could have cut through the woods and fallen, maybe hitting her head."

"Yeah, but someone had to have found her. She was gone for an entire month. She wouldn't have survived two weeks in the woods. It gets cold at night. She'd have died of hypothermia or starvation."

"But she didn't." Jillian looked up. "I want to go to the school and attempt to retrace Julia's steps."

"It's getting dark outside."

"Please. I won't go far and we can start at the curve in the road. The last place Mrs. Tillman saw Julia."

Though he didn't like the idea of Jillian out at night, wandering around in the woods, Chance reasoned that he would be there and could protect her. So far the threats had involved another vehicle or her house. If they didn't stay until it got really dark, they should be okay.

Jillian leaned forward as Chance drove down the road leading into the school yard. He made a circle where parents dropped off their children in the morning and then drove to the back of the building, where trucks delivered supplies for the kitchen and the administrative staff. He parked and got out.

Jillian exited and stood beside him, her hand reaching for his. "This is where it all started."

"I can't imagine a little girl walking home, not a care in the world, and poof. Gone." Chance's hand tightened on hers. "It's a parent's worst nightmare."

Jillian nodded. "How frightening for little Julia." She stared across the school yard, past the playground equipment to the soccer goals and farther toward where she could see the slim ribbon of a road. "That street doesn't connect to the one coming in or out of the school campus." She tugged on his hand. "Let's drive around to the curve before it gets too dark to see."

"It's about that dark now," he said, but got into the car with her and drove away from the school. Once off school property, he turned right and connected with the road leading up to Jillian's house. The sun had sunk below the horizon, leaving the land bathed in dusk gray, that time of day when shadows consumed the light.

Jillian swiveled in her seat, looking back at the school yard. She touched his arm. "Stop here."

Chance pulled to a stop on the shoulder.

Jillian got out and stared back at the school. She moved several feet farther down the road, looking back every so often until she came to a halt. "At this point, Mrs. Tillman couldn't see Julia." She turned toward the woods and squinted, wishing she could see her house through the brush. "If Julia wanted to get home in a hurry, she probably cut through the woods, and if she was busy looking at the music box she was carrying, she could have lost her way."

Chance came to stand behind her and rested his hands on her shoulders. "Your point?"

Jillian sagged. "It's too dark to look now, but tomorrow I'd like to come out and walk through the woods."

"She could just as well have walked home by the road. Someone could have driven by and forced her into the vehicle."

Jillian shook her head. "Call it a gut feeling, but I don't think so."

"Why?" Chance asked, though he couldn't argue with instinct. It had saved his butt on more than one occasion.

"She knew she wasn't supposed to walk through the woods, but she was so excited with her gift, she probably took the shortcut anyway."

"Okay. We'll come back tomorrow when it's daylight and we can see two feet in front of us. In the meantime, we need to see if your house is habitable. We might be staying in town tonight if there isn't water."

Jillian nodded. "You're right. It can wait until tomorrow. In the daylight. No. Wait. It'll have to be the day after tomorrow. I'm working in the morning and meeting with Molly in the afternoon for the final dress fitting."

"Okay."

"And I'll want to drive through the trailer park, as well."

"That's the same trailer park where we dropped Daryl, right?"

Jillian nodded, chewing on her lip. Finally she asked the question that had been gnawing at her. "Do you think Daryl had anything to do with Julia's disappearance?"

Chance didn't answer right away. When he did, he said, "I really don't know Daryl enough to make that call. The man cried over a lost dog. I can't imagine he has a mean bone in his body."

"Yeah. That's what I think. He'd never spray paint graffiti on the walls or cut the rails. And he can't drive, so he couldn't have been the one to crash into us."

"Or can he drive and he's putting on a front?"

Jillian shook her head. "I don't know what to think anymore. Let's head back to town and grab something from the café for dinner. I can call my contractor while we're in town. If he says the water's on, we'll go back to the house. If it isn't, we'll find a place to stay in town."

Chance turned around in the middle of the road and headed back into town. As soon she had reception on her cell phone, Jillian called Bob.

"I'm glad you called," he said.

Jillian braced for bad news.

"The septic system is fine and functioning. The plumber cleaned it out and finished running the new pipes. The water's on throughout the house, and we didn't find any leaks. You're in business."

Jillian let go of the breath she'd been holding. "That's the first good news we've had all day. Thank you." She ended the call and beamed at Chance. "We're staying at the house tonight."

He nodded. "Okay. Let's get dinner and eat it at the house to celebrate coming home."

Jillian sat back in her seat, realizing how good it felt to have someone with whom to share her triumphs as well as her struggles. It felt natural to include Chance. Some of her happiness faded at the thought of his departure after the wedding. She pushed it to the back of her mind, determined to enjoy his company while he was there.

At the café, they ordered two steak dinners to go, telling Nora about the steak Mortimer had insisted they give him in exchange for information.

"Well, at least he knows we keep good steaks in our refrigerator. He needs to come out of the woods more often."

"Does he work anywhere?"

Nora nodded. "He's a writer. What he writes, I haven't a clue. I believe he uses a pen name to keep anyone from stalking him."

Jillian laughed. "I don't think he has to worry about that. That wolf of his would keep the stalkers away."

"I couldn't even bribe it with the steak," Chance added.

"Hmm." Nora's brows lowered. "I'll have to remember that. No more steaks for that man. He can come to the café for the next one. What did you learn from Alan Thompson?"

"He isn't involved." Jillian accepted a cup of coffee from Nora and sipped the fragrant brew. "Chance checked his references for last night. He was where he said he was. And I just don't think he would do it."

"I remember when Julia was missing." Nora poured a cup of coffee for Chance and one for herself. "No man looked harder or longer than Alan Thompson. He loved that little girl, and he loved Sarah. I wish he could have gotten his act together before he lost them."

"Yeah, he's still beating himself up over their loss, even after all the years."

"Did he know where Sarah and Julia ended up?" Nora asked.

Jillian shook her head. "No."

Nora left them to check on their meal and returned with two covered plastic plates and plastic utensils. "You sure you don't want to stay and eat here?"

"Thanks, Nora," Jillian said. "I need to get back to the house. I hope that with me staying there, whoever vandalized it won't try it again."

"I'll make sure Tom sends a unit by to check on you."

Chance smiled. "It's nice having connections. Tell him thanks from us."

Jillian's heart fluttered and heat filled her insides. Chance had said *us* as if they were together. She quickly squashed that thought. She'd only known the man a couple days and slept with him once. That didn't constitute a lasting relationship. It would be foolish of her to hang her hopes based on that short a time frame.

With a house and herself under attack, she didn't really have the time to dedicate to falling in love with a stranger.

They made the drive back to the house in silence. As they cleared the tree-lined drive and the headlights shone on the structure, Jillian sighed in relief.

"Why the big sigh?" Chance said as he shifted into Park.

"No new graffiti, and the house is still standing. I'd say that's a plus in my favor." She grabbed the two plates and stepped out of the vehicle.

The construction crew had been careful to clean the path to the house, so she didn't have to worry about tripping over discarded lumber or tools. The vehicle headlights stayed on long enough to light their way up to the front porch before the automatic off switch engaged, plunging them into darkness.

Jillian handed the food to Chance and dug in her pocket for her keys. After several attempts to insert the correct one into the door lock, she opened the front door and reached inside to switch on the lights. The front entrance lit up, chasing away the darkness.

Jillian checked the kitchen. "I still don't have cabinets and my table is buried beneath all my other furniture, so I suggest we eat in one of two rooms habitable at this time."

"And that would be?"

She pointed up the stairs. "My bedroom." The butterflies in her belly took flight. "Unless you want to find some boards or an empty paint bucket to sit on. Or we could sit on the toilet and the edge of the bathtub in the only other room that is functional at this time. However, I think my bed will be more comfortable. I had the guys move it upstairs when they finished painting the room."

"I'll check all the windows and doors before we go up."

Jillian found her box of linens and grabbed towels, sheets, pillows and a blanket.

Chance made a quick run through each room on the

ground floor and a trip to the basement to secure the two small windows there.

With no desire to start up the stairs to the second floor without him, Jillian waited until Chance was done with his security check. She hated to pander to the element of fear that had taken root since the wreck, but she wasn't ready to go it alone yet.

Chance appeared in front of her. "Ready?"

She nodded, handed over the linens and let him take the lead while she followed with the plates of food.

They made their way to the master suite at the end of the hallway, stopping in every doorway long enough to check for intruders and test the locks on the windows.

"Are we good for the night?" Jillian asked.

"We're good." He tossed the linens on the mattress. "I don't know about you, but I'm hungry."

"Me, too." Jillian handed a plate to him and removed the cover from hers. The smell of grilled steak made her mouth water.

They ate in silence, Jillian avoiding the elephant in the room, afraid to bring up the fact there was only one bed and two of them. It was one thing for passion to bring them together in the same room at the McGregor B and B, but sharing a bed without the requisite fore-play only made it awkward. Hell, he might not *want* to sleep with her.

"If you're worried about the sleeping arrangements, don't," Chance said. "I have a sleeping bag in the back of the car. I'll be sleeping on the floor."

Hiding her disappointment, Jillian protested, "It's not right. You're doing *me* a favor by staying here. It's only right for *me* to sleep on the floor and you take the bed."

She didn't offer to share the bed. Since he'd suggested

sleeping on the floor, he probably hadn't been sufficiently satisfied by their lovemaking to ask for a repeat performance. A lead weight settled on top of the steak and baked potato she'd just consumed, making her wish she hadn't eaten almost all of it.

Chance finished his food first and replaced the top on the empty plate.

"You can have the first shower. I'll need my bag from the car for my toiletries and clothes." He nodded and left the room.

Jillian followed him to the landing and stood at the top of the stairs as Chance descended. She tried not to admire the breadth of his shoulders or the way his waist narrowed into the waistband of his jeans. Hell, she wasn't fooling anyone, especially not herself. With and without clothes, the man was too sexy to ignore.

When he disappeared out the door, she spun on her heels and returned to the bedroom to make the bed. She had the fitted sheet on and was smoothing the top sheet over it when Chance returned carrying both his bag and hers, and the dreaded sleeping bag.

Well, damn. He really was going to sleep on the floor.

"Need a hand?" he asked, reaching for the other corner of the sheet.

"No," she said, the answer coming out a little harsher than she'd intended. A bit of anger made her snap the sheet tight. "I can handle it. I'll let you test the water. Hopefully the hot water heater has had time to heat."

Chance ditched her bag and carried his into the adjoining bathroom, closing the door behind him.

Damn again. If she'd held out a hope that he would invite her to join him in the shower, she could forget about it. That door was closed.

Jillian finished making the bed and spread out the sleeping bag on the floor beside it, laying a pillow at the head. Though she was hurt and disappointed by his decision to pass on sleeping with her, she didn't like the idea of him on the cold hardwood floor.

A moment later, the door to the bathroom opened, emitting a waft of steam. "Hot water is great. I saved some for you." He came out with the towel around his neck, wearing a pair of sweatpants and nothing else.

Jillian couldn't look away. The man's bare chest was like a magnet, making her want to reach out and touch it.

He twisted the towel and popped her with it. "Your turn."

Heat rushed into her cheeks. Jillian grabbed her bag and made a run for the bathroom. How embarrassing to be caught staring like a drooling teenaged girl. She turned on the shower, stripped down and stood beneath the hot spray, wishing she had the nerve to invite Chance to join her. But she couldn't handle the potential rejection. She had to be sure that was what he wanted, not just something she wanted. Wanted so badly her body ached.

She'd have to seduce him the old-fashioned way. Not too openly, but obvious enough he'd get the hint. With a plan in mind, she finished showering, dried her hair and sprayed her skin with a tantalizing body spray advertised to set any man's blood on fire. Then she dressed in the filmy nightgown that had seemed to do the trick the night before.

Armed with every bit of feminine ammo she had in her overnight bag, she opened the door to the bedroom and stood there, letting the light from the bathroom silhouette her nakedness beneath the sheer baby-doll nightgown.

The pallet of sleeping bag and pillow she'd laid out on the side of the bed facing the bathroom was gone.

Moving into the room, Jillian looked for the missing man. He wasn't anywhere in the room. That niggling stab of fear rippled through her. She ran to the door, jerked it open and nearly tripped over the man lying at her feet, cocooned in the sleeping bag, his hands crossed behind his head.

He propped one eyelid open. "Everything okay?"

Jillian could swear the corners of his lips twitched for a nanosecond before his face lost all expression except that of polite curiosity.

"Yes. Everything is just peachy." She slammed the door, stomped to her bed and climbed in. Alone. Wearing a nightgown that left her cold and cranky.

"Men. Who needs them?" She rolled onto her side, facing the bathroom, not the door behind which Chance lay. If that was the way he wanted it, so be it.

Jillian lay still, counting the number of breaths she took. When that didn't help, she rolled onto her back, her eyes closed, trying to focus on going to sleep. She should be exhausted, but her body hummed with a need she couldn't satisfy.

Damn the man. He had to know she wanted him, and yet he'd purposely positioned himself out of her reach.

As she lay there stewing, her anger eventually faded. Maybe he was actually doing her a favor and letting her down easy. She should thank him.

Yeah, that wasn't going to happen.

After a while she gave up trying to sleep and lay there, staring at the ceiling, thinking of all that had happened that day. They'd questioned so many people, and what did they have to show for it?

A better understanding of little Julia and her family. Both parents loved her dearly and had sacrificed everything for her.

Jillian wanted to find Julia and her mother to let them know how much Alan Thompson regretted letting them down. Jillian closed her eyes, an image of a little girl lost in the woods, scared, alone and cold, materializing in her head.

A child's cry echoed through her mind. Not until it sounded again did Jillian realize the sound wasn't just inside her head. It was outside in the night.

She leaped out of bed, her body shaking, a lump of fear lodged in her throat. Torn between alerting Chance and looking out the window, she opted for the window. If it was all in her mind, she didn't want to disturb her bodyguard. If it was real, she was safe on the second story of her house and had time to get to Chance, if she needed him.

Inching her way to toward the curtainless window, Jillian dragged in a shaky breath, peered out into the night and screamed.

Chapter 17

The scream pierced the light web of sleep to which Chance had finally fallen victim. He tossed back the sleeping bag, shot to his feet and burst through the bedroom door.

Before he could ask what was wrong, Jillian threw herself into his arms, her body trembling so badly it shook him, too.

He held her, his hands spanning her lower back, his gaze scanning the room, taking in every detail. Nothing appeared out of place. "What's wrong?"

She shook her head and pointed to the window. "I saw...a...ghost."

"Stay here and let me look." He tried to pry her arms from his body, but she wasn't letting go. "Okay, show me."

She eased away enough to walk with him to the window.

Chance looked out. That crazy fog the locals called the devil's shroud had crept in, surrounding the house, thick enough that it blocked the view of the nearby trees. Yes, there was fog, but as far as Chance could see, there were no ghosts. "Do you see it now?"

Jillian leaned toward the window, her body quaking. Then she let go of him and stared down at the ground. "It's gone. It was right there next to the house, all white and scary." She shivered.

"Are you sure you saw someone down there? You weren't walking in your sleep?"

"I never went to sleep. I wasn't even remotely sleepy when I heard something outside. That's why I got up to look."

Chance didn't like the idea of someone playing tricks on Jillian. If there was someone down there, he'd put a stop to it now. "Stay here."

Jillian grabbed his arm. "Do you have to go?"

"If someone is trying to scare you out of your home, we need to catch him in the act."

"But it looked like a ghost, not a person."

"You'd be amazed at what illusions people can conjure with a little face paint, smoke and mirrors. The fog played right in with it." He captured her arms in his hands. "Now, are you going to stay here, or are we going to let this guy get away with terrorizing you?"

She bit her lip and stared into his eyes, her usually light blue ones having darkened to the steely shade of storm clouds. "Be careful." She released him and wrapped her arms around her middle.

Chance walked out of the bedroom and turned. "Lock this door behind me." He pulled the door closed and waited for the sound of the lock engaging. Jamming his feet into his shoes, he dug in his sleeping bag for his flashlight. It was the heavy kind of flashlight that could be used as a club. He also pulled out the Glock he'd been issued when he'd gone to work for SOS. With the flashlight in one hand and his gun in the other, he eased down the steps without turning on the flashlight. Because of the fog outside, very little light came through the windows. A safety night-light had been installed near the base of the stairs, illuminating the first step and three feet around it. That one light gave him enough visibility to navigate the ground floor.

Moving as quickly as possible, Chance slipped out the kitchen door and rounded to the back of the house, where the master bedroom overlooked the stunning waters of the bay.

Nothing moved and he didn't see anyone lurking around the building. But then he could only see a few feet into the fog. He had turned back toward the house, ready to consider the ghost sighting a figment of an overstressed mind, when the sound of an engine revving found its way through the fog to him.

He switched on the flashlight and ran around to the front of the house. Stopping for a moment to listen, he could hear the crunch of gravel on the drive.

Damn. He'd left the car keys upstairs. Chance did the only thing he could. He ran, hoping to catch the intruder or at least get a description of the vehicle or a view of the license-plate number.

He sprinted all the way to where the driveway emptied onto the paved road before he stopped to drag in deep breaths. Whoever had been there was gone. Apparently Jillian hadn't been dreaming. Someone had purposely visited her house in the middle of the night, and it hadn't been a ghost.

He jogged back up the driveway and entered the side door he'd exited moments earlier. Again, he checked the doors and windows throughout the first floor and the basement before he ascended the stairs to the second floor.

Before he reached the master bedroom, a voice called out through the door panel, "Chance?"

"Yeah, it's me, baby."

Jillian flung the door open and stood there, her eyes wide. "I thought you'd never come back. I was about to go looking for you."

He smiled. "I wasn't gone that long."

She pulled him through the door and closed it behind him. "Did you see anything? Was it all in my imagination?"

"I didn't see anything."

Jillian's shoulders sagged.

"But I heard a car engine pulling away down the driveway. That's what took me so long. I tried to catch up to it before it got away."

"Are you crazy? He could have run you over." She slipped her arms around his waist and pressed her cheek against his chest. "Though it would have been good if you'd seen who it was, I'm glad he didn't see you."

"You have got to get a phone in here. I could have called the police and had them watching for a car entering town."

"I know. I'll check the status of the installation tomorrow while I'm in town working."

He held her for a while longer and then set her to arm's length. "You'd better get some sleep."

She curled her fingers into his T-shirt and stared up at him, her eyes two deep pools of blue. "Stay with me."

Chance swayed toward her, wanting more than anything to do as she asked. "I can't."

Jillian glanced toward the window and back. "I promise not to make a pass at you. You can sleep on the bed, and I'll sleep on the floor."

He released his hold on her arms and tipped her chin up with his finger. "Really, I can't."

"Why? Was I that horrible in bed last night that you can't even stay in the same room with me?" She gave him a weak smile. "It's okay to tell me. You won't hurt my feelings…much."

He pulled her against him and smoothed a hand over her hair. "Just the opposite. You're making it really hard for me to walk away from you."

"It's only a couple more nights before you leave Cape Churn. I won't expect anything from you."

"That's not it. Sleeping with you is too dangerous."

She stood still, her head tipped to the side. "Dangerous? What do you mean?"

He let go of her and sighed. "Since I came back from the war, I've had really bad dreams."

"I have bad dreams, too," she said.

"My dreams can be extremely violent. I almost killed a guy during one of them."

Jillian's eyes widened. "But you slept with me last night, and you didn't have any dreams."

He nodded. "That's rare. The norm is nightmares at least every other night."

"How long has it been since you returned from the war?" she asked.

"Over a year." He ran a hand through his hair. "Some

nights I think I'm getting better, then I'll have another bad night and feel like I'm back at square one."

Jillian tipped her chin upward. "I'm willing to take the chance."

He cupped her cheek and kissed her forehead. "Darlin', I'm stronger than you. I could easily overpower you. I was trained to kill. That's not something that goes away."

"You don't know that. You could be dream-free sleeping with me and not a threat at all."

"I'm not willing to risk your life on possibilities." He lifted her hand and pressed a kiss into her palm. "And you were amazing last night."

Her hand curled around his fingers. "Would you at least stay until I go to sleep?"

He hesitated but finally decided he couldn't hurt her if he left before he fell to sleep. "Okay."

With his hand in hers, she led him to the bed, climbed in and patted the mattress beside her. "I promise I won't make any moves on you. Just sit here. I'll go to sleep as quickly as possible."

Chance sat on the edge of the bed while Jillian settled beneath the sheets and pulled the comforter up to her chin. She smiled, closed her eyes and rolled onto her side, away from him. "See? I'm not even trying to tempt you."

Hell, she didn't have to try, and he was beyond tempted. Fighting the urge to touch her, to feel her warmth against his hand, Chance had to be satisfied with watching her, studying the way the light from the nightstand shimmered in her golden hair.

A shiver shook her body. She pulled the blanket closer and shivered again. Once the tremors started, she couldn't seem to shake them and Chance couldn't ignore her discomfort.

He really tried not to get too close to her, but after the first five minutes, he couldn't stand it any longer. Chance slid beneath the blanket and sheets, gathered her body close and pressed her back to his front.

Soon, she ceased trembling and fell asleep.

Chance held her until his eyes started to droop. At which point he slipped out of the bed, retrieved his sleeping bag and laid it out in front of the bedroom door on the inside, instead of the outside.

As soon as he crawled inside the bag, he closed his eyes, going over everything they'd learned that day. He was angry that someone had been there trying to frighten Jillian away. He vowed to check every inch of the house and the nearby grounds the next day, hoping to find whatever it was someone was determined to keep secret.

What could be so important someone would try anything to get Jillian to pack up and move out?

Jillian woke in the wee hours of the morning, cold and disoriented. She'd left the light burning on the nightstand to chase away the shadows. The blanket wasn't keeping her warm enough, and she was getting colder by the minute.

Her gaze went to the sleeping bag in front of the door. She bet the floor was hard, but inside the bag was probably toasty. A man like Chance generated heat.

Gathering her blanket, she wrapped it around her and slipped out of the bed. As she crossed the cool hardwood floor, she shivered, wishing she'd thought to turn on the heater before going to bed. Now she couldn't get to the thermostat with Chance's body blocking the door.

For a few seconds, she stared down at the man, willing him to wake and invite her in. When he didn't, she eased herself into the bag beside him and added her blanket to the top, congratulating herself on not waking Chance. She lay for a long time, absorbing his warmth and memorizing every detail of the man—his shape, the smell and the feel of him beside her.

He rolled onto his side and spooned her body, draping an arm around her waist.

Jillian snuggled close, content to be held. She'd do her best to sleep lightly in case he had a bad dream. After a while, she drifted off, falling into a deep sleep, free of dreams and ghosts.

She didn't wake until the sounds of men's voices and the roar of the generator woke her. When she opened her eyes, she realized she was back in her bed, buried in the covers, and Chance was nowhere to be found.

What the hell? Had she slept through him waking to find her in his sleeping bag? And how had he carried her to the bed without waking her? She stretched her arms, debating whether to leave the warmth of the blankets and go find Chance or snuggle deeper and go back to sleep.

A knock on the door made her pull the sheet up to her chin.

Without waiting for her answer, Chance pushed the door open and entered with two steaming mugs of coffee. "Thought you could use some caffeine. And I turned on the heater."

"You are an angel." She sat up, giving him a good eyeful of her sexy nightgown, fully aware of the men working below. She didn't care. He'd rejected her the night before; he might as well see what he'd missed.

Chance handed a mug to her and sat on the edge of the bed. "What are your plans for the day?"

"I have some work to do at my office in town, and then I'm having lunch with Molly. We're going to the tailor in Portland afterward for the final fitting and hopefully to pick up the wedding gown. I'll be busy most of the day—if you have something you need to do, today would be a good day for it. Not that you have to baby-sit me all the time. Since it will be daylight and I won't be at the house, you don't have to follow me around."

"What? You just want to get rid of me?" He stood, fully dressed in black jeans, a black T-shirt and his shoes. "I'll leave you to get dressed. I want to take a look around the house and the yard."

Jillian glanced toward the window at a dismal gray sky. "I take it the fog cleared."

"It did, but it looks like rain. See you downstairs when you're ready." He grabbed a leather jacket from his bag and left the room.

No good-morning kiss. No "I'm glad you slept with me after all last night." Jillian sighed. The attraction might well be only one-sided. She'd have to accept that and move on. At least she had a busy day to take her mind off the man who'd been so much a part of her thoughts for the past few days.

Setting the coffee mug on the nightstand, she threw back the blanket, grabbed tailored gray trousers and a soft white figure-hugging sweater, and headed into the bathroom.

Ten minutes later, dressed, brushed and wearing sufficient makeup to hide the faded dark circles beneath her eyes, she emerged from the bedroom, ready to take on the world. Shrugging into her charcoal-gray leather jacket, she descended the stairs into a cacophony of construction noise.

She was happy to see the old linoleum gone from the kitchen, the hardwood floors sanded and the old cabinets gone, making way for the new upgrades. The original hardwood floors in the living and dining rooms were being sanded. Her heart lightened. The house would be beautiful, warm and inviting soon. All she needed was to find who was causing her grief and put a stop to it.

Jillian stepped out onto the front porch and glanced up at the clouds choking the sunshine out of the day. It wasn't unusual for there to be clouds on the Pacific Northwest coast. She refused to be affected by the gloom. Pasting a smile on her face, she descended the steps.

Chance appeared from around the side of the house. "Ready?"

She nodded and headed for his SUV, the ugly red paint an angry reminder of the continued assault on her house and person.

When she reached for the door handle, Chance swept her hand aside and opened the door for her.

"Thank you." Jillian slipped into the seat and her gaze followed Chance around to the driver's side. Her heart thumped against her ribs. He was gorgeous, muscled, a gentleman and basically everything she could dream of in a man. The woman who finally tamed his nightmares would be lucky to have him in her life. Jillian wished it could be her.

Chance slid behind the wheel and started the vehicle.

"Did you find anything noteworthy?" she asked.

He shook his head. "Nothing. I searched the perimeter a hundred yards out. Nothing stood out. If there's an unmarked grave, it blended with the landscape."

Jillian's heart fluttered. "You think there's someone buried out here and that's why I'm being chased away?"

He tossed her a crooked smile. "I can't think of any other reason for someone to want the owner of a house to leave."

A chill rippled across her skin. "Maybe we've been focusing too much on Julia Thompson and we should have been asking about unsolved murders."

"I was thinking the same. While you're working, I think I'll pay a visit to Chief Taggart and the local library and look for any murder cases in the past seventeen years the house has sat empty."

"I'd help, but I have a couple of showings this morning and some new listings to post to MLS. My afternoon is completely devoted to Molly and the wedding." She shook her head. "I don't want any of what's happening to me to detract from Molly and Nova's big day."

"Got it. Just promise you'll call me when you're ready to go back to the house."

Jillian nodded, her mind on the tasks filling her day, pushing aside the troubles she'd encountered since starting the renovations on her house. One thing she couldn't push out of her thoughts was the man sitting beside her. Maybe once he was out of sight, he'd be out of her mind, as well.

Ha. That's not going to happen.

Chapter 18

After giving Jillian his cell phone number and strict instructions on contacting him or the police immediately if she thought she was in danger, Chance dropped her at her office. He wasn't comfortable with the idea of her showing houses. After she explained that she knew the customers personally and would be meeting them at her office and leaving from there in her clients' vehicles, he was more willing to let her handle it on her own.

Jillian hated being on guard all of the time. She leaned back into vehicle one last time before he left. "I hope you find something in your digging today." She smiled. "As long as it's not a body in my backyard."

His grim expression didn't leave her feeling better about the day. All morning she worked, trying to catch up after taking the previous day off to chase after the ghost of Julia Thompson, who might not even be dead.

Two showings and setting up the listings on the Multiple Listing Service took up all of her morning. Jillian was just posting the last house to the website when Molly sailed through the door.

"Hey, sweetie, wrap it up. You and I have a lunch date." Molly was all smiles, her cheerful attitude just what Jillian needed.

Jillian stood and gave her friend a hug. "I'm done." She grabbed her purse and jacket and followed Molly to the door. "Seaside Café?"

"Since we have to drive into Portland for the final fitting, I thought we'd eat lunch there. It gives us a few more choices than here in Cape Churn. That's if you can wait that long to eat?"

"I can wait," Jillian said, although the breakfast bar she'd had earlier had long since worn off. The drive to Portland would give her time to go over all the preparations for the upcoming wedding, nailing down the last-minute details. She slid into Molly's SUV and buckled her seat belt.

Molly got in and started the car. "When will your car be fixed?"

"I need to call the adjuster and see what the damage is. Thanks for the reminder." Jillian called and got the adjuster's voice mail. She left a message and settled back in the SUV, prepared to enjoy the rest of the day with her friend. "Are you ready for the wedding?"

Molly laughed. "I'm ready for it to be *over* so we can enjoy our honeymoon in Hawaii, far away from all the chaos of the wedding." She gave Jillian a sad kind of smile. "As soon as we get back from our honeymoon, Nova has to go back to work. It's been nice having him here these past few weeks. I'll miss him when he's away."

"How do you feel about him going out on dangerous missions?" Jillian asked. "Won't you worry?"

"Hell, yes." Molly's fingers tightened on the steering wheel. "I'll worry about him every time he goes away."

"And you're okay with that?"

"It's his job. What he loves to do. I wouldn't take that from him. Besides, it'll make his homecomings that much more intense." Molly's eyes narrowed. "Why do you ask? Are you thinking of snagging a secret agent for yourself?"

Jillian's cheeks heated. "No, of course not."

Molly's foot left the accelerator. "Oh, my God! You're falling in love with the best man, aren't you?"

"I don't know." Jillian looked away, afraid Molly would see in her face something she wasn't ready to admit to anyone, even herself. "We've only known each other a few days."

"A few *intense* days. That's all it took with Nova and me. He's more than I could ever have hoped for in a soul mate."

Soul mate. Jillian chewed on that phrase. Was that what she was feeling? Chance was the kind of man she could spend the rest of her life loving, if she let herself. And if *he* let her.

"So what's wrong?" Molly demanded.

Jillian's head jerked back to her friend. "Nothing."

"You have that look like someone just kicked your kittens." Molly grinned. "And for the record, Jack and Jill are fine. Nova is quite good with animals and keeps them entertained when I need to get work done."

"I'm sorry. I shouldn't have dumped them on you. I can take them home with me tonight."

"You will not. Those kittens have been a godsend.

They keep Nova out of my hair for long stretches at a time. And now that his family is here, they are helping entertain them, as well."

"How's that going?"

Molly laughed. "I love his family, but after being just me and Gabe for so long, all the family time is a bit overwhelming. That's why I was so looking forward to this trip to Portland. I can escape for a few hours. Just you and me. Now, tell me what's wrong between you and Nova's hunky best man."

Jillian took a deep breath and then admitted, "You're right. I'm attracted to Chance."

Molly took her hands off the wheel long enough to clap. "I'm so happy for you."

"Well, don't be." She reached out to steady the steering wheel.

Resuming her control of the vehicle, Molly asked, "Why?"

"Chance doesn't want a relationship."

"Is he already committed to someone else?"

"I don't think so."

"Then he only needs to be shown that he really does want to be in a relationship. With you."

Jillian shook her head. "He's serious."

"There's no way any right-minded man could pass on a dish like you, Jill. You're stunningly gorgeous, smart and independent. Just the kind of woman a secret agent needs in his life."

"Apparently not."

"Then there's something wrong with Chance, if he doesn't like you."

Jillian smiled. "Oh, he admitted to liking me."

"Then what's the big deal?"

"He's afraid of sleeping with me. Afraid he'll hurt me in one of his violent nightmares."

"Oh." Molly stared ahead for a while. "PTSD can be pretty bad in some veterans. Nova says that being on guard at all times, as well as being shot at and bombed, screws with your head."

"I told him I was willing to risk it. But he's not."

"Well, damn. I thought for a moment there we might have a double wedding."

"Molly! Chance and I barely know each other." Jillian's heart beat faster at an unbidden image of two brides walking down the aisle to their grooms.

"Again, it didn't take long for me to know Nova was the one for me."

"It doesn't matter. When the wedding's over, Chance will be on his way back to Virginia. That's on the opposite side of the continent. It's not like we'd see each other."

"I'm sorry," Molly said, her happy smile sliding off her face.

"Enough about me. This is your week and your wedding. I refuse to be morose when my very best friend is about to marry the love of her life." Jillian squared her shoulders and forced a smile on her face.

The rest of the way to Portland and during their lunch, Jillian and Molly talked through the final planning for the rehearsal dinner, the wedding and the reception.

The fitting went well, the dress perfectly shaped to Molly's gorgeous figure. Jillian cried when she came out of the dressing room wearing the beautiful mermaid dress with the sweetheart neckline.

"Good grief, Jillian." Molly laughed. "Are you going to cry at the wedding, too?"

Pressing a tissue to her nose, Jillian nodded. "Damn right I am. Don't worry, I'll tuck tissues into my bra so that I don't drip on anything important." She winked and helped Molly out of the dress. The attendant packaged the beautiful gown and they were on their way back to Cape Churn before sunset.

Jillian was tired but happy for her friend. Molly, so intent on getting home, forgot to stop in Cape Churn to drop Jillian off with Chance, bypassing the turnoff to Main Street and heading straight for the road leading to Jillian's house.

Jillian texted Chance, letting him know she would be at her house and that she would be fine. He could take his time, or not come at all. She sent the text before she could change her mind, hoping he would ignore her silent offer to stay away, if he wanted. The thought of sleeping alone in her house made her insides quake. With a nutcase running around trying to scare her with ghost sightings, car crashes and the sabotaged railing, Jillian wasn't confident in her ability to sleep through the night.

As Molly pulled up in front of the old house, she frowned. "We can just wait in the car until Chance gets here." She shifted into Park.

Before she could shut off the engine, Jillian covered her hand. "I'll be fine for the few minutes he's not here. You need to get back to the B and B. Your houseguests will be expecting you back by now."

"My mother and sisters-in-law are taking care of dinner. I'm actually looking forward to it. They're cooking a traditional Mexican dinner complete with homemade tamales. Nova's mother promised she'd share the recipe."

"Your guests love everything you cook." Jillian gathered her purse and opened the door the SUV. "If it makes you feel better, the construction crew is here if I need anything."

Molly glanced at the clock on the dash. "If you're sure. I would like to get back and hang the dress before it gets any more wrinkled."

Jillian leaned across the console and hugged her friend. "I'll see you tomorrow when they deliver the chairs for the ceremony."

"Okay." Molly stayed where she was until Jillian entered the house. Then she turned around and left.

Jillian found Bob in the kitchen, inspecting the floors that had been sanded and cleaned.

"We're just about done for the day. The cabinets will be here in two days. Countertops, sink and appliances will be here next week."

"Really?" Jillian grinned. "I didn't expect them to come that soon. That's wonderful."

"We're cleaning up some of the mess, then we'll be heading out. Is there anything you need?"

For Chance to get here before you leave. "No. Thank you for everything."

"Our pleasure. It's nice to see old places like this get a makeover. It has good bones." Bob patted the wall beside him. "Just needs a little TLC."

"Do you think it's haunted?" Jillian asked.

Bob's brows puckered. "Excuse my French, but hell, no. I don't believe in ghosts."

"Me either." Although she'd thought she'd seen one last night. Based on Chance's scouting, she'd been corrected—someone driving a vehicle had pretended to be a ghost to scare her.

"We'll be back early in the morning." Bob tipped his ball cap. "Good night, Miss Taylor."

The men piled into the crew cab truck and Bob started the truck, backed up and turned around.

"Hey, wait. Aren't you missing someone?" Jillian waved to Bob. "Where's Daryl?"

Bob poked his head out the truck window. "He's out back stacking lumber. I didn't think he'd be working today since he wasn't at the café, but his mother brought him by around ten this morning. Mrs. Sims will be by to pick him up today." With that explanation, Bob and his crew left.

Jillian walked around the porch to the back of the house.

"Hi, Miss Taylor," Daryl said, continuing to work. "I'll only be a little longer."

"Thank you, Daryl. If you need anything, I'll be in the house. Just yell."

"I will." He continued to sort and stack boards and pieces as Jillian went back into the house. She opened the box the deliveryman had left and was happy to see the dresser she'd ordered online. Unfortunately, it needed assembly. With nothing else to do but kill time until Chance showed up, she changed into jeans, a sweatshirt and tennis shoes, found her toolbox, took out the instructions, and started reading through them. As she tore open a package of nuts and bolts, the bag came apart faster than she expected, scattering the items over the floor. Jillian scooped them up and was stuffing them into her front pocket when she heard a knock on the front door.

Thinking it was either Daryl or Chance, Jillian jerked the door open.

"Hello, Miss Taylor." Mrs. Sims stood in the doorway, wearing old jeans, a flannel shirt and a heavy coat.

"Good evening, Mrs. Sims. Daryl's out back, stacking lumber. Come in while I get him." Jillian stood back and waved the woman into the house.

She remained standing on the porch. "I can go around on the porch. No need to track my dirty feet through your home." The woman looked past Jillian. "Are you alone?"

Jillian smiled. "Only for a little while."

Mrs. Sims tilted her head. "Has anyone ever told you that you look like the woman who used to live here?"

"Really?" Jillian shook her head. "Are you talking about Sarah Thompson?"

"Yes. She was about your height and had blond hair."

"I have one more thing in common with her."

"What's that?"

"We both love this house." Jillian glanced around. "I felt like I was at home the moment I stepped through the door."

Mrs. Sims eyes narrowed, and she stared at Jillian for a long time. "Where did you say home was?" she asked.

"Here, now." Jillian drew in a deep breath. "I came here for a short vacation a couple years ago and felt like I knew this town, like it was the home I never found in Portland." She laughed, a little self-conscious at revealing so much about her decision to stay in Cape Churn to Mrs. Sims. "Anyway, I'm here now and hope to make new memories in this house."

"Do you have family back in Portland?"

"My mother and stepfather died in a small airplane crash the year before I found Cape Churn. I have no siblings and nothing to take me back to Portland. This is home."

"You sure you want live here? Some say the place is haunted by that little girl who disappeared."

"I don't believe in ghosts, Mrs. Sims. And the little girl was found. She didn't die in this house. But I am concerned that that person who took her was never captured and put away."

"That should be enough to scare away most people," Mrs. Sims said.

"Most people, but not me. I refuse to be frightened away from my first home." Jillian balled her hands into fists. "It's mine. I'm not going anywhere."

The older woman studied her for a long moment and then nodded. "Well, don't let me keep you. I'll get Daryl and we'll be on our way."

"Okay." As Mrs. Sims turned to walk around the porch, Jillian closed the door. She tracked the woman's progress through the windows that had no curtains until she moved out of sight.

Jillian went back to the task of assembling the dresser.

A knock on the kitchen door at the side of the house interrupted her in the middle of twisting a screw into the wood. She set the screwdriver on the floor and wove her way through Sheetrock boards, a generator and tools to the door. When she opened the door, Mrs. Sims stood there, a frown digging deep grooves in her forehead.

"Daryl wasn't there. By chance did he come inside?"

Jillian stared out at the encroaching fog. "No, he didn't. I hope he didn't get lost."

Chance spent the morning at the library, combing through page after page of newspaper articles dating back seventeen years. Julia Thompson's was the only missing person case that was still unexplained. And he found five murders reported in those years, but all the bodies were found in their homes, none of which was Jillian's house.

By early afternoon, his eyes were crossing and he'd developed a headache. Since Jillian was in Portland for the rest of the day, Chance drove out to the B and B to see Nova.

As soon as he drove up the driveway and parked in front of the mansion, Nova stepped out on the porch, a huge smile on his face. "Chance, amigo! I was beginning to think you'd skipped town and wouldn't make it to the wedding." He dropped down off the porch and enveloped Chance in a back-pounding hug.

"I've been busy," Chance offered.

"Busy keeping up with the pretty Realtor?" Nova winked. "She's *muy linda*, isn't she?"

Chance climbed the steps to the porch and sat in one of the rocking chairs. "Yes, she is. And that's becoming a real problem."

"Why? Don't you like her?" Nova dropped into the chair next to him.

"Yeah. Too much." Chance glanced at his friend. "I want her, but I can't let myself get involved."

"Because of the nightmares?" Nova's face lost the happy smile and turned serious. "You can't stop living because of your dreams. Have you thought of getting help?"

"I've been to the shrinks and therapists. I'm armed with all the techniques for coping with PTSD. Most of them say to give it time and the dreams will fade away."

"And have they?"

"Some."

"Then what's stopping you from pursuing the pretty maid of honor?"

"I don't want to hurt her. Physically or mentally."

"From what Molly said, you slept with her the night you stayed here. How'd that go?"

"No nightmares." Chance rocked out of the chair and stood. "But one night isn't enough to know if I'm over the violent reactions."

"You won't know unless you give it a shot."

"And risk Jillian's life on maybes?" Chance shook his head. "I can't do that to her. I'd never forgive myself if I hurt or, God forbid, killed her."

"It's been over a year since you choked that guy. You haven't had a recurrence."

"Because I haven't allowed myself to sleep in the same room with anyone else."

"Until Jillian." Nova nodded. "Does she know why you don't want to start something with her?"

"Yeah, I told her last night."

"And?"

"She's willing to risk it."

"Did you sleep with her last night?"

"Yes and no."

Nova laughed. "To me, that should have been one or the other. Either you did or you didn't."

"I held her, but I didn't sleep." He dragged a hand over his face. "I want to be with her, but I need to sleep."

"She's with Molly all afternoon. Why don't you find a lounge chair in the living area and catch some *z*'s? I just lit the fire."

Chance glanced through the windows. "I thought you were overrun by family?"

"I sent them to town. Dave Logsdon promised to take them deep-sea fishing. They'll be gone all day. You can sleep in complete silence."

Chance smiled. "I'm going to take you up on that offer."

"Go. I have a honey-do list a mile long that will keep me busy for most of the afternoon. Just watch out for Jack and Jill. They think the furniture is their territory. You might have to share."

Chance found a recliner near the crackly blaze in the big fireplace. He stretched out and closed his eyes, his mind going over all he'd learned and all he'd read, disappointed he didn't have any more than he'd started with. When Jillian returned from Portland, she'd be disappointed. But he couldn't magically produce the one piece of information that would solve all of her problems.

Before long, exhaustion claimed him and he slept so soundly, he didn't wake until a phone rang somewhere in the house. It rang seven times, finally pulling him from the warm, restful cocoon of a dreamless sleep.

Chance pushed to his feet, followed the sound of the ringing and found Nova, out of breath, answering the phone. He turned toward him and said, "Oh, good, you're awake. It's Royce. He says he tried to call your cell, but couldn't get through." Nova's lips twisted. "Big surprise out here, huh? Anyway, he has some information that might help."

The gray fog of sleep vanished as Chance took the phone from Nova. "What do you have?"

"We found records of Sarah Thompson's legal name change in the Social Security database."

"What did she change it to?"

"She changed her name to Sandra Warren. Using that name, we checked court records in Portland and found record of her marriage to a Robert Taylor. He then adopted her daughter, Jillian, who we assume was little

Julia. We also found death certificates for Sandra and Robert Taylor from three years ago."

Chance's blood chilled. Jillian Taylor was the little girl who'd disappeared seventeen years ago and had no memory of the incident or who abducted her.

"Thanks, Royce. I have to go." Chance ended the call and stared for a moment at the telephone. How the hell was he going to tell Jillian she was Julia? God, it all made sense now. She'd told him she didn't remember anything before the fifth grade. The town of Cape Churn and the house she'd purchased all felt like home. Though she didn't know it, her deeply buried memories had led her back to the place that had stolen them.

"Nova, I'm home," Molly's voice called out from the front door.

Chance jerked his head toward the window. The sun, hidden by the clouds, must be well on its way toward the horizon, and one of those deadly fogs had crept in while he'd been asleep.

Molly entered the house carrying a long garment bag, smiling at Nova. "I have my wedding dress. I can't wait for you to see me in it."

Nova pulled her into his arms and kissed her soundly. "I can't wait to see you out of it."

Molly swatted his chest. "Nova, we have company." She looked past him to Chance. "How was your day? Jillian and I had the best afternoon."

"Does she need help carrying anything in?" Chance asked.

Molly's brows dipped. "No, she's not with me. I dropped her at the house."

Chance's heart slammed against his ribs. "You what?"

"The construction crew was still there. She said she'd

be fine. She texted you when we got back in town." Molly's lips twisted. "If you've been out here all afternoon, you probably didn't get the text."

"Gotta go." Chance hurried past Molly and Nova. "I'll be at Jillian's house if you need me." Once out the door, he raced for his car, jumped in and screamed out of the driveway, kicking up gravel. The clock on the dash indicated it was past six. The construction crew had been gone from the house at five thirty the previous evening. Which meant Jillian might be alone now.

The thought of her alone and exposed to whoever wanted her out of her house scared Chance more than any Taliban fighter ever had. If the person who'd abducted Julia had any clue she was the grown-up little girl, he might not only scare her, he might kill her to keep her from ever remembering him and turning him in to the police.

Chance drove at breakneck speed through the thickening fog, desperate to get to Jillian, kicking himself for being so weak as to sleep through the afternoon instead of being vigilant and there when Jillian needed him.

His gut feeling wasn't good. And damned if his gut wasn't always right. He prayed that for once it was wrong, and he'd find Jillian painting a wall or taking a shower, which he would happily join.

Damn it to hell. Could the fog be any thicker?

Chapter 19

Jillian stood in the doorway to the kitchen, staring out at Mrs. Sims, a shiver of apprehension rippling through her. "Daryl wasn't stacking wood out back?"

Mrs. Sims shook her head. "I couldn't find him."

Jillian walked around to the back of the house where she'd last seen Daryl. The wood was piled neatly, but Daryl was nowhere to be seen.

"Daryl?" Jillian called out. Dusk had mingled with the overcast skies, settling over the property while she'd been working on the dresser. Along with the shadows, the devil's shroud had crept in from the ocean.

A chill racked Jillian's body. She should have put on her jacket, but she hadn't planned on being outside long. "I have no idea where he could have gone. You're welcome to look inside the house, but I've been working on the first floor since last I saw him and no one has come inside."

Mrs. Sims pressed her lips together. "That boy is always wandering off when he shouldn't be." She turned and stared into the woods. "I'll honk my horn. Sometimes that reminds him to come. He's so easily distracted." She left Jillian on the deck and walked around to the front of the house. A moment later, the sound of a car horn cut through the shadows and fog.

Jillian stared at the woods, hoping the man would appear, but even after the honking, Daryl didn't materialize out of the fog.

Mrs. Sims rejoined her on the porch, her hands in her pockets. "I'm afraid for the boy. If it gets any foggier, he could get lost trying to get back to the house. He could walk off a cliff and we'd not find him until too late." She started toward the woods. "I guess there's nothing else to do but go look for him."

"Let me help you." Jillian stepped down from the porch and followed the woman to the edge of the woods. She wished Chance would arrive before they got too deep into the underbrush. Though she didn't want to depend on him to bail her out of tough situations, it was nice having a man like him around. Especially when it came to finding a developmentally challenged individual in the woods, in the fog.

Mrs. Sims seemed to be a woman on a mission. She marched into the forest, plowing ahead. "I hope he didn't go too far. The fog's getting really thick."

Jillian worried about visibility, too. Though it wasn't completely dark yet, the fog was making it hard to see ahead or behind. Rather than compound the problem of one lost person in the woods, she decided to leave a trail to make it easier to find her way back in the fog.

With no bread crumbs to drop, she reached into her

pocket for the loose nuts and bolts she'd stuffed there earlier and dropped them every few steps. When she finally got back to her house, she'd have to come up with a whole new set of nuts and bolts to assemble the rest of the dresser. But it was a small sacrifice to keep from getting lost.

Mrs. Sims was well ahead of her. Jillian had to hurry to catch up with the older woman. She wasn't even sure which direction they were headed. At least if they started going around in circles, Jillian should find her trail of shiny bolts.

With the ever-thickening fog pressing in on her, Jillian momentarily lost sight of Mrs. Sims. She picked up her pace until she burst through the stand of trees into an opening and almost pitched over the edge of a cliff.

"Mrs. Sims?" Jillian called out. Dear God, she hoped the woman hadn't fallen over the ledge. She gazed over the edge but couldn't see more than five feet down. "Daryl?"

The tinny sound of music echoed in the darkness.

Jillian straightened, her body stiffening. She'd heard that tune before. But where? She dug in her memory, the answer seeming to slip just out of reach. She closed her eyes and listened to the haunting melody, one she'd heard a long, long time ago. An image of something small and dark emerged in her mind. A shiny black box, decorated with bright paintings of men and women dancing.

Jillian gasped, feeling as if all the air was sucked out of her lungs. She opened her eyes, straining to find the source of the music. She knew that song. The first time she'd heard it, she'd been carrying a black Russian porcelain music box home through the woods. *Oh, God.*

Her knees wobbled and tears filled her eyes. These

woods. She'd been on her way home to show her mother the box her teacher had given to her as a gift.

"I'm Julia," she whispered and turned in a circle as if seeing the world for the first time. "I'm Julia Thompson."

Mrs. Sims stepped out of the fog and held out the Russian music box. "Do you remember this?" she asked.

Jillian nodded. "Mrs. Tillman gave it to me for helping her to clean the boards after school." She held out her hand. "Where did you get it?"

"What else do you remember?"

Jillian pinched the bridge of her nose, a stabbing pain shooting through her head. "I don't know. I was on my way home to show it to my mother, but I fell. I must have hit my head because when I woke, I was in the dark."

Her eyes widened as everything came back to her. "I didn't remember anything. I woke up and didn't remember who I was, where I lived. Anything." Her body shook. "I was so scared."

"And who took care of you?"

"A teenager. He kept me in a dark cellar or something, along with a menagerie of cats and dogs. He said his mother wouldn't let him keep them at home so he brought them to the cellar and hid them."

"Where were you?" Mrs. Sims asked, her eyes gleaming, her expression intent.

Jillian shook her head, wondering why the woman was so adamant. "I don't know. I can't believe I remember as much as I have. It's been a very long time."

The older woman stepped up to Jillian, coming toe-to-toe with her. "Tell me where you were!" she demanded. "You have to tell me where you were."

Automatically backing up a step, Jillian held up her hands. "I can't. I don't know where I was."

"You have to remember. I have to find and destroy his hiding place."

"Whose hiding place?"

Mrs. Sims clutched the box to her chest, her eyes glazing and blotchy red flags of color rising high in her cheeks. "For seventeen years, I've lived in fear of this day. After all this time, I thought we were safe. Then you showed up, bought that damned house and ruined everything."

"I don't understand."

"Julia disappeared. No one could find her because my son hid her. Daryl has a place he hides all the strays he rescues. You were one of his strays. When my son came home carrying this box, I knew he had you, but I couldn't find where. I still don't know where he hides things. You have to tell me. I need to know so that I can protect him."

"Mrs. Sims, I remember carrying the box and falling. But I can't remember where the cellar was. I must have wandered out and somehow found my way home."

"You're lying!" She charged Jillian and shoved her.

Jillian staggered backward, her arms flailing to the side. She grabbed Mrs. Sims's arms to keep her balance. So close to the edge of the drop-off, Jillian couldn't risk taking one more step backward. "I'm not lying, Mrs. Sims. Please believe me."

Mrs. Sims's face flushed red and her eyes glowed like an animal possessed. "I can't let you tell anyone else what you know. If the police find out Daryl was the one to keep little Julia Thompson for thirty days, they'll take him away, lock him up in a mental hospital, and that would leave me all alone." She shoved at Jillian. "I won't let them take him away from me. Do you hear me? He's all I have. I'm his mother, damn it." With the strength of a much younger woman, she slammed into Jillian, knocking her backward.

Still holding onto Mrs. Sims's arms Jillian fell backward, landing on her butt on the very edge of the escarpment. Mrs. Sims landed on top of her and grabbed for Jillian's throat, squeezing as hard as her bony fingers could.

Jillian struggled to break the woman's hold, but she couldn't. The advancing fog was just a part of the gray haze filtering into her vision, making it even darker.

She had to hold on.

Chance skidded to a stop on the gravel drive in front of Jillian's house. Another vehicle stood out front, an older-model tank of a car with peeling paint. Lights shone through the windows, but he couldn't see any movement inside the house. He slammed the shift into Park and leaped out of the vehicle, running for the house. Skipping the steps, he leaped up onto the porch and burst into the house. The first thing he noted was the door was unlocked.

"Jillian!" he shouted. A quick run through the first floor netted nothing. He took the stairs two at a time to the second floor. Jillian wasn't in the master bedroom, bathroom or any other room on the second floor. Back down he went and checked the basement. She wasn't there.

Forcing himself to think calmly, he looked around the living area. Nothing seemed out of place except a half-assembled piece of furniture. It wasn't the kind of thing the construction crew would be responsible for building. A perky pink tool bag sat beside the wood panels and an assortment of slides and brackets. Jillian had been at work assembling this item when she'd been interrupted. By the owner of the dilapidated car out front?

Where had they gone?

Chance ran outside and stopped on the edge of the porch. He heard a faint cry, but he wasn't certain from which direction it had come. He waited to hear it again. It sounded as though it came from the side of the house. With darkness descending, and the fog getting so thick he couldn't see more than five feet ahead, Chance needed something else to get around. He ran back into the house and up to the master bedroom, where he'd left the flashlight.

Outside, he shone the light on the ground and worked his way toward the cry he'd heard. A shout sounded in the distance. Chance picked up the pace, his flashlight swinging left and then right. He was afraid to move too fast for fear of running into a tree or over the edge of a cliff.

As he swung the light back the other way, he caught the flash of light on something metal. He bent to examine what it was and discovered a small shiny bolt. One that could be used to assemble a piece of furniture.

He walked forward several steps, swinging the flight, pointing at the ground. After a couple more steps, he found another bolt. After the fourth bolt, Chance knew—Jillian had left him a trail to follow.

He built up a controlled speed, stepping through spongy moss, patches of large rocks and phalanxes of old-growth timber, but he still felt as if he was moving far too slowly, tracking the shiny bolts all the way to an opening in the trees and a rocky ledge.

Ahead he heard a woman scream and another cry out.

Chance ran as fast as he could, praying he wouldn't be too late.

Two shadowy figures struggled ahead. One plowed into the other and both fell.

Chance shone his flashlight toward the rocky ledge. The figures had disappeared. "Jillian!" He ran to the edge of a drop-off and leaned over. He couldn't see more than five feet down the sheer face of a cliff. "Jillian," he called out, his heart sinking to his shoes. He waited, straining to hear even the faintest cry for help.

"Chance?" Her voice came to him from what seemed like a long way down.

"Sweetheart, are you okay?" He squatted down on his haunches and tried to see her, but couldn't.

"I landed on a ledge. I'm not sure, but I think Mrs. Sims landed farther down. She hasn't made a sound."

"Can you hang on until I get help?"

"I can. It's a small ledge, but enough for me to balance on. I'll be okay, I'm just afraid for Mrs. Sims."

"Hang tight. I'll be back as soon as I can get help."

Chance hated leaving her, but he couldn't help her without a rope. He didn't know how steep the cliff was or how far down she'd landed. He followed the nuts and bolts trail back to the house, knowing he'd have to drive halfway to town to get help.

When the big old house loomed in front of him, another figure took shape out of the fog. A man stood next to the old car that belonged to Mrs. Sims.

"Daryl? Is that you?" Chance asked.

"Yes, Mr. McCall. My mama is picking me up to take me home. Her car is here, but I can't find her."

"She and Miss Taylor have had an accident. They fell

over a cliff. I need to get to town to get a rope or someone to help get to them."

"I have a rope," Daryl said."

"It might have to be a really long rope to get all the
way down the cliff to where they are."

"My rope is as long as a football field."

Chance grabbed Daryl's arm. "I need it now. I don't
have time to go all the way to your house to get it."

Daryl smiled. "You don't have to. It's close by. In my
treasure cave."

Making a snap decision, Chance grabbed the man's
arms. "Show me."

"It's a secret. You have to promise not to tell."

"I promise, Daryl. We have to hurry. I'm afraid Miss
Taylor and your mother are hurt."

Daryl's brows drew together. "Follow me." The man
led Chance into the fog. Chance soon struggled to keep
him in sight—Daryl moved quickly through the woods
as if familiar with his way, even in the choking fog.

Engulfed in the devil's shroud, Chance began second-
guessing his decision to trust Daryl's ability to judge the
length of a rope or find his way through the woods to
some alleged treasure cave. Chance might have been better off driving toward town and calling 911. Then he'd
have the full contingent of rescue personnel to help him
get to Jillian and Mrs. Sims.

"Daryl," Chance called out. "We should go back."

"Why? We're almost there." He kept moving, faster
than Chance could keep up.

They were far enough away from the house that
Chance wasn't so sure he'd find his way back. Apparently, Daryl didn't need a bread-crumb trail to find his

way through the fog. If Chance turned around to find his own way back, he might not make it.

Daryl disappeared into the haze.

Chance shone his flashlight, the beam bouncing back at him, reflected by the moisture in the air. He almost walked into a rocky bluff before he saw it. "Daryl?"

"Here," he said from somewhere in the maze of jagged boulders.

Chance wove his way between them and found Daryl rolling a boulder to the side. Beneath it lay a solid metal trapdoor.

A dog's bark sounded from beneath the door.

Daryl grinned. "That's JT. She likes it when I bring her food." He pulled on a metal ring and flung the trapdoor open.

A set of wooden stairs led down into an underground cave nestled into the rocky hillside.

JT, the dog they'd rescued from the animal shelter, bounded up to Daryl, tail wagging and happy to see her master.

Daryl grabbed a battery-powered lantern from a hook near the top of the steps and led the way into the cave.

Chance followed, amazed at all the stuff the man had accumulated in the cavern. An old wingback chair sat against one stone wall with an area rug in front of it. A fold-up cot with a thin mattress was completely made up with sheets, several blankets and a pillow. Stacks of boxes lined another wall farther back.

"This is my pirate's treasure cave. Do you like my treasure?" Daryl turned toward Chance, a smile on his face, proud of his collection.

"It's very impressive. What about the rope?"

"Oh, yeah." He hurried to the back of the cave and

dug into a box. He lifted a huge coil of rope out and carried it across to Chance. "Will this be long enough?" he asked. "We should go. Miss Jillian and Mama need us."

"Yes, they do." Chance started for the stairs and stopped with his foot on the first one. "Daryl, did a little girl ever live in this cave?"

Daryl nodded. "JT. I found her in the woods, all cold and shivering. I brought her here and warmed her up. I would have taken her home, but she was lost and couldn't remember how to get there. So I let her live here until she left."

"Her name was JT?"

He nodded and hurried to the makeshift bed, reaching beneath it to pull out an old cookie tin. He opened it and sifted through buttons and old coins and finally found what he was looking for, a pendant with the letters *J* and *T* engraved on the back. "See? JT. I named my dog after her."

"Had you met JT before she came to live here?"

Daryl shook his head. "No."

"Why didn't you tell someone that JT was living here?"

"Mama doesn't like me to talk to anyone, especially little kids. She doesn't like me to bring anything home with me either. She would have been mad. She *was* mad when she found the music box JT gave me. She took it and wouldn't give it back."

Chance's chest tightened as Daryl told him the story of the little girl who'd come to live in his pirate's treasure cave. Sweet heaven. Julia Thompson had been here for thirty days. Daryl had been the one who'd unwittingly hidden her.

He couldn't dwell on the past. Jillian and Mrs. Sims needed his help now.

"Daryl you did such a good job getting us to this place, can you get us back to Miss Taylor's house?" Chance hurried up the stairs.

"Yes, sir." Daryl climbed out of the cave. "Stay, JT. I'll be back in the morning." He closed the trapdoor and rolled the boulder back over the top of it, effectively hiding it from view.

Then Daryl headed back to Jillian's house.

Chance kept his flashlight trained on the ground, searching for the little nuts and bolts. He wasn't sure where he was, but if he found the nuts and bolts, they would lead him to the cliff Jillian and Mrs. Sims had fallen over.

After what felt like forever, Chance caught the glint of metal in the mossy ground. "Daryl, wait!" he shouted. "Come with me. I know where they are." He turned and let the little pieces of metal lead him back to the point at which he'd left Jillian.

"Jillian?"

For a moment she didn't response. Then the sweet sound of her voice drifted up to him. "I'm still here."

"Hang on, I have a rope."

He tied the rope to a tree trunk near the edge of the cliff. Then he tied a loop in the other end and tied the flashlight to it. "I'm going to lower the rope. It has a flashlight on it. Help me guide it to you when you see the beam."

"Will do." Jillian's voice shook. "Hurry. I can't see Mrs. Sims. I don't know what happened to her."

"Lowering the rope now." Chance fed the rope over

the edge of the cliff, releasing ten, twenty, thirty feet. "Can you see the light yet?"

"Maybe."

He lowered another ten feet, then another.

"There! I see the flashlight." Jillian's excitement gave Chance renewed hope. "Move it to your left and down another five or ten feet."

He moved the rope to his left and lowered it another eight feet.

"Another four feet to your left," she called.

Working blind, he could only hope he was getting close enough for her to catch it.

"Got it!"

A rush of joy washed over him, but he reminded himself she wasn't up yet. "Are you hurt in any way?"

"Bruised a bit, but nothing's broken."

"Slip the loop over your head and beneath your arms."

"Okay."

"We're going to pull you up."

"Wait," Jillian said. "Can you lower me first? I think Mrs. Sims is just another twenty feet below me. I can't be sure."

"Let us bring you up, then I'll come back for Mrs. Sims."

"No. If she's hurt, I might be able to help immediately. Please, lower me. If she's not twenty feet down, you can bring me up and come down yourself," Jillian called up to the top of the cliff.

"Daryl, I'm going to need your help," Chance said. He instructed the man how to wrap the rope around his waist and take the weight of the person below by leaning back. When he was sure Daryl was ready, he backed twenty feet from the edge, held on to the rope and called out to Jillian. "Okay, going down. Walk backward down the cliff."

"Walking." Jillian's weight tightened the rope.

Chance and Daryl eased toward the edge until they'd used all twenty feet of slack.

"I found her," Jillian called up and the rope loosened. "She's unconscious, but alive," she said. "Leave me here and go for help."

"Are you in a safe place?" Chance called out.

"I am. Go!" Jillian shouted, the sound seeming to come from a long way down.

Too far down for Chance's comfort. "Daryl, stay here and talk to Miss Taylor. I'll be back with help."

"Okay."

Chance followed the metal trail back to the house. As he emerged into the yard, he spotted an SUV pulling up next to his. He almost cried out in relief when he saw the emergency lights on top.

Gabe McGregor stepped out and shone a flashlight in his direction. "Chance? Is that you?"

"Thank God you're here. We need a rescue crew and an ambulance here, ASAP."

"What's going on?"

Chance gave him the necessary information and waited while Gabe called it in. "How in hell did you find your way in and out of the woods?"

"Jillian left a trail of nuts and bolts."

"Well, let's make it a little easier to see." Gabe reached into the back of his vehicle and pulled out a roll of yellow police tape. "Lead the way."

Between Chance and Gabe, they marked the trail to the cliff and stayed to talk to Jillian until the first responders arrived with mountain-climbing equipment and a stretcher.

Chance waited a few steps back, a lump lodged in his throat, struggling to breathe normally until a member of the rescue team popped up over the top with Jillian in front of him.

His knees nearly buckled in his relief.

They wanted to put her on a stretcher and carry her out, but she refused.

Chance chuckled and wove his way through the people working the rescue efforts until he stood in front of Jillian and opened his arms.

She fell against him and wrapped her arms around his waist. "Thank you for coming to find me."

"I wouldn't have stopped looking until I did."

The team brought Mrs. Sims up from below and carried her back along the police-tape trail. Gabe hooked Daryl's arm and walked with him back to the house.

Chance slipped an arm around Jillian and helped her over the rough ground. Whatever reservations he had about being a part of this woman's life were pushed to the very back of his mind. When he thought he'd lost her, his world felt as if it had come completely apart. Now that he had her back, he didn't want to let her go. Ever again. He'd find a way to overcome his nightmares. Hopefully, Jillian would be willing to work with him as he resolved his issues with PTSD.

Chapter 20

When they emerged beside the house, Molly and Nova were there. They enveloped Jillian in hugs, shocked at what had almost ended in disaster.

Jillian returned their hugs but then pushed through to the ambulance, where Daryl stood as they loaded his mother in the back.

"Daryl, are you okay?"

"Yes, JT."

Jillian's eyes rounded. "You knew?"

He nodded.

"Why didn't you tell me?"

Daryl shrugged. "You didn't remember me."

"I do now." She touched his arm. "Thank you for helping me when I was a little girl."

"Mama said if anyone found out I helped you, they would take me away."

Jillian hugged Daryl. "No one is going to take you away. You saved my life."

"I did?" His face brightened.

"Yes. You're my hero." She kissed his cheek.

The medical technicians nudged them aside and lifted Mrs. Sims into the ambulance.

Gabe joined them. "Daryl, I'm going to take you to the hospital and see that you get home afterward."

Daryl nodded. "Can I come visit you when your house is all done, JT?"

"You bet." Jillian hugged him again and then turned toward Chance, Molly and Nova, her heart swelling. Her friends were her family, and she was damned lucky to have them. They looked out for her and made sure she was happy.

As exhausted and banged up as she was from the stress of the day and the fall over the cliff, she refused to let it get her down. She squared her shoulders and marched toward her future. Whether it included Chance or not, she wasn't afraid. She could handle anything.

Two days later

"Everyone line up! They're coming!" Jillian shouted. She rushed down the two rows of guests, handing out bags of birdseed. The bruise on her cheek was barely noticeable beneath her makeup.

Chance smiled and snagged her around the waist, pulling her up beside him as Molly and Nova emerged from the McGregor B and B as Mr. and Mrs. Casanova Valdez.

Molly's cheeks glowed and her eyes sparkled with excitement. Every time Nova glanced at his bride, Chance could see the depth of his love for this woman. He'd been happy and proud to stand beside his friend as he married the woman who had become a part of his heart.

Chance glanced at Jillian tossing birdseed and laughing, her joy for her friends, for her life and for the town she called home shining through like a beacon.

Over the days he'd been in Cape Churn, Chance had found a community of people who cared about one another. Old and new friends came together to help each other.

Since the night Jillian had learned she was the little lost girl, Julia Thompson, she'd pushed aside the drama of her life to focus on bringing Molly and Nova together in holy matrimony, refusing to dwell on the secrets, the trauma and the revelations of what had occurred.

Molly and Nova climbed into his SUV decorated with Just Married across the back windshield and strings of tin cans tied to the bumper. They pulled away amid shouts of well wishes and showers of birdseed.

The local members of the SOS team had all been there, including Nicole Steele, who'd flown in from her assignment in Guatemala, arriving in time for the rehearsal dinner and bachelor and bachelorette parties. Creed Thomas stood with Emma Jenkins. Once the bride and groom left, they gathered around Jillian and Chance.

"Now that you've been here for almost a week and had a chance to look around and get to know some of the locals, are you going to join the West Coast office of SOS?" Nicole asked. Dave Logsdon stood beside her, his hand resting on her waist.

Chance had been with Jillian for the past couple of nights, sleeping in her house and her bed. He'd had dreams of his tours in Afghanistan, but he hadn't had any violent outbursts, and Jillian had been more than willing to risk the effects of PTSD.

Mrs. Sims was recuperating in the hospital, soon to be transferred to jail to await her trial for attempted murder. Even if she ended up with a light sentence, at least she would get the mental health care she so badly needed.

Jillian empathized with the older woman and had actually visited her in the hospital, reassuring her that Daryl would be all right and she wasn't going to press charges against him for holding her in his pirate's cave when she was a child. The community would look after him.

With the threat against Jillian neutralized and Mrs. Sims in custody, everything was quiet in the small town of Cape Churn.

He had nothing to draw him back to Virginia, and his assignments could take him anywhere in the country or the world.

"Well, are you?" Jillian asked.

He leaned close to her and whispered, "Remember when I said you were making it really hard for me to walk away?"

She smiled up at him, beaming like a ray of sunshine on a foggy day. "I remember."

"I'm not walking away."

She flung her arms around his neck and kissed him full on the lips. He held her close, deepening the kiss until Nicole cleared her throat next to him.

"I'm staying," he announced to the others.

His teammates hugged him and pounded him on the back, welcoming him to life on the West Coast. He'd never felt more at home and accepted than he did at that moment.

When the party broke up a couple hours later, Chance drove Jillian home to the house she'd grown up in and that had been in her family for years. Jillian sat back in her seat next to him, a smile playing across her lips, her eyes half-closed with exhaustion. "It was a beautiful wedding."

"Yes, it was. And you did a great job organizing it."

"It was an honor to help. Molly and Nova are my family. Molly was one of the first people I met when I came to Cape Churn. That was shortly after my parents died. I thought I was alone in the world, and I was sad. She helped me see Cape Churn as my home, and she and her brother welcomed me."

"Now that you know you're Julia Thompson, you realize you have a father still living?"

She nodded. "I do."

Chance cast a glance her way, watching the play of emotion across her face.

"When everything settles down, I want to make a trip down to see him. I think I'd like to get to know him."

"You know, I feel like we skipped some parts in our relationship."

She turned to look at him. "Have we?"

"Yes, ma'am. And now that I'm going to be around for a while, I feel like I need to remedy that oversight. I don't believe we've had our first date."

Jillian laughed, the sound pure joy. "You're right."

"I'll make a reservation at the Seaside Café for tomorrow night. I'll pick you up at six."

"I'd like that." She reached across the console for his hand.

"If you want, I can get an apartment in town and let

you get used to idea of having me around." He squeezed her hand. "You might decide I crowd you."

"No way," she said. "Jack and Jill are a joint responsibility. Besides, they like how you feed them better."

Chance winked. "All you have to do is add a little tuna juice to sweeten their cat food."

"You do it so much better. And no, I don't want you to move into an apartment. I kinda like having you around."

"Good, because I like being around."

As he pulled up to the old house still in the throes of a massive overhaul, Jillian sighed. "Chance?"

"Mmm?"

"Do you believe in love at first sight?"

His hand tightened on hers and then he released it to shift into Park. "No."

She shot a worried glance his way. "No?"

He shook his head. "If you recall, you didn't like me when you first met me."

"I remember." Her lips twitched. "Do you believe two people can fall in love in less than a week?"

He got out of the SUV and rounded to the passenger door, opening it for her. He helped her down and pulled her into his arms. "Darlin', I believe if we aren't already there, we're well on our way."

* * * * *

COMING NEXT MONTH FROM

H HARLEQUIN

ROMANTIC suspense

Available June 7, 2016

#1899 CAVANAUGH COLD CASE
Cavanaugh Justice • by Marie Ferrarella
Playboy detective Malloy Cavanaugh is on the case when
bodies are unearthed in a cactus nursery. But it's medical
examiner Kristin Alberghetti who poses the greatest threat
to his heart.

#1900 A BABY FOR AGENT COLTON
The Coltons of Texas • by Jennifer Morey
FBI profiler Trevor Colton isn't looking for a family beyond
his recent reunion with his siblings, but when his partner,
Jocelyn Locke, announces she's pregnant, he's thrown into
the role of protector while they chase a dangerous serial
killer.

#1901 DELTA FORCE DESIRE
by C.J. Miller
When Griffin Brooks rescues a computer programmer from
being kidnapped by cyberterrorists, he marvels at his client's
beauty *and* brains. But the classified project Kit worked on
threatens both of them and their burgeoning relationship.

#1902 A SEAL TO SAVE HER
To Protect and Serve • by Karen Anders
A wounded navy SEAL and a hunted US senator run for their
lives in war-torn Afghanistan. Their pursuers: her security
detail. Their mission: get out alive!

HRSCNM0516

REQUEST YOUR FREE BOOKS!

2 FREE NOVELS PLUS 2 FREE GIFTS!

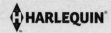

ROMANTIC suspense

Sparked by danger, fueled by passion

YES! Please send me 2 FREE Harlequin® Romantic Suspense novels and my 2 FREE gifts (gifts are worth about $10). After receiving them, if I don't wish to receive any more books, I can return the shipping statement marked "cancel." If I don't cancel, I will receive 4 brand-new novels every month and be billed just $4.74 per book in the U.S. or $5.49 per book in Canada. That's a savings of at least 12% off the cover price! It's quite a bargain! Shipping and handling is just 50¢ per book in the U.S. and 75¢ per book in Canada.* I understand that accepting the 2 free books and gifts places me under no obligation to buy anything. I can always return a shipment and cancel at any time. Even if I never buy another book, the two free books and gifts are mine to keep forever.

240/340 HDN GH3P

Name	(PLEASE PRINT)
Address	Apt. #
City	State/Prov.	Zip/Postal Code

Signature (if under 18, a parent or guardian must sign)

Mail to the **Reader Service:**

IN U.S.A.: P.O. Box 1867, Buffalo, NY 14240-1867
IN CANADA: P.O. Box 609, Fort Erie, Ontario L2A 5X3

Want to try two free books from another line?
Call 1-800-873-8635 or visit www.ReaderService.com.

* Terms and prices subject to change without notice. Prices do not include applicable taxes. Sales tax applicable in N.Y. Canadian residents will be charged applicable taxes. Offer not valid in Quebec. This offer is limited to one order per household. Not valid for current subscribers to Harlequin Romantic Suspense books. All orders subject to credit approval. Credit or debit balances in a customer's account(s) may be offset by any other outstanding balance owed by or to the customer. Please allow 4 to 6 weeks for delivery. Offer available while quantities last.

Your Privacy—The Reader Service is committed to protecting your privacy. Our Privacy Policy is available online at www.ReaderService.com or upon request from the Reader Service.

We make a portion of our mailing list available to reputable third parties that offer products we believe may interest you. If you prefer that we not exchange your name with third parties, or if you wish to clarify or modify your communication preferences, please visit us at www.ReaderService.com/consumerchoice or write to us at Reader Service Preference Service, P.O. Box 9062, Buffalo, NY 14240-9062. Include your complete name and address.

With the pregnancy test long ago thrown in the trash, Trevor paced from one end of the living room of Jocelyn's condo to the other. She sat on her gray sofa before the stacked gray rock wall, a fresh vase of yellow lilies on the coffee table, reminding him that her chosen profession missed the mark. What hit the mark was what had him pacing the room. Her. Pregnant. Raising babies in a warm, inviting home like this one, in a gated community with a pool and clubhouse.

He knew what he had to do. He just couldn't believe he actually would.

He stopped pacing in front of the sofa, looking at Jocelyn over the tops of cheery lilies. "We have to get married."

That blunt announcement removed her annoyed observation of him digesting the idea of his impending fatherhood. Now shock rounded her eyes and parted her lips with a grunt.

"Will I be at gunpoint?" she asked.

She felt forced into this. He understood that. So did he.

"Love isn't important right now. The baby is what's important. No child of mine is going to be raised in a broken home."

She stood up. "Nothing's broken in *my* home."

She kind of went low on that one. His home was broken. Did she mean him or his dad? Both, probably.

"I won't get married just because I'm pregnant," she said. "I want love. Love is important to me, equally as much as this child." After a beat, she added, "And I thought you didn't mix personal relationships with your professional ones."

"I don't, but a baby changes everything. I won't be my father. I won't tear apart a family and destroy the lives of my children. I'll give them support and the best chance at a good life as I can."

Nothing in the world held more importance than that. He'd do anything, go to any length to avoid turning out like his father. He was no murderer. He had sanity. And he was on the opposite side of the law from his father. That was where he'd stay.

Don't miss
A BABY FOR AGENT COLTON by Jennifer Morey,
available June 2016 wherever
Harlequin® Romantic Suspense
books and ebooks are sold.

www.Harlequin.com

HARLEQUIN®

A Romance FOR EVERY MOOD™

Love the Harlequin book
you just read?

Your opinion matters.

Review this book on your favorite
book site, review site, blog or your own
social media properties and share
your opinion with other readers!

Be sure to connect with us at:
Harlequin.com/Newsletters
Facebook.com/HarlequinBooks
Twitter.com/HarlequinBooks

THE WORLD IS BETTER WITH

Romance

Harlequin has everything from contemporary, passionate and heartwarming to suspenseful and inspirational stories.

Whatever your mood, we have a romance just for you!

Connect with us to find your next great read, special offers and more.

f /HarlequinBooks

🐦 @HarlequinBooks

www.HarlequinBlog.com

www.Harlequin.com/Newsletters

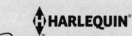

♦ HARLEQUIN®

A *Romance* FOR EVERY MOOD™

www.Harlequin.com

HARLEQUIN®

A *Romance* FOR EVERY MOOD™

JUST CAN'T GET ENOUGH?

Join our social communities
and talk to us online.

You will have access to the latest
news on upcoming titles and special
promotions, but most importantly,
you can talk to other fans about your
favorite Harlequin reads.

Harlequin.com/Community

f Facebook.com/HarlequinBooks

🐦 Twitter.com/HarlequinBooks

📌 Pinterest.com/HarlequinBooks